Different Kind of Forever

Dee Ernst

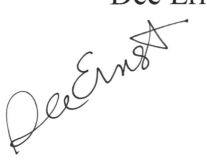

Books by Dee Ernst

Better Off Without Him

Author's Note

I wrote this book a number of years ago. It did not get published, but it did get me a great agent, Lynn Seligman. It was also read by a number of friends and co-workers, whose kind words took the sting out of all those rejection letters. So I'd like to thank them all, the Tabor Ladies and the great folks at Barnes and Noble, who cheered me on when I really needed it.

I'd also like to thank Carole Williams for her good eye and generous spirit.

This is a work of fiction, so, I'm sorry, but there is no real Michael. However, I was inspired by Dan Futterman, Jon Bon Jovi, and Elijah Wood. I have never met any of these fine gentlemen, but if any one of them would care to get in touch with me for any discussion of Michael's character, please. Email me. Any time. Really.

And, as always, comments from my readers make my day.

dernst2010@optonline.net

CHAPTER ONE

Diane Matthews came out of sleep as one swimming upwards, a slow brightening, an awareness of sound. Dog barking, slow ticking, a long deep breath. It was Tuesday morning, so no classes till after lunch. Tuesdays were her mornings to play, run errands and sometimes write. She sighed, moving deeper into the covers. Her first challenge: sleep another half hour, or get up now and get an extra jump on the day? She opened her eyes: empty room, quiet, pale curtains, alone. The cat, Jasper, a long, rangy calico, leapt lightly onto the bed. Good morning.

She rolled out of bed and stepped into the shower. She could hear the girls upstairs, the faint footfalls coming through the sound of water. Emily would have gotten up first, rousing her younger sister with her own bathroom noises. A school day, the regular routine.

"Mom, you need to sign this." Emily stood before her in the kitchen, holding a sheet of paper that looked vaguely official. Diane sipped coffee, squinting. Emily let out an exaggerated sigh and reached for Diane's reading glasses on the counter, handing them over with a small shake of her head.

"Some day, you'll be old and I'm really going to enjoy it," Diane grumbled, putting on the glasses and reading. A permission slip for the Science trip in June. She signed quickly, then marked the calendar. Megan came up behind her and gave her a quick kiss on the cheek and a mumbled, morning, while reaching for cereal. Then, both girls froze. The sound of the radio, coming from the living room, caught their attention. They both grabbed for their cellphones and waited as the DJ droned on. Tickets for the concert. Of course. They had been in a frenzy for weeks, trying to win free tickets for NinetySeven, local boys made good, for their last show of the current tour. The question hadn't been asked yet, but it didn't matter. Between the two girls, they knew every bit of trivia about the band there was to know.

"This one's easy," the DJ was saying. "How did they get the name NinetySeven?"

"Oh God, I know that, I know that." Emily had her cell phone to her ear. Diane looked at Megan and raised an eyebrow.

Megan had her cell phone in one hand and poured cereal with the other. "That's the number they came up with when they added up all their ages, right after Mickey Flynn joined the band. He was the youngest, only 15."

Emily was shaking her head. "How do people get through?" she howled. "It's impossible. This is so unfair. I mean it. Mom, you should go down to the radio station and complain. It's totally impossible."

Diane studied her daughter's face. Long, thin, deep-set eyes. Not a beauty, but arresting, intense. Completely different from Megan, who was so open and sunny. Emily was scowling now. She slammed the phone onto the counter as the DJ announced they had their caller. Megan shrugged and turned off her own phone, but Emily, as always, was taking it personally.

Diane winced as Emily stormed around the kitchen. Was she that self-involved at 16? She didn't think so, but it was quite a while ago. Her oldest, Rachel, had been very quiet and self-assured, focused on becoming an actress since the age of ten and never wavering. Emily was flighty, over-dramatic and irrational in reacting to perceived slights. As for Megan, at 14 she was following Rachel's footsteps, thank God.

"Mom, did you get Dad's okay?" Emily asked suddenly.

Diane frowned. "For what?"

A heavy sigh. "If we get tickets. Did Dad say we could go to the concert?"
Diane sipped more coffee, thinking quickly. Her ex-husband had the girls on weekends, picking them up every Friday evening.

"No, I didn't say anything to him yet, but he knows how important this would be to you. He wouldn't give you a hard time. Why don't you call him yourself, and give him a heads up?"

Emily cocked her head at her mother. "He'd let me go, but not alone. You'd have to come with me. So what about Megan? If we win this contest, it's only two tickets." Emily started pacing again. "It's not fair, Mom."

Megan raised her eyebrows at her sister. Diane took a deep breath.

"Em, why don't we wait until you actually have tickets before we start to worry about your sister, okay?"

Emily turned abruptly and left. Diane turned and looked at Megan.

"Is there really a 15-year-old in the band?"

Megan put her bowl in the sink. "He's not 15 now, Mom. That was like, ages ago." Megan lifted herself onto the counter and sat, legs swinging slightly. "See, Joey Adamson and his two cousins and his best friend had this band, and they were, like all twenty or twenty-one or something, then Joey's brother met Mickey's sister, and Joey heard him sing and asked him to be in the band, and he was only 15, but really good, you know? So then Mickey started playing with them and they changed the name to NinetySeven and then they became really known, and got a record deal and stuff, and now they're, like, famous." Megan smiled. "He's cute."

"Mickey?"

"Oh, yeah, him too. But Joey? He's the drummer? He's really cute, but old, you know? Like thirty or something."

Diane put down her cup. "Yeah. Old."

Megan hopped off the counter and headed out as the house phone rang.

Diane checked the caller I.D. and grinned. "NinetySeven Central," she answered.

"If I never hear about this stupid band again, I'll die a happy camper." Sue Griffen said over the line. "I may have to lock both kids in a closet."

Diane laughed. Sue's daughters were the same ages as Emily and Megan, and were close friends. "Have yours put the radio station on speed-dial?"

Sue snorted. "Oh yes. Thank God for cell phones or I'd never see my landline. I should have let them camp out and get the friggin' tickets. This is way too much aggravation."

"Hey, there's only what, three more weeks of this? Then we can relax till the next round. I remember Rachel doing this to me last time these guys were on tour, what, five years ago? I think it was the same radio

4

contest - maybe the same DJ. Can you come over for coffee? I've got the morning free."

"Nope, not me. That's why I called. I've got the dentist in like 20 minutes. Ask Megan to swing by and get Becca, okay?"

"Sure. Later." Diane hung up and grabbed a yogurt from the fridge. Sue Abbot lived two doors down. They had moved into the neighborhood within months of each other, and had their youngest in the same week.

Diane went to the bottom of the stairs and yelled up. "Megan, you've got five minutes. Pick up Becca on the way to the bus stop, okay?

Diane sat on the couch and stared out the window, listening to her daughters get ready. She was pretty, with dark, intelligent eyes and a shy, lovely smile. Her hair was dark, curling, brushing her shoulders. She had been divorced for almost five years.

"Mom?" Emily came down the stairs, her face set. "Can you listen to the radio for me?"

"Emily, what the hell do I know about these guys? You're the NinetySeven expert, not me."

Emily rolled her eyes and pushed out the front door. Seconds later, Megan came down. She bent and kissed her mother's cheek.

"She's just really worked up about this, that's all." Megan made a small face. "You know how she gets. She wants to be the one to go, 'cause nobody else got tickets and it would be a big deal."

"I know." Diane smiled at her youngest and watched her leave, listening to the vague squawk of the radio. She spent the rest of the morning quietly, doing laundry, straightening books. She didn't often venture upstairs, but as she carried a basket of towels into the girls' bathroom, she threw a quick look into the two bedrooms. Megan's room was a mess. Clothes on the floor, bed unmade, a pile of shoes spilling out of the closet. It always looked cluttered, even when clean, because there was not an inch of white, empty wall. All the flat surfaces were covered with posters – television and film actors, bands, and unicorns.

Emily's room was slightly better – she took care of her clothes and they were never left on the floor. Her room was dominated by a single, life-sized poster of the band, NinetySeven. Diane looked at the faces. *They are all so young,* she thought. *Well, maybe not. They have been around for a while. They might even be over thirty.* She stepped closer. Except Mickey Flynn. She remembered the poster that Rachel had of the same group, years ago. Mickey Flynn had been a kid, small, innocent-looking, with big blue eyes and a sweet smile. He was taller now, lean and wiry, brows heavier, his face all angles. Behind him was, she assumed, the handsome drummer. Joey. Very handsome and muscular in a tight black tee shirt and jeans.

"I'd do him," she said aloud. Jasper the cat wrapped around her ankles, purring.

"What do you think, baby," she asked him. "Could I get a rock star?"

The cat sat and began to lick his front paw.

"Didn't think so," she said, and got ready for work.

She drove through the early afternoon. Her first class was not until two. If she was lucky, and no one saw her sneak into her office, she could have almost an hour alone to work on her play. It had been accepted for production at Merriweather Playhouse, a small, private theater connected to Franklin-Merriweather University. She taught at Dickerson College, a liberal arts college whose campus adjoined the University.

She had gotten the idea for "Mothers and Old Boyfriends" five years before, when she went to Ohio without her daughters to attend the wedding of her college roommate. She had been invited to spend the night before the wedding at Judy's, with two other women, Judy's sister and her childhood friend. Diane had not met the other two women before, but they all clicked immediately, and after the rehearsal dinner, they sat in Judy's living room and talked about their younger college days, and about their mothers and all of their old boyfriends.

When Diane decided to take Sam French's playwriting class a few years later, she wrote about the four women coming together: but in addition to those four characters, the four different mothers and all those ex-lovers became part of the story, stepping in and out of conversations, and having discussions of their own that ran counterpoint to what the women had to say. Only in theater could the line between fantasy and reality be so easily crossed. Diane wrote steadily, her fingers tripping over each other in her eagerness to get the words down, and Sam French loved the result, doing the piece the following year as a read-through in a Master's workshop. Then he asked if he could direct it in full as part of the winter schedule. Franklin-Merriweather had never done an original work before. This would be a first.

It would be a busy summer for her. In addition to the play, she would be teaching a graduate level class the following year, beginning in January. Normally, she would spend at least part of the summer traveling, but this year she would be home with her daughters for the whole three months, working.

She was lucky when she got to work. She slipped into her office unnoticed and began to read through the notes Sam French had left for her. Act 1's second and fifth scenes were dragging. She made the changes, working on the hard copy before putting changes into the computer. She lived in terror of the computer losing everything, and would print out any and all changes in addition to saving them onto a disk.

Marianne Thomas poked her head in a few minutes before class. She was 50, almost six feet tall, and the most beautiful woman Diane had ever known. Part Chinese, part African-American, Marianne was brilliant, a lesbian, and had been Diane's good friend for years, besides being her boss.

"Can I have a minute?" she asked.

Diane nodded, hit the save button, and turned to her friend. "Ten minutes. What's up?"

"I'm thinking of using Torino's for the picnic. You've had their food, what do you think?"

Diane pursed her lips. Every year, at the end of spring term, Marianne invited all Dickerson's faculty to a picnic at her old farmhouse. It had become something of a tradition, and Marianne took it very seriously.

"They're good, but they're kind of a small operation. Can they handle that many people?"

Marianne looked thoughtful. "Good point. I'll have to think. I may get a country western band to play instead of a DJ. I think it would be a hoot. Can you imagine Peter Ferrell trying to line dance? It might be worth the thousand dollars for that alone."

Diane grinned. "You're awful. He is a perfectly nice man, why do you pick on him so much?"

"Because he honestly believes the spaceship is due back any day now. Isn't that why you stopped dating him?"

"No. Well, maybe. He was a little too cerebral for me."

Marianne snorted delicately. "And this from a woman who reads Tibetan poetry for fun. How about a movie this weekend? Something in English, please?"

Diane nodded. "Sure. Saturday night. But we'll have to make it late. Megan's car-wash fundraiser is Saturday, and I've got the afternoon shift."

"You'll be washing cars? In public? Lord, Diane, surely you could just write a check?"

Diane began to gather up her books. "I'm a single parent, remember, trying to live on a professor's salary. I don't have the disposable income of certain, unencumbered people. Besides, it'll be fun, out in the sunshine, playing with hoses and soapy water."

"Playing with hoses? God, I could never be a parent."

Diane smiled. "Maybe not. Can you walk with me? I have an issue, I think, with my class."

They walked across campus, Diane explaining her problem with trying to get an outline together. Marianne agreed to get a meeting together next week, they picked a movie for Saturday, and parted. Diane had two classes, both senior seminars. They were her favorite classes, and they sped by. Afterwards, she ran into the grocery store and then hurried home to her daughters.

The week went by quickly. On Friday morning, Emily mentioned that her father would be picking the girls up early. Diane looked at her suspiciously.

"What? What are you cooking up now?"

Emily rolled her eyes. "He just needs to talk to you, okay? It's not such a big deal."

Diane looked at Megan, who lifted her shoulders and shook her head. "Sorry Mom, not a clue."

Emily huffed and ran back upstairs. Diane looked back at Megan, who was putting her cereal bowl in the sink.

"Megan, tell me," Diane asked. "Please? Whenever she gets that look in her eye, I know there's trouble."

Megan twisted her lips together. "She was talking to Alison about the shore this summer."

Suddenly, Diane knew. "Okay. Not a problem."

She was on good terms with Kevin, her ex-husband. Theirs had not been a dramatic divorce. They had just grown apart. He would have probably been willing to go on indefinitely, but Diane found herself increasingly unhappy, and they finally separated. He had since re-married, to a much younger woman, who was expecting their first child in September. He had also been talking about buying a house on Long Beach Island, and spending the summer there. Diane could imagine that the idea of spending the entire summer within sight of the ocean, not to mention all those boys, would be irresistible to Emily. Diane smiled ruefully to herself. She would have loved it at that age. Hell, she'd love it now. Diane chewed her lip for a moment. It would be interesting to see how Emily would approach her.

That afternoon, when Kevin came to pick up the girls, Emily sat beside him on the couch. Diane looked at him fondly. He was a quiet, attractive man, just over fifty, who still had a great deal of affection and respect for his ex-wife. Kevin put his arm around Emily's shoulder.

"Well, I want you to know that Victoria and I have gone ahead and bought a shore house. It's small, just a summer bungalow, but it's on the beach block. Victoria is going to be living there all summer." He smiled at Megan, then at Emily. "So, Em, do you have something to ask your mother?"

Emily's jaw dropped and she looked at her father, stricken. "Dad, I thought you were –"

Kevin shook his head. "You stay with me every weekend and for three weeks in August. If you want anything else, it's up to your mother."

Diane raised an eyebrow. Emily glared daggers at her father, and then turned to her mother, carefully re-arranging her face.

"Mom, I'd like to spend all summer at the shore - with Dad and Vicki. Is it okay with you?"

Megan jumped up. "Wait, what about me?"

"Honey," Kevin said soothingly, "of course this includes you. It's just that Emily brought it up a few weeks ago, so she and I have been discussing it."

"Well," Megan sputtered, "what about Mom? I mean, she'll be here all alone. I don't want to leave Mom alone. What would she do? She's not even going away this summer. She'll have nothing to do without us here."

Diane tightened her lips to hide a smile. "Megan, thank you for thinking of me, but I'll be working all summer. I've got a new class to prepare, and there's the play."

"Then it's okay?" Emily asked.

Diane fixed her eye on her. "What about the job you were going to get this summer to pay for all the driving you're supposed to be doing next year?"

Emily squirmed. "I can get a job down there. I can wait tables at the shore just as easily as I can here. And I can walk or ride a bike there, and I can't here, not really. And besides," she added, as a final stroke, "I can help Victoria take care of the house. She's sick because of the pregnancy and needs me."

Kevin pursed his lips in a silent whistle and met Diane's eye. Diane had to cough.

"Really? You're going to help Victoria? Does that mean you'll be cleaning and doing the cooking for all of you?"

Emily squirmed again, looking thunderous. Diane didn't let her off the hook.

11

"How are you going to take care of a house and work? You're always complaining I do a lousy job of both, that dinner is never ready, that you have to do your own laundry, and numerous other transgressions. Do you think you'll do a better job?"

Kevin stood up and turned away, running his hand through his hair.

"Well, Mom, I could help," Megan offered. "I do stuff around here. I'd do the same chores down there, if Em wanted. I could, you know, set the table and stuff."

Emily stood up and stormed around the room. "You're only saying no to be mean to me, because you never got to spend the summer anywhere cool, you were always moping around dumb Ohio, helping your father, so you just don't want me to have the greatest summer ever to prove some stupid point, right?"

"I didn't say no," Diane said calmly, stopping Emily in her tracks. "I just asked you a question. If you do get a job, and save one thousand dollars, which is what we had talked about before, I see no reason for you not to go. The fact that you're going to be doing so much for Victoria is just an added bonus. I had no idea you were so concerned about her welfare."

Emily opened her mouth, realized the trap too late, and shut it again. Clearly torn between feeling grateful at being allowed to go, and being angry at herself for being put in the position of helpmate, she did the smart thing.

"Thanks, Mom."

"Sure. Now, Meg, do you want to go as well? It's up to you."

Megan grinned. "I want to go. It will be so cool, going to the beach every day. Will I have to get a job, too?"

Diane shook her head. "Not unless you want extra pocket money. I'm sure you could baby-sit somewhere down there, right, Kev?"

Kevin nodded, once again amazed at the way Diane danced through the minefield that was their middle daughter. Often, Emily would reduce Diane to tears, but Diane had been prepared for this one, and played it just right.

"Okay, let's go." Kevin shouted, clapping his hands together. "Move out the troops." The girls scampered out as they had done when they were babies, when any trip with their Daddy was an adventure. Kevin kissed Diane on the cheek, and followed the girls out.

The next day, the car wash was cancelled out by a day-long spring downpour, so Diane called Marianne and met her for dinner. Afterwards, they went to the movies, then stopped in to a local pub for a drink. Diane was feeling tired and sipped club soda, while Marianne knocked back a straight scotch and lamented the current state of American cinema. Suddenly, she leaned toward Diane and whispered.

"That man at the bar has been staring at you since we got here. Should we invite him over?"

Diane looked at her friend in surprise. "How do you know he's not staring at you? You're taller, thinner, and a lot more gorgeous than I am."

Marianne raised her eyebrows in exasperation. "Diane, I'm a lesbian, remember?"

"True," Diane admitted. "But you're not wearing your 'Bug Off Creep, I'm A Dyke' sweatshirt."

"That man is white. Why would he be staring at me?"

"Because he's not a racist?"

Marianne sighed. "You are such a Pollyanna, Diane. At times, it's endearing, but it tends to wear thin. I sometimes wonder how we remain friends."

"Well for my part, you happen to be very politically correct. So many minorities rolled into one. I don't have to feel guilty about having so many straight WASP's for friends with you on the roster. I think you like me because when we're together you can feel superior without having to be too condescending."

Marianne lifted her eyebrows and made a polite noise. "You may very well be right. Now, about that nice man-"

"No. Forget it."

"Why, are you dating anyone?"

Diane shook her head. "Nope. Not this week. How about you? What happened to the travel agent?"

"She was a racist."

"I thought she was black."

"She was. She didn't think I was black enough."

"Sorry. I liked her."

"You like everyone. It's disgusting how nice you are to people. I bet you know the grocery clerks by name."

"Evelyn, Maggie, Sophia, Lorraine, -"

"Oh, stop it. Now, you're just showing off. Do you worry about not having someone in your life? At your age?"

Diane shrugged. "I have lots of people in my life, Marianne - you, my kids, my friends, Evelyn, Maggie, Sophia. I don't have a man in my life, but that's fine. I'm really very happy, you know that."

"Yes," Marianne mused. "You are a very successful single person. That man at the bar also looks very successful. Are you sure?"

Diane gathered her purse. "I'm tired. Doing nothing all day wore me out. Are you ready?"

Marianne drained her glass, and they left. Diane went home, watched TV with Jasper purring on her lap, and fell asleep on the couch. Sunday was another rainy day. She worked on her play, called her mother in Ohio, and napped until the girls came home.

The week began again, and another Tuesday. She ran errands in the morning, the dry cleaners, the library. She decided to treat herself to Moe's, a small, crowded deli with great sandwiches. Standing in line, she wavered between corned beef and pastrami, but it was Moe himself who made the choice, wincing at her corned beef request. She picked up a cream soda, and then headed out to Bloomfield Park, a large, green oasis. She parked her car and walked toward a picnic table under a barely leafed-out maple tree, next to the duck pond. She was alone in the park except for a man and a dog playing out on the ball field.

She opened her sandwich and took a bite, then opened her soda. She needed to work on the second act this week. It was running way too long. She was running lines in her head when she heard someone yelling. She looked toward the noise, and jumped up in alarm. The dog that had been romping playfully in the ball field a few moments ago was racing toward her. The animal's owner was running behind.

"He wants your sandwich," he yelled. Diane stared at her sandwich, then at the rapidly approaching dog. It was huge, shaggy, long ears streaming back. No way was the owner going to catch it. She grabbed her sandwich in both hands, scrambled on top of the picnic table and stood, waiting.

"He wants your sandwich," the man yelled again, so she stuck out her hand and the dog bounded up, snatching the sandwich from between her fingertips and landing gracefully a few feet away. Diane stared at the animal in amazement, then turned as the owner came running up to her. He was completely winded, gasping, bent over with his hands on his knees, trying to catch his breath.

"I'm so sorry," he panted. "But my dog really loves pastrami."

Diane stared at him. "That's the silliest thing I've ever heard."

The owner of the dog nodded his head. "Oh, I know," he gulped. "It's probably the silliest thing I've ever had to say."

Diane began to laugh, a tickle that began in her throat and bubbled up. She felt tears streaming from her eyes. No one would ever believe this. The owner started to laugh with her. He seemed very young, dark hair cut short and as he lifted his smiling face, she saw startling blue eyes, an angular jaw. Suddenly, she stopped laughing.

"Oh, my God. I know you."

He was still breathing heavily. "I'm Michael Carlucci, and this is Max." The dog had finished and was sitting quietly at his master's feet. Michael gazed up at her. "I'm very sorry. Can I help you down?"

"Oh. Yes, please." She felt suddenly awkward, and reached down to take his hand. She climbed down off the table carefully, her skirt riding to mid-thigh, heels unsteady on the grass. They were suddenly eye to eye. He was not much taller than her, slim, in a white polo shirt tucked into faded jeans, a thin belt around his waist. His arms and hands were beautiful, she noticed, sculpted and strong-looking.

"I'm sorry," she said, smoothing her skirt. "I thought you were somebody else. You look just like Mickey Flynn."

He grinned sheepishly. "Yeah, that's me. Michael Flynn Carlucci. I was named for my Irish grandfather."

"I thought it was you. There's a life sized poster of you in my daughters' bedroom. Your hair was longer."

"Yeah." He ruffled his hair with his hand. "Well, it's the end if the tour. I can lose the look." He stuck his hands in his pockets. "Are you okay? I mean, he didn't get your hand or anything, did he?"

"What? No, no I'm fine. This is the most excitement I've had in a month. My daughters are never going to believe this." She stared at her hand. "They will never let me wash this hand again," she said solemnly.

Michael laughed again. His breathing was back to normal. Max yawned, and began sniffing the grass. "Are they fans?"

"Are you kidding? They've been trying to win tickets for weeks. Some contest going on. It's amazing how much trivia there is out there about you guys." She leaned toward him. "Do you know what your drummer's wife's maiden name is? I do."

He reached over and brushed something from her shoulder. "God, I hate those damn contests. Our publicist drives us all crazy. Do you want tickets? I could have some sent over."

Diane took a half step away from him. There seemed to be a heat radiating from him, an energy that she could feel.

"Really." His eyes were serious. "It's the least I can do." That grin again, sudden, a full blast of charm. "My dog stole your lunch."

"You can do that? Just get tickets?"

"Hey," he said with a cocky tilt of his head, "I'm in the band. Of course I can. How many daughters?"

"Three. But only two are home. Megan and Emily."

"How old?"

"Old? Sixteen and fourteen"

"My nieces are that age. Do yours travel in packs, too?"

Diane smiled. "Yeah."

He nodded. "Okay, so I'll send over tickets. Your daughters can each bring a couple of friends. You and your husband want to come?"

"I'm divorced."

"Okay, your date. I wouldn't expect you to take teenage girls to a concert unprotected."

"That would be wonderful." Diane was taken by surprise. "You have no idea what that would mean. They'd clean their rooms for months."

"No problem. Do you have a pen or something? Write down your address and I'll get them to you."

She turned and rummaged through her purse, dragging out a pen and note pad. She wrote her name, address and phone, and handed it to him.

"Diane Matthews," he read. He stuffed the paper into his pocket. "So, tell me, Diane Matthews, are you a fan, too?"

She opened her mouth to lie, then caught the glint in his eye. "No, actually, I'm not. Nothing personal - I happen to think you guys are really talented. I was a big Motown fan. I never liked rock and roll." She grinned. "Except, of course, the Beatles."

"Of course. So who was your favorite?"

"Paul. Naturally. I had his picture everywhere. I was devastated when he got married. I spent years obsessing over the fact that I was too young for him. Who knew I'd end up being too old for him?"

Michael laughed in delight. "God, that's great. I have to remember that for my sisters. They all loved Paul too."

"How many sisters?" Diane sat back on the picnic table top, propping her feet on the bench.

"Three, all older than me. The youngest was ten when I was born."

"You must have been spoiled rotten," Diane said. "I bet you had them all wrapped around your little fingers."

He sighed. "Oh, you are so right. I can't believe some of the things I got away with. They are such great women." His face changed. "My mother died when I was a kid. They all raised me."

"I'm so sorry. But I bet they loved it, raising you."

"Yeah." He nodded his head. "My oldest sister, Marie, she used to get so upset when people would mistake me for her son, instead of her brother. She would yell at them, you know? But when she got home, we would all laugh about it."

They were silent a moment, Diane staring at the tips of her shoes, and when she looked back over to him he was staring right at her, and she once again caught the force of his personality. A second later he shrugged and smiled.

"He's still living here, my dad, in the same house we all grew up in. It's great coming back."

Diane was surprised. "You're from here? I thought the band was from over in Hawthorn."

"The rest of the guys, yeah. But I was born and raised right here in West Milton."

"Wow. Did you go to Carver Mills High?"

"No. Fabian's." Fabian Academy was a very exclusive, private prep school. He noticed her raised eyebrows. "Before that it was Catholic school," he added, shrugging. "For all of us. Saint Kate's. Those nuns were ball-busters, I'll tell you."

"Me too. Catholic school, I mean. Not Saint Katherine's. I'm from Ohio, originally, but I think Catholic School nuns all come from the same planet."

Michael sat next to her on the picnic table. "Did you have a Sister Elizabeth Immaculatta?"

"No, but I had a Marie Celeste."

"Moustache?"

"One eyebrow and the mole on the chin."

"Yes, yes!" They were laughing again.

Diane cupped her chin in her palm and looked hard at him. "You're not what I expected in a rock and roll god."

"Ouch." He made a face. "Rock and roll god? Please. I'm a guy from Jersey who took piano lessons from a lady named Mrs. Foster and wore a uniform to school. I put together model cars."

"Oh, my God. You were a geek."

"Yes," he said grinning ruefully, "and you must swear to never tell."

"Might ruin your image?"

He snorted. "Are you kidding? I'd never get laid again." He glanced at her and shrugged. "Sorry. That was a very stupid, rock-and-roll-god kind of thing to say. Hey, would you like some lunch?"

"What?"

"Lunch. We could go to Weatherby's, it's right on the other side of the park."

"What about Max?" She looked down at the dog, who lifted his head at the sound of his name. Besides," she said, looking at her watch, "I have class in about an hour and a half."

"Well, that leaves Chickies." He slid off the table and looked at her expectantly. "It's close and we could eat outside. Are you hungry?"

Diane stared at him. "Are you serious?"

"Sure, why not? I owe you lunch."

His eyes were incredibly blue. Diane smiled.

"Lunch would be great."

They walked to a small, roadside stand that opened directly onto the highway. They sat at a round plastic table under an umbrella, eating hot dogs and fries, while Max wolfed down a few well-done hamburger patties.

"So, what do you teach?" Michael asked her.

Diane shook salt on her fries and looked at him suspiciously. "How do you know I teach?"

"Well, you have class, right? You're too well dressed to be a student."

"Hmm. How diplomatic of you. I teach at Dickerson. English. This afternoon I have two senior seminars, one in Eighteenth Century Drama and one in Contemporary American Theater."

"Wow." He looked impressed. "Nothing like a little light reading in the afternoon."

"It's great, actually. I love drama and theater, and the kids are really into it."

They started talking then, about books, then music, then traveling, which she loved and he hated. He was attentive, she was relaxed, and they laughed often. He had an animal vitality that she could feel as he leaned toward her, and he seemed to be listening closely to every word she said.

She looked at her watch. "Oh shit. I can't believe it's this late. I've got class." She began to pick up her empty paper cup.

"No, let me do this if you're late." He put his hand on top of hers to stop her. She froze. His skin was warm. She stared at his hand covering hers. She lifted her eyes and saw that he was watching her.

"Thank you for lunch," she said faintly. He seemed very close to her. He had not let go of her hand. "This was an unexpected pleasure, meeting you."

"Me too." He pulled back his hand. He was still looking at her. "About the concert - do you think you guys would want to come backstage after the show?"

"Are you kidding?" She blurted. "They'd be thrilled."

"Okay then. I'll see you next week." He stood, hands pushed back into his jeans' pockets, Max standing obediently at his side.

Diane nodded. "Thank you." She turned and walked away, back across the road to the park. She thought he would be staring after her, and she wanted to turn to see, but she kept going, got into her car, and did not see him standing perfectly still, watching her drive away.

CHAPTER TWO

She found herself slightly unnerved by the incident, and was distracted and moody during class. Her Tuesday seminars were usually lively and enjoyable, but not today. After assuring yet another student that she was feeling fine, just thrown off balance by being late, she started for home. The girls would already be there, waiting for her, starting dinner. She wasn't going to say anything about what happened, she decided. He probably wouldn't send the tickets anyway. He had a million other things to do, and she didn't want to get the girls' hopes up.

She entered the house and could smell garlic. Good. She was starving. Maybe that was what was wrong with her.

"Hey, whatcha cooking? I'm famished."

"Lemon chicken," Emily called from the kitchen. "With noodles. There's something here for you."

Diane walked back to the kitchen. Emily was there, stirring something in a frying pan. Megan was diligently dipping chicken breasts into egg and bread crumbs.

"What are you talking about?" Diane asked, giving Megan a quick hug.

"Some guy dropped this off," said Emily handing over a large manila envelope. Diane opened the clasp and emptied the contents onto the counter. There was a long white envelope and a number of white badges on black cords. She fumbled in her purse to find her glasses. She picked up a badge. Fleet Bank Arena Guest Pass. She turned it over. The NinetySeven logo. Double Dutch Tour.

"What is it?" Emily asked. "Did we win the lottery?"

"No." Diane said in amazement. "Tickets to the concert, and back-stage passes."

The girls both screamed. Megan grabbed the badge from Diane's hand.

"Mom, how did this happen? Did you win the radio contest?"

"No." Diane had opened the envelope. "I met Mickey Flynn in the park." There were eight tickets inside, and a note on plain white paper. Emily read over her mother's shoulder.

"Hey Diane, here are tickets and passes. Show your stubs to security and they will take you up to the VIP section. You should ask them to escort you back stage as well. Things get crazy after the show and I'd hate for you to be wandering around in all that madness. Michael." Emily clutched the note in both hands. "Oh, Mom, eight tickets? Can I ask Allie? And Chloe? And Jordan?"

"You may each ask the Griffen girls and one other friend." They both ran out of the kitchen, shrieking. "When you call Allie or Becca, I want to talk to Sue," Diane called after them. She stood in her small, warm kitchen, smiling to herself, the black mood gone. She took a deep breath, pulled off her jacket and turned to the chicken, abandoned on the counter. He had done it.

She nodded her head to some unseen melody, sliding the chicken into the olive oil, checking to see if the large pot of water was boiling. She began the automatic motions of coming home – into the bedroom to take off her shoes, on to the den to dump her books and briefcase, then back to the kitchen. She checked her pots and pulled dishes from the cabinet.

There was a clamor at the front door – Alison Griffen and her sister Rebecca were calling, running upstairs. Moments later, Sue Griffen came into the kitchen. She was tiny, short and slender with wild dark curls shot with gray. She leaned her hip against the counter and picked up one of the badges.

"You got these tickets how?" she asked.

"I met Mickey Flynn in Bloomfield Park. Michael. His dog stole my pastrami sandwich. He felt bad and sent them over."

"His dog stole your pastrami?" Sue echoed. "Holy shit. Are you kidding?"

Diane giggled. "No. It was hysterical. I was laughing so hard I almost peed my pants."

There was more pounding of footsteps and all four girls crowded into the kitchen. Emily now had a serious look on her face.

"Mom, tell us everything that happened. You actually met him? Mickey?"

Diane turned down the heat under her dinner and took a breath. "Michael. I was having lunch in Bloomfield, over by the duck pond. He was there with his dog, which is huge, by the way, and the dog must have smelled my pastrami sandwich and raced over. I jumped up on the picnic table. The dog grabbed the sandwich from my hand. Michael was very sorry and offered the tickets as an apology. End of story."

The girls were staring at her, open-mouthed.

"Oh, Mrs. Matthews," Alison breathed. "Was he nice?"

"Yes, he was very nice. Charming." Diane leaned close in to Alison. "He had charisma."

Alison sighed and closed her eyes. "Charisma," she repeated. Her eyes flew open. "What was he wearing?"

Sue rolled her eyes and started to speak, but Diane looked thoughtful.

"Well, he had on jeans, and a white polo shirt, you know, the kind with buttons at the neck?" The girls were all staring, nodding. "And black sneakers, and his hair was cut short, not a buzz cut or anything, but short, and he had some kind of string bracelet thing on, and a silver chain around his neck. And a very expensive watch."

"Was he hot?" Alison asked.

"Allie!" Sue admonished.

Diane nodded. "Very hot."

"Mom," Emily sighed.

"What? He was hot. Not very tall, but adorable." She leaned into Alison again. "Great butt."

"Oh, Mrs. Matthews," Alison breathed.

"Okay ladies," Sue barked, "we're outta here in ten. Make your phone calls."

They swarmed out, all talking excitedly, and Sue raised her eyebrows.

"Great butt?"

Diane nodded. "Oh, yeah. His jeans weren't tight or anything, but you could tell, you know?" Diane flashed a grin at her friend. "Nice arms, too."

Sue looked at her closely. "You seem to have remembered this in great detail."

"Hey, how often do I get to meet such a cute young guy?"

Sue looked at her sternly. "You teach at a college, Diane. Don't you see cute young guys all the time? Like, in your class?"

Diane shook her head emphatically. "None of my students ever looked like him."

Sue burst out laughing. "Oh God, you fell for him!"

Diane returned to the stove. "He was sweet. If I weren't old enough to be his mother, I'd say yeah, I fell for him. So, want to come with me? Friday night? I am going to need help keeping these girls on a leash."

"Sure, I'd love to go, but I think you need a date, maybe with a real man? When was the last time you saw a little action, anyway?"

"I had a perfectly nice dinner with a perfectly nice dentist a month ago and he never called back. You know I can never manage to get past a third date." Diane glanced over her shoulder. "Please? We'll get to go backstage."

"Sure, I'll go. I used to be quite the groupie."

"I never was, but I figure I'm scoring big with my kids, especially Em. It'll be nice to be the Mom that got her backstage, instead of the Mom who can't do anything right."

"I hear you there. You seem terribly pleased with the whole thing. You haven't stopped smiling since I got here."

"Because I didn't expect him to come through with the tickets, and I've been kind of beating myself up all afternoon thinking he was going to flake out. It's nice to meet somebody who does what they say they're going to do."

Sue moved closer and leaned back against the counter. "Did you have, like, a real conversation?"

"Yeah, we did. A lot of conversation." She looked to make sure the girls were still upstairs. "We had lunch."

"He bought you lunch? Wow. Where?"

"Chickies."

Sue snorted. "Oh, you're kidding!"

"He wanted to go to Weatherby's, but I had class, and there was the dog. So we sat outside at Chickies. It was fun."

"What a cool thing to happen. And now we can all stop listening to that god-damned radio station." She stepped back into the hall. "Griffen kids, let's go." She yelled, then winked at Diane. "Way to go, kiddo."

After Sue left, Diane finished making dinner, calling down her daughters. They set the table, noisy, happy. Emily actually gave her a hug and a thank you. The meal was eaten quickly, and the girls cleaned up as Diane went back into the den, laying out her books, getting ready for the work ahead for the night. Finals were coming up, and she had lots of prep work to do. She would have to call Kevin about the concert.

"Kev, hi, it's me. How are things?"

"Good. Victoria is a little out of sorts, but that's expected. What's up?"

"Believe it or not, we have tickets for the concert next Friday night."

"Good Lord, Di, how did you manage that? Emily must be ecstatic."

"Yes, as a matter of fact, she is. Is it any problem?"

"Oh, of course not. Victoria will enjoy a quiet Friday evening. We may even go out. Are they around?"

"Sure. Hold on." Diane called upstairs, waited to hear the upstairs line pick up, then sat down to work. She accomplished quite a bit, her mind very clear. The girls said goodnight at ten, and she settled herself into the couch and began proofreading the freshmen final. When the phone rang, she was startled. The girls' friends knew not to call this late.

"Hello?"

"Hi. Is Diane there?"

She recognized his voice. "It's me."

"It's Michael. Did you get everything okay? Dave said he sent a packet over."

She sat up, feeling herself starting to smile again. "Yes, we got it. I can't tell you how excited they are. You have scored major points here. Seriously. If there's such a thing as the karma scale, you are way on the plus side. You can be miserable to the next ten people you meet, and you'll still be ahead. Thank you again."

He started laughing."Is there really a karma scale?"

"Oh, I haven't a clue. Maybe. But my daughters are grateful, and so am I."

"So, about the concert," Michael began, "you don't have to worry about any crazy shit backstage. We're pretty boring after a show, actually. We're generally too tired for anything more than a chicken wing and a beer."

"You're sure you won't mind us back there? I mean, these girls are going to ask for autographs and all that."

"Sure, that's fine. Look, it's part of the game. We love it, all of us. Besides, all the guys will have people there, it'll be fun."

"Okay. I'll see you then."

"Yes, unless you'd like to have dinner."

She felt suddenly off balance. "What do you mean, dinner?"

"Dinner. It's a meal. With food, plates and silverware. Sound familiar?"

She smiled. "Isn't that from a movie?"

"Probably. I'm usually not very glib. So, how about dinner? With me. Friday night?"

"Yes, that sounds great. No, wait. I have a meeting at six. I'm teaching a graduate class next year. I have to go, and it might run late." She chewed her lip. "I could meet you somewhere?"

"Sure. How about Marcos, about eight?"

"I love Marco's. But if I'm late, we'd lose the table."

"Don't worry. Friday then?"

"Yes."

"Good."

And she hung up, thinking that maybe she had fallen for him after all.

She did not tell anyone she had a dinner date with him. The girls certainly did not need to know. Sue Griffen casually mentioned her seeing a movie Friday night, but she begged off, using her meeting as an excuse.

The meeting ran long. Marianne Thomas kept pushing the other faculty members from other issues to Diane's problem, but it was a tough sell. When the room finally began to clear, Marianne sat by her friend as Diane began gathering her files into her briefcase.

"What the hell is wrong with these people?" Diane muttered to Marianne. "It's Friday night, for God's sake. Don't they have anything better to do than argue about copy paper?"

"Of course not," Marianne said mildly. 'They're academics. They don't have a life. Why would they agree to a Friday evening meeting in the first place if they had someplace else to be? You, on the other hand, have got a hot date."

Diane glanced at her friend. "And how can you tell that? Crystal ball?"

"You're wearing a silk pantsuit on a Friday. You look fabulous in that color, and you know it, and your perfume is fresh. I don't have fifty-two different degrees for nothing."

"Fifty-two?"

"Whatever. Where are you going?"

"Out to dinner."

"Anyone I know?"

"He's a musician."

"That's interesting. What kind of places does he play?"

"Oh, you know. Arenas, stadiums," Diane shrugged. "Madison Square Garden. I'm going to be late. See you Monday."

"I want details," Marianne called after her. "Serious details."

She was late after all. It was after eight-thirty when she walked in to the restaurant. It was packed, as always on a Friday night, and the bar was full of patrons waiting for a table. She looked for Michael, but could not see him seated in the dining area. Her shoulders slumped. She fought her way to the front desk, where the maitre'd looked up expectantly.

"I'm late. I was meeting somebody." She paused. Would he have made the reservation under Mickey Flynn? Maybe not. The maitre'd looked at her closely.

"Are you Diane?" he asked.

"Yes," she answered, surprised.

"Come," he said courteously, and led her through the bar.

Michael was sitting toward the back of the restaurant, at a small, corner table, an older man sitting across from him. They stood up as she approached, and Michael took her arm, kissing her lightly on the cheek.

"Hello. Diane, this is my uncle, Marco Carlucci."

Diane held out her hand with a smile. "Of course, I've often seen you here. I love your food." She turned to Michael. "A Grammy may be a big deal where you come from, but holding a table at Marco's on a Friday night? Now I'm impressed."

Michael grinned and Marco bowed and kissed her hand. "That is the ultimate compliment. Please," he held his chair for her and she sat down. "What would you like, my dear?"

Diane thought "Vodka martini please. Straight up, with an olive."

31

Marco nodded graciously. "I'll have it sent over. Michael usually trusts me with his meal, but would you like a menu?"

"No. I'll take my chances. I'm sure I'm in good hands."

"The best." Marco bowed again and turned to Michael. "Tell Denise my Noelle will call her, yes?" Michael nodded, and Marco gave him a hug. "It was a pleasure meeting you. I'll check in later," he said graciously to Diane, then left.

Michael sat down and smiled at Diane. "You look great." He was wearing jeans, a button-down blue shirt and a gray linen blazer. His eyes looked very blue.

Diane stared at him. She had tried not to think about him during the week, and she was struck with again how attractive he was, not just the strong lines of his face, but the energy and charm.

"Thanks," she replied, faintly. "I'm sorry I'm late. I was afraid things would get hairy. Academics are a pain in the ass to deal with." A drink was set down in front of her, and she murmured her thanks. She picked up her glass.

"What shall we drink to?" she asked.

Michael picked up his red wine. "How about being in good hands?"

They clinked glasses gently and she took a healthy gulp, feeling the vodka immediately take the edge off the vague, nervous feeling she had had all day.

She looked across the table at Michael. He was watching her, a faint smile on his lips. "So, you're Italian?" she asked.

He sounded slightly defensive. "Yeah."

"It's just that I am too, and I know that whole only son Italian thing. How the hell did you talk your father into letting you sing in a band?"

He chuckled. "It was a tough sell, believe me.

32

My sister Denise did the whole thing. That's how she became our manager."

"Okay, I'm confused. Your sister?"

"Sorry. I just assume sometimes – I mean –." He looked flustered. "It's just that there's been so much stuff written, and I've given so many interviews, well, I'm usually not talking to somebody who doesn't know my whole life story. That sounds really arrogant. I'm sorry."

"Don't apologize. I'm just not used to having dinner with famous personages."

He blushed faintly. "I'm not a famous - ." He saw the look on her face. "Okay. So, are you going to bust me all night? Can't we pretend I'm, say, a nice bus driver?"

"Like Ralph Kramden?" she asked.

"Who? No, wait, I know who he is. Okay, like Ralph Kramden."

"Fine, but if somebody asks for an autograph, I may get suspicious."

"Deal. So, what do you want to know? I'll be happy to tell you everything."

"I don't think I'm ready for everything, but tell me about your sister and the band."

"Okay. Denise is twelve years older than me. She's my middle sister, and the last to get married. She stayed home and took care of me and my Dad. My father was getting crazy, kept asking her why she wasn't married – well, you're Italian, you know – then one day she comes in with this guy, Dave Adamson, and says they're in love and want to get engaged. Well, my Dad is happy because Dave is an electrical engineer, and he'll always have a job, right?"

"Right - the first priority for an Italian father. The guy may have one eye and sleep with his sister, but as long as he's gainfully employed, he's a keeper."

"Exactly. So, right after this, Dad goes off on some business trip, Denise invites Dave over and I find out the real story. Dave was managing his brother Joey's band on the side, and what he really wanted was the band to be successful enough to quit his day job. Now, Dave had been telling Denise that the band was great, terrific potential, all that shit, but they needed a second vocalist and maybe a keyboard player. So Denise drags him over to our piano and makes me sit down and play for him. I'd been playing the piano for years, and I was really into the whole thing, writing and all sorts of shit, plus I played guitar and I'd been singing forever. Dave thinks she's crazy, till he hears me. So he calls Joey, Joey comes over with Seth, and we are just going to town. I mean, Joey's a big R&B fan, and so am I, and we were kicking serious ass. So Dave figures I'd fit right in."

"Wait a minute. What about the whole geek thing?"

"That was a problem. I was fifteen, but I looked about twelve. I was still really short, skinny, I wore glasses. It was awful."

Diane smiled. "Oh, God, I can just see it. The mild mannered Catholic schoolboy."

"Oh, big time. The rest of the band finally came over, we all got along great, but we couldn't figure out how to get me on stage without the audience laughing out loud."

"So, what? How did you do it?"

A waiter appeared with a basket of warm, fragrant bread. Michael broke off a piece and dipped it into a bowl of olive oil.

"Try this," he urged, "it's incredible." Diane followed his lead. It was delicious.

"You're trying to distract me with food," Diane said accusingly. "What did you do? A wig? A Nixon mask? Lifts in your shoes?"

"Close. We figured I'd just grow my hair really long so you couldn't see my face and I'd sit at the keyboards so no one would notice I was only three feet tall."

"Okay, that would work, but what about your Dad?"

"Well, he came home, and Denise told him the whole story, and of course, he freaked out. He's a lawyer, and he wanted me to go to law school, right? Plus, he doesn't want me around all the drugs and alcohol and everything else that went with rock-and-roll. But Denise said she'd make sure I kept up my grades, and she'd be with Dave at all our shows, and she promised my father that there would be no drugs or drinking."

"Wow. Isn't that why guys want to join a band in the first place?"

"Hell, that's why I wanted to join."

"So she went on the road with you?"

"Yeah. It was pretty bad for a while. She wouldn't let those guys do shit. No beer, pot, coke, nothing. She'd follow them into the men's room and flush stuff down the toilet."

"What a woman. So that just left sex, right?"

"No. Thanks to me, she cracked down on that too."

"Oh, Michael, what did you do?"

"I don't know you well enough for that story."

The waiter took away their plates and brought Diane another drink. She looked startled.

"What's wrong?" Michael asked.

"I usually don't have two of these," she explained. "I may end up dancing naked on the bar."

Michael grinned. "Then I'll ask Teddy to keep them coming."

Diane made a face. "You may live to regret it," she said taking a sip. "I tend to ask embarrassing questions when I've been drinking."

"Ask away. My life is pretty much an open book anyway."

"Okay." She took another long drink and sat back. She could feel a little buzz in the back of her head. "Do you like your life being an open book?"

"No," he said quickly. He shrugged. "I don't. But it's part of the package. You can't be somebody like me without having to put up with some bullshit. It's invasive. I love the fans, I really do, but I don't think they have a right to know every single thing about my life."

She finished her drink and felt her lips go numb. She looked at him carefully. His eyes were very blue. "Are you wearing contacts? I can't tell," she asked.

"No. Why?"

"You said you wore glasses."

"Oh, I did. I had laser surgery. Really amazing."

"Yeah?"

"Yep. A couple of years ago."

Diane tilted her head. "Do you get laid a lot?"

Michael blinked. "Excuse me?"

Diane was blushing furiously. "I can't believe I just asked you that. I am so sorry. See, I told you." She buried her face in her hands. "God," she muttered.

He was laughing. The waiter had returned, placing in front of them two salads.

"Diane," Michael said, "please, eat some salad. It looks terrific."

Diane dropped her hands and stared down at her dish. "I'm sorry."

"Don't be." Michael took a bite of salad. "I used to. Get laid a lot. It was amazing, after that first album. There were girls everywhere. I was only eighteen, and Denise stayed home, and Dave came on tour with us and man, all I had to do was point and smile. After a while, I started looking for more, ah, permanent relationships. But the women in this business, they just assumed that every date would end up in bed. I'd meet them for coffee and automatically stay to breakfast. I didn't even like some of them. Most of them." He shrugged. "Seth used to say there was no such thing as a wasted condom, but I don't know. It gets old. Finding somebody to go to bed with is easy. Finding someone to wake up with, now that's hard."

Diane lifted her fork and started eating. "So, how many times have you been in love?" she asked, looking up at him again.

He thought. "Three times. My first great love was Theresa Milano. She moved next door to us when I was in the third grade. She was in public school, and I was in Catholic school, but I was determined to make it work. I proposed to her half-way through the fourth grade, but she had become infatuated with a shortstop. She broke my heart. But we stayed friends. She's an intern now, at Columbia Medical School. I still see her."

"How sweet."

"There was an actress. We dated for about a year. Then I stopped touring and we lived together for six months. All that togetherness was a big mistake." He sipped more wine. "And then there was a week ago Tuesday."

Diane looked puzzled, then broke into a smile. "Oh?"

"Yes. I'd ask you to spend the rest of your life with me, but I have to go to Philadelphia tomorrow."

"Well, I'm crushed, of course, but I understand. Especially since I would never go to Philadelphia."

Michael smiled and shrugged. "That's what I figured." The salad plates were gone, and were replaced by bowls of steaming risotto.

"Oh, this is fantastic," Diane exclaimed. "So, do you have a show in Philly?"

"Yes, Sunday and Monday. We've got promos and interviews tomorrow. Seth likes to be there when they set up the equipment, even though our road manager has been doing it perfectly for years."

"Denise doesn't do that stuff anymore?"

"No. David oversees everything now. Denise is our lawyer. She takes care of contracts, investments - all that stuff."

"Good for her. This risotto is amazing. So the famous Marco and your father are brothers?"

"Yes. My father is the oldest of five brothers. They're all great men, all great success stories." Michael gestured with his fork. "Look, another drink," he said wickedly.

Diane pushed it firmly away. "No. I refuse to embarrass myself further."

"Does this mean no dancing? Oh, well. Now you tell me."

She looked puzzled. "Tell you what?"

"Well, let's start with how many times you've been in love."

Marco approached the table. "How is everything so far?" he asked.

"Oh, Mr. Carlucci, everything has been delicious. Really." Diane smiled happily.

Marco leaned in. "Would you like to try the veal?" he asked her. She nodded. He patted her hand. "It's perfect tonight. Just wait."

Diane sighed after he left. "I'm going to have to walk at least fifteen miles when we're done. I just know it."

"Okay. So, we'll walk. But now, how many times have you been in love?"

So she told him. And as she told him, and as they ate, she found herself leaning toward him more, watching him closely. Once or twice her hand accidentally touched his, and she felt a warm rush in her cheeks. She was smiling at the end of the evening, her hand propping her cheek, thinking she had probably said too much. The effects of the vodka had worn off, but she was still feeling light and absurdly happy.

They left around eleven, having thanked Marco, and they walked in the cool, spring evening, past darkened shop windows. They were shoulder to shoulder, not touching, still talking. She stopped in front of her car, and she leaned her back against the door, breathing deeply.

"I had a terrific night, Michael. Everything was just wonderful. Thank you."

Michael stood, hands in his pockets. "Me too. Listen, I won't be back until Tuesday, no, probably Wednesday, and things are going to be crazy. But I want to see you again."

Diane nodded. "I'll see you Friday night. We'll come backstage." She took a deep breath. She wanted to touch him. "I've got to go. It's late." She leaned over and quickly kissed his cheek, then turned, reaching to open the car door.

Michael put his hand on her shoulder and turned her back around, pulling her toward him. He kissed her, and his arms went around her, and when he let her go she was out of breath, blood drumming in her ears, her face flushed.

"I'm going now," she whispered. His face was very close and his lips brushed her cheeks, the corner of her mouth.

"Okay," he whispered back

She had been gripping the smooth fabric of his jacket, and she let go suddenly, smoothing out the wrinkles with her hands. She could feel him, still close, his hands against her back, hot against the cool silk of her blouse.

"Good night." Her voice was hoarse. She was looking into his eyes and she brought her hands up and into his hair, soft and thick, and they kissed again. She leaned forward, her whole length against him, feeling the slim strength of his body, and when she finally pulled away she had to take a deep breath, her eyes closed, as she pulled the world back into sharp focus.

"I have to go," she said softly.

"Yes. You mentioned that." He kissed her cheek, the soft spot below her ear, her neck.

She opened her eyes and took another breath. "Really. It's late."

"Okay." He cleared his throat and stepped away from her. "Good night."

She got into her car and drove away.

CHAPTER THREE

On Friday night, they piled into Sue Griffen's Suburban and inched their way into the parking lot of the Fleet Bank Arena. The younger girls had been in a frenzy all afternoon. They had arrived at Diane's house after school with armloads of outfits and spent hours screaming, laughing and arguing the merits of each article of clothing. Diane vetoed Megan once and Emily twice. She had no control over what the other girls wore, but her own daughters were not going anywhere in anything too tight or showing too much skin. Sue brought over boxes of pizza, and sent her own oldest daughter home to change. Diane chewed pizza, and put on jeans and a white tee shirt under a black leather blazer. She brushed her hair, refreshed her mascara and lipstick, and they were off.

She had gone on the Internet the night before and typed in the name of the band. The number of sites available shocked her. She read reviews. The first album eight years ago had been a stunning breakthrough, nominated for five Grammy Awards, winning two. The last album was considered their best yet. She read a few interviews. The band mates had nothing but respect and affection for each other, and there wasn't even a rumor of back-biting. There were sites dedicated to individual members, Joey Adamson having a large, rabid following of women who speculated in chat rooms about everything from the state of his marriage to the size of his penis. Seth Bascomb had been engaged six times to six different women. The Martone brothers, Monty and Phil, were happily married to sisters and their children were born three months apart.

The pages for Mickey Flynn were mostly divided between women of all ages who wanted to either knit him a sweater or have wild with him sex on stage. He

41

was also widely discussed as a songwriter, with a few fan sites devoted entirely to that aspect of his life. Although the band received credit as a group for all original material, Michael did most of the writing. Before he had joined them, the band had been called Mitchell Street, and they had been known as an R&B cover band. Once Michael came on board, and they began to play his original material, things had taken off.

The current tour was considered a financial and critical success. Their concerts were called old-fashioned block parties, with everyone up and rocking. The new material was well-received, but also included plenty of old favorites, and at the end of every show, Mickey Flynn would tell a story. It had apparently started when the band went on their first major tour. They had no material for a second encore, so Michael had gone out and told the crowd one of the funnier stories of the road, then sat down and played an old blues number that no one had ever heard of, but had received a standing ovation. After that, every concert ended with a story and a song from Mickey Flynn.

Diane had not seen a concert in years, and had never been to the Arena. She dutifully showed a red-shirted security guard her ticket and pass, and they were lead through the swarm to the center section, second row. The place was massive, the stage looming before them. Speakers were everywhere, a giant screen across the back of the stage. They had all gotten programs, and she bought her two daughters' tee shirts. She and Sue settled into folding seats, keeping an eye on their charges.

"We should have roped them all together," Sue said, directly into her ear, and Diane nodded with a grin. They could easily get lost in the vastness of the arena. She couldn't imagine how they were going to get backstage.

She heard someone calling her name, and turned to see another security person. He was very tall and broad, with several earrings and a ponytail. She stood up and moved to the end of the aisle.

"Are you Diane?" The guard yelled into her ear.

She nodded, and the guard stuck out his hand.

"Michael is worried you guys will take a look around and give up on coming backstage."

She shook his hand. It was huge. "I was thinking about that, actually."

"Yeah, well, don't worry. After the lights come up, just stay in your seats, okay? I'll come and get you. You follow me back."

"Thank you very much," she shouted.

"Thank Michael."

Sue looked at her, questioning, as she made her way back into the seat. When Diane explained what the guard had said, Sue lifted an eyebrow.

"That's pretty considerate of him, isn't it?" she asked.

Diane nodded. She had not told Sue about their dinner. She had not told anyone. She wasn't sure how to explain it, exactly. It was only a dinner, but he had been on her mind for a week, his smile, his kiss, and she was anxious about seeing him again. The arena was filled, the buzz of the crowd intense. The lights flickered. The screaming started, and the clapping in time. There was no opening act. The house lights went down, the stage blazed with light, and the band walked on.

The cheering was intense, a wave of sound that Diane could feel pressing behind her. Her own daughters were screaming, clapping. Diane stood with them, applauding, watching as Michael came on stage.

He was behind Seth Bascomb, a tall black man with a shaved, beautifully shaped head, in red leather

pants and a white silk shirt. Michael wore jeans and a
short-sleeved Sponge-Bob tee shirt. He walked up
steps to the keyboards, waving once to the audience.
Diane had been holding her breath. He had seemed
dwarfed by Seth, who was at least six feet tall. The
equipment seemed to loom around him. His head was
turned, speaking to Joey Adamson, who was settling
behind the sprawling set of drums.

Seth Bascomb was standing before the
microphone. He held up his arms and yelled, "It's great
to be home!" The crowd roared in response. Monty
Martone slipped the strap of his guitar over his head.
His brother, Phil, did the same with his bass. The
brothers were very much alike, slight, long blonde hair,
in jeans and open-necked shirts. Seth waited as the
crowd began to quiet down.

"Me and the boys are glad to be here. It's been a
bitch of a tour, but we promise tonight will be a blow-
out." The crowd started up again. Seth was grinning.
He looked back at Michael and said something.
Michael grinned in response and nodded. Joey
Adamson, long hair flying, began a tap on the drum.
Phil Martone picked up the beat. The keyboards began,
and Michael began to sing.

Diane had heard the music before, of course. All
three of the band's CD's had been copied to all
available iPods and other players. They even had their
own station on Pandora. She knew Michael's voice. It
was deep and pure. Seth Bascomb sang with him,
higher, a rock and roll voice, rough and sexy. The band
was all about good-time rock. The music was fast and
furious, heavily influenced by R&B. They played their
own music, of course, but covered Chuck Berry,
Credence Clearwater Revival,and Springsteen. The
crowd never sat down. They were up, dancing and
moving, hands clapping. Diane was amazed at the

quality of the sound. The performance was infused with drive and energy. Michael no longer appeared lost. The moment the music began, the blast of his personality blew across the stage and into every corner of the arena. She found, much to her surprise, that she was having a lot of fun.

There was camaraderie on stage that was a joy to watch. Seth was everywhere, sometimes playing rhythm guitar, singing solo, backing up Michael. He was the star, and everyone knew it, but Diane could not take her eyes off Michael. He seemed to be having a blast. More than that, he was obviously a serious musician who gave one hundred and ten percent of his talent to the audience.

Halfway through the concert, Seth stood before the mike, arms out, waving the audience to silence. Other members of the band drifted off-stage. Michael came back onstage with an electric guitar, and he and Seth did a few numbers together. Michael's playing was big and bluesy. His voice and Seth's melded beautifully. Then Michael walked offstage, and the Martone brothers came back. They did a number with Seth, a ballad, one of their biggest hits.

The second set began, Michael on guitar for most of the numbers. For their encore, Michael sat behind the keyboards and Seth sang "Great Balls of Fire", as well as one of the bands' first hits. Seth took a bow, and the stage lights went off, and Diane could hear the crowd chanting. The stage remained dark, but no one moved from their seats.

Diane looked expectantly up at the stage. She could hear the crowd more clearly now. *Tell a story. Tell a story.*

A single spotlight lit center stage and Michael stood alone. He had changed to a plaid, button down shirt, and sweat was pouring down his chest, fabric clinging to his body. He put his hands in his front pockets and said into the mike, "I've got a four year old niece who says the same thing every time I see her."

Laughter, and then the crowd got quiet.

"Well, tonight I've got two new stories for you." There was a burst of applause. Michael grinned. "That's what you get for being the hometown crowd." The applause rolled again, died down. "I'll start with Max. I have a dog named Max. We never figured out what he was, exactly. We think part Irish wolfhound and part Alaskan brown bear. He was a gift from this woman I knew for a while."

"Gretchen Miles," someone yelled from the audience.

"Bitch," someone else yelled.

Michael shook his head. "Man, you guys are harsh." More laughter. "Anyway, the only real people food Max ever ate was pastrami, because my niece fed him about a half a pound of the stuff one afternoon." Diane took a quick intake of breath as the audience laughed. "And from that moment on he could smell pastrami from a mile away, and whenever he did he went crazy."

He took his hands out of his pockets to pull the front of his shirt away from his chest. "So, last week, I'm back home and I figure I'll take Max out to Bloomfield Park. I got the Frisbee, I got tennis balls, we're ready for anything, you know? So, we're on the ball field, the park is practically empty, we're having this great old time, and suddenly the wind shifts. Max freezes, and takes off like a shot and I know, man, I just know." He paused and dropped his voice. "Shhhiiiit. It's pastrami."

Diane sank lower into her seat as Sue hit her excitedly on the arm.

"So Max is flying, and I am pounding after him, and there's one, lone woman, sitting at a picnic table, eating a sandwich." Laughter. "I yell, 'he wants your sandwich', and the woman jumps up on the picnic table, and she sticks out her hand and Max leaps like a gazelle, gets the sandwich, and it's gone." The audience started to clap and cheer. Michael was shaking his head, one hand on his hip. "So I'm looking up at this woman." He got in closer to the mike, and dropped his voice again. "Sensational legs." Diane glanced over at Emily, who was open-mouthed. "And this great tattoo right above her ankle."

The crowd roared and hooted. Diane felt the blood drumming in her ears.

"Since she didn't say anything about suing me," Michael went on, "I bought her lunch and invited her to the show." He shaded his eyes and looked down at them. "Are you girls having a good time?"

Megan, Emily and all their friends shrieked and waved excitedly. Michael nodded.

"Good." He turned to the stage hand that had walked onstage with another microphone and an acoustic guitar. "Thanks, man." He slipped the guitar strap over his shoulder and adjusted the mike.

"Now I'm going to tell you all about my sisters. I have three, all older, and they were all into music, and I spent my whole childhood sneaking into one of their rooms, and listening to whatever they were listening to. That's how I began to love music. That's when I decided to make it a part of my life."

His voice had dropped, grown softer, and Diane could feel everyone leaning in, straining to hear.

"When I was five, I started taking piano lessons, because everyone in my house took piano lessons. But I wanted to play guitar. Angela, my youngest sister, was taking guitar lessons. I made a deal with my Dad

47

that I'd go to my piano lesson like a good little boy, if I could also go with Angela. So she took me along with her, I'd sit in the corner and listen, then we'd go home and practice together, and that's how I learned to play the guitar. Angela had this big, old Lennon-McCartney songbook, and we learned every song." The crowd burst into applause. As they quieted, he went on.

"My sisters all loved the Beatles, especially Paul. I would play and they would sing along. And that is just about as perfect a memory you could have." He had been looking down as he spoke, his hands folded over the curve of the guitar. He suddenly lifted his eyes and his smile went out across the audience. "I had forgotten. Diane with the sexy tattoo reminded me. I want to thank her for that. So this song is for the Carlucci girls, who are responsible for so many of the good things in my life."

He began to play 'And I Love Her.' Diane felt a rush of tears to her eyes, and she clamped her hand to her mouth. Michael's voice was deeper than Paul McCartney's had been, and he sang the words slower, not to a lover, but with gratitude and a touch of sadness. The guitar had a different touch, but still exquisite. When he was done he quietly said good night, and the stage went black, and a deafening roar went to the ceiling and Diane sat dumb, tears streaming down her cheeks.

The house lights went on suddenly, and Diane blinked against the brightness. She wiped tears off her face and turned to look at Sue.

Her friend shook her head. "Oh. My.God. You have just become a piece of NinetySeven history. The Web is going to be on fire with this."

Diane looked past Sue to Megan further down the row. She was talking excitedly with Becca and Joann.

Then Diane turned her head toward Emily. Her other daughter was staring at her.

People were beginning to move. She felt a tug on her sleeve. Megan was reaching over.

"Mom, are we going backstage?"

"Yes. Wait for the guy. Yes, we'll go." Her breathing was returning to normal. She fingered the pass around her neck. In minutes, the arena had become chaotic. She was being pushed, jostled. They waited ten, fifteen minutes. She saw the security guard waving to her. She and Sue herded the girls together, and they followed him as he shouldered effortlessly through the crowds. They went around to the side of the stage, then through a series of doors, until they were in a long corridor. There were people everywhere, all with passes dangling from their necks. They turned a corner, and there was Michael.

He was leaning against the wall, his head tilted back as he drank from a large bottle of water, a white towel draped across one shoulder. A man was standing beside him, talking intently. Michael pulled the water bottle away from his face and the water spilled over his face and neck. The man was still talking, but Michael was shaking his head, turning away from him. He caught sight of Diane. He smiled and wiped his face with the towel.

"Hey." His body seemed drained, his face white and pinched. "You all have fun?"

Diane took a deep breath, smiled and put her arm around Emily. "These are my daughters, Emily and Megan." Megan crowded against her mother's side

"Hello. I'm Michael," he said easily. They immediately started talking. They gushed about the show, the music. They introduced their friends. Sue Griffen stood quietly, watching her friend. Diane's

49

eyes never left Michael. He did not look at her, just concentrated on the young girls, flirting just a little. *He could really work a crowd,* Sue thought. It also seemed to her that he was very aware of Diane, and when he finally turned to her, their eyes met and Sue could feel a jolt. *Holy shit,* she thought to herself.

"Come on back." His voice was very light. "There are a bunch of people here, lots of food." He reached toward Diane, his hand catching her arm, sliding up to her shoulder. Sue pursed her lips. Michael moved his hand to the small of Diane's back, and they walked into a noisy, crowded room, people everywhere, and the smell of food. The girls bunched together, and Sue moved them toward a long table set against a back wall, laden with platters and steam trays.

Diane felt his hand on her back. She half turned toward him and rested her hand lightly against his chest.

"You look exhausted," she said softly. "Are you sure you want us here?"

His eyes focused on her sharply. "Yes, I want you here. What did you think of the show?" His eyes were very close and serious. His hand left her back, and he was running his fingers lightly down the back of her arm. Diane's hand went to the collar of his shirt, and she brushed her fingers across the smooth V of skin at his neck.

"You were fantastic. I never thought it would be so much fun." She broke into a grin. "The music was amazing, and you're a great storyteller, Michael.   And talking to Meg and Emily like that, it was very generous of you." She moved slightly, and now she was facing him squarely, their eyes level, and as she spoke, she pressed the palms of her hands against his chest, and she could feel the pounding of his heart, the heat of his skin through the damp fabric of his shirt.

"Generosity had nothing to do with it." His hand was under her blazer, resting on her hip. He pulled her closer. She touched his lower lip with her finger tip. It was full and very soft. He was smiling at her, looking tired and very young.

"I was scoring points. I figured if I did good, maybe I could see you sometime tomorrow."

Diane felt her heart start to race. "I would love to see you tomorrow."

"I've got some stuff to do, but I'll call." He had dropped his hands from her and put them into his front pockets. *Our faces were too close,* she thought. She didn't want her daughters to see. But she did not step away.

"I thought about you a lot this week," she said.

"I thought about you, too. Your friend Sue seems nice." Michael said. His breath warmed her ear and neck, and her hand plucked the front of his shirt. "So, no boyfriend?"

"No boyfriend. The men my age seem to want women who are, well, your age."

He laughed softly. "Then men your age are fools." He reached to brush the fall of bangs from her forehead. His fingers trailed through her hair, touching her cheek, and when she turned her head, he held the curve of her face in his hand.

Diane forced her hands at her sides and took a half-step away from him. He reached inside her blazer again, to pull her back to him, but she caught sight of someone, coming behind him, and stepped back quickly as a woman came up, smiling and holding out her hand.

"Hi, I'm Denise, Mike's sister. You must be Diane." She shook Diane's hand warmly. "He told us about you. God, I wish I could have seen it, that damn dog running you down. What a riot." She was attractive, friendly, and looked very much like Michael.

51

"I just met your friend and all the girls. Your daughters are lovely. Did you like the show?"

"It was great." Diane was grateful that her voice sounded so normal. She put her hands into the pockets of her blazer. "These guys are terrific."

"You bet. But we have you to thank for bringing down the house, and reducing all of us to tears. Mike usually doesn't get so sentimental on stage. Marie is still recovering." She kissed her brother. "Mike, be a good host, let her get something to eat." She turned back to Diane, shaking her head. "He's suffering from post-concert brain freeze. It happens every time. Come with me. Have some food. He'll get in gear in a few minutes." She took Diane's arm and drew her into the room.

Diane allowed herself to be led. She met Michael's oldest sister, Marie, who was close to her own age. She couldn't meet the other sister because, Denise explained, Angela was home with a sick little girl. Diane started shaking hands. There were husbands, and then cousins. Members of the band – Seth Bascomb, tall and smiling, Joey Adamson oozing charm as his blonde wife clung to his arm. Denise finally excused herself, asking Diane to stay as long as she liked. Diane thanked her. Sue came and stood beside her, and they tracked the six girls across the room as they moved like a small herd.

Diane kept glancing toward Michael. He spoke to everyone, smiling, and his vitality seemed to return. When he made his way to where Diane and Sue were standing, he was more relaxed. The man that had been with him in the hall came up, serious and impatient.

Michael sighed. "Ladies, I have to attend to Sammy here, or he'll stroke out and things will get ugly. Are you going to be around for a while?"

Diane shook her head. "It's after midnight now, and we've got to get going. Look, you have business to take care of. It was a wonderful night, really. Thank you so much."

Michael was looking at her, his eyes very still. He opened his mouth to speak, when Megan ran up, plowing into her mother, Becca and Joann giggling behind her.

"Mom, can we go backstage with that guy, the one in the green shirt?"

"No." Sue and Diane both answered at once.

"We've got to get going anyway," Sue said smoothly. "Come on girls, let's find the others. Diane, why don't we meet you out in the hall?" And she pushed the girls back, moving them directly into the puffing Sammy, who backed away to let them through.

"Can I call you tomorrow?" Michael asked quickly.

"Yes. Anytime. I'll be home all day."

"Okay." He was gone and Diane walked into the hallway to wait for Sue. She leaned back against the wall, her legs suddenly shaking. She could hear Emily's voice, loud, complaining. Why did they have to leave? Alison was arguing with her mother. But Sue led them all out into the hallway, turned on them sharply, and shushed them all.

"Okay, ladies, shut up now. You are six of the luckiest girls in West Milton and you should all be humble and grateful instead of whining and complaining. It's time to go. Now. Walk to the end of the hall and wait under the exit sign and not another word."

The girls looked shamefaced and filed silently away. Sue watched them for a moment then turned to Diane.

"Are you okay?"

"Of course. Why shouldn't I be?"

"You're still blushing." She looked at her friend thoughtfully. "Listen, what's going on with him?"

Diane lifted her shoulders. "Who?"

Sue looked disgusted. "Hey, it's me, okay? And I know fireworks when I see them. Shit, I was waiting for the two of you to rip your clothes off right there in front of everybody. No wonder his sister swooped in."

"Sue, you're ridiculous."

"You're not fooling me, kiddo."

"Did the girls notice?" Diane asked, concerned.

"No. There was too much else going on. Why would they want to look at old Mom?"

"Old Mom. Oh, God. Do you know how old he is?"

"Yeah. Good for you. Are you seeing him again?"

"He's going to call."

"I bet he is." She turned and walked back toward the girls.

They said very little after that. All during the long ride home, Sue hummed along with the radio, while Diane stared out the window into the darkness. She remembered feeling this way before, the powerful rush of wanting. She had stopped feeling that way about Kevin during those last years. She often wondered if the lack of desire had been the reason for the failure of her marriage, or if it had been the other way around. She had loved sex, reaching for her husband often. But it wasn't just the physical longing that had waned. As she had slipped from raging passion to quiet affection she had stopped wanting his conversation, caring about his day. They both loved the girls, but that had not been enough for her.

"Sue, are you still madly in love with Pete?" she asked quietly.

Sue glanced into the rearview mirror. "You mean do I still call him to come home for a nooner?"

Diane chuckled. "Yeah, I guess."

"Yes. I'm still madly in love with my husband. I still smile every time he walks into a room. I still touch him whenever I can. He's still the person I want to spend the most time with." She glanced over at Diane. "You didn't have that with Kevin, did you?"

"No. Not for a long time. I think I figured every marriage just kind of faded out to something else, like mine had."

"I can't imagine putting up with all the shit that being married and having kids means without feeling the way I do about Pete, even when he's part of the shit. He still makes me feel like a silly nineteen year old. When he gives me a certain look I get all wet and itchy. I figure it's God's reward for fighting the good fight, you know?"

"You're lucky."

"Pete and I are both lucky."

"Yes."

They drove a few more miles. The girls in the back were starting to quiet down. Diane turned and looked back into the van. Megan, Becca and Joann were all texting. The older girls, in the very back seats, were talking quietly together.

"We went out to dinner," Diane told her, her voice low. "Last week. Last Friday."

"Diane. You did? And you didn't even tell me? Did you have a good time?"

"I had a great time. He's smart and interesting to talk to. He had me laughing all night. And he's a terrific kisser. I swear, my knees buckled."

"Holy shit. I knew something was going on. This is so cool."

"Yeah, well it's all new to me. Did anything like this ever happen to you? Instant physical attraction?"

Sue smiled in the darkness. "Lust at first sight?"

"Yes. My whole body was all tingly, you know? And that good, achy hurt you get right in your, well, you know where."

"From just a kiss? Where were his hands?"

"Sue," Diane pleaded, "be serious. Please?"

"Okay. Yes, that exact same thing happened to me." Sue checked the rearview mirror again. "With Pete. We had a blind date, left before dessert, and spent three days in bed. And look how we turned out."

Diane closed her eyes and leaned her head back against the seat. All she could see was Michael's face, and hours later, as she tried to sleep, she could still feel his skin against hers.

CHAPTER FOUR

Michael Carlucci had always known he would be a star. His sisters had been telling him so since he was a baby, and they wouldn't lie to him. When he was eight, his mother died of cancer. She had been sick most of his life, and had always been a fragile, inconsistent presence in his life. He had loved his mother, worshipped his gentle, silent father, but he depended on his sisters for strength, confidence and support, and they had never failed him.

The year his mother died, his piano teacher told his grieving father that Michael's talent needed more guidance than she could provide. Marie found someone else, and Denise took the train to Manhattan with him every week for the next five years. Angela had already bought him a smaller-sized guitar, so his tiny hands could more comfortably reach around the neck. By then, her guitar instructor had taken Michael under his wing, and all the girls knew they had something special on their hands.

He had sat with them since he was old enough to toddle down the hallway into their bedrooms. At first, they thought it was cute, the way he remembered the words to every song they played on their stereo. Then they realized that he was not only singing the words, but remembered melodies and harmonies. His voice, for such a little boy, was huge. It was also always on key.

He was always the smallest kid in his class. The Catholic School bullies pursued him mercilessly, so he learned to be the toughest kid as well. He played piano in the concert band, made straight A's, collected model cars and waited for his sisters' dreams for him to come true.

Dave Adamson had stared at Denise in disbelief when she asked him to consider Michael for his brother Joey's band. Joey had put together Mitchell Street with his best friend Seth Bascomb, and they were starting to get something of a reputation in the wide open North Jersey club scene. But the band was just a cover band, and lacked the extra kick that could mean success. Besides, Denise Carlucci was beautiful and sexy and when they were in bed together, he couldn't say no to her. So, he agreed to listen to Michael. And he had been blown away.

Getting the band to accept Michael had been easy, once they heard him play and sing. Getting Anthony Carlucci to agree to let his underage son go on the road had been another story. But Denise had kept up her end of the bargain with her father. Michael's grades never dropped. He never had a beer with his band mates, never smoked a joint.

Three months after he began performing with the band, just days after he turned sixteen, a twenty-three year old fan followed Michael into the unisex bathroom in a bar in Ithaca, New York. As he came out of one of the stalls, she was waiting for him, bare breasted, and she pushed him back into the stall, gave him a blow job as he stood balanced up on the toilet seat, then left without saying a word. Denise came in moments later to find her sweet, beautiful little brother fumbling to zip his jeans while a hard-looking blonde rinsed her mouth out at the grimy sink. Denise never said a word to him. She never had to. One look at the disappointment on her face was enough for him. It didn't happen again.

Michael graduated high school the following year. He had been accepted to Princeton. He had been rejected by Julliard. The band was asked to go on tour with BonJovi. Anthony Carlucci traveled down to Princeton and received the personal word of the head of the Department of Mathematics that his son would be more than welcome the following year should he choose to take some time off to travel the country. So NinetySeven went on tour. Denise and Dave had married that spring, so Denise traveled with them while David continued to work at home and pay the bills.

When the band received an offer from PolyGram records, Michael told his father he wasn't going to Princeton after all. Michael had grown up, filled out, and was no longer a skinny awkward kid. His youthful confidence had grown to a real power. Everyone could see it, especially his father. Anthony took one look at the contract the band had been offered, tore it up, and drew up another that at least would assure his son a shot at some real money. Anthony then took all the savings that had been earmarked for his only sons' Ivy League education and offered to send Denise to law school, providing she specialized in entertainment and would look after her brothers' business affairs. Denise agreed, and after the release of the first album, Dave went out with the band on tour.

In six gleeful months, Michael tasted every formerly-forbidden fruit. Drugs did not appeal to him. He didn't like the feeling of being out of control, and worse, the loss of creativity. Too much alcohol made him physically sick. Women, however, had no distasteful side effects. With his beautiful blue eyes, blazing smile, and adorable face, he found himself drowning in them. He was careful, respectful, and considerate. He thought he had been in love a couple of times. But when he had looked into Diane Matthews' big, brown eyes, he knew he had lost his soul.

He couldn't believe how lovely she was. Not one of the usual beauties that drifted in and out of the vague world known as show business. Most of the women who had appealed to him until now had been model-thin, with translucent skin, straight, streaming hair and serious, intense eyes. Diane's skin was dark and warm, her hair thick and curling. She had smiled and laughed when she could have been shrill or severe. Her face was all ovals - large, bright eyes, full, smiling lips, high cheekbones. Her body round as well. When he held her, she was soft and yielding, no hard bones and angles. And her lips had been soft, sweet and warm. On top of all that, she was smart and funny. He could not get her out of his head.

Saturday morning after the concert, he started calling her at nine in the morning. No answer. He left a message, then tried calling again after fifteen minutes. An hour later he went to his computer, downloaded directions to her address, and was on his way. She had said she would see him. She had said she would be home. No point, he thought, in wasting the day.

Her house was in an older neighborhood, the streets lined with shade trees and brick sidewalks. He pulled into number 17, a white, expanded Cape Cod, with green shutters, and lots of daffodils blooming. The front door was closed. A Subaru wagon was in the driveway, and the garage door was open. She was home. He went up the walk and rang the bell. There was no answer, but he could hear music. He walked around the house, past the garage. A post and rail fence surrounded the back yard, and as he pushed through the gate, he could hear the faint jingle of a brass bell that was attached to the gate. It should have announced his coming into the yard, but the sound was drowned out by the music that blasted out of open French doors.

Diane was toward the rear of the yard, trying to dig up an oversized azalea bush. He could see she had already prepared a new hole for it, right beside a large, slate patio. She was dressed in overalls, faded and baggy, caked with dirt. She was wearing a sleeveless tee shirt underneath, and her hair was pulled up and off her face in a spiked ponytail. She had been working for a while, and had almost completely dug up the bush, but it was stuck, and as she strained to uproot it, he could see the muscles on her arms tighten from the strain. Sweat trickled down the side of her face, soaked the neck of her shirt. She pushed against the shovel with all her weight, grunting with the effort, but the bush did not move, and as her arms began to tremble she threw up her hands.

"Fuck," she said very loudly. Michael broke onto a grin.

She was wearing green canvas gloves, and she pulled them off and threw them down.

"Fuck." She turned away from the azalea bush, then walked back to it and tried to kick the shovel with her foot. She missed, and stumbled, off balance.

"Fuckfuckfuck."

Michael walked toward her. "Would you like some help with that?" he called, trying not to laugh.

She whirled and stared at him, her mouth open in surprise.

"Michael. God. Hi. What are you doing here?"

"I tried calling, but you weren't answering, so I thought I'd take a chance on just coming over. You said you'd be home."

The blood rushed to her cheeks. "Oh, right. My ex picked up the girls early, so I've been out here all morning. I can't hear the phone, especially with the music. I'm sorry. I should have brought out the cordless. I knew you were going to call." She wiped her hands against her thighs. "I was trying to keep busy. I didn't want to be hanging over the phone all day." She looked away from him, biting her lip

"Oh." He was watching her closely. When she looked back at him, he grinned. "So, do you want some help?"

"That would be so great. I was starting to get a little frustrated."

"So I heard."

She looked sheepish. "Not exactly appropriate language for an English professor, is it?"

"No, I thought it was perfectly appropriate. Do you have a pitchfork?"

"Yes." She walked back toward the house and picked up a pitchfork from off the grass. He took it from her, and plunged in into the moist dirt. He worked quickly, using his weight, and in a few minutes, the bush heaved and flopped sideways. He and Diane lifted it into a wheelbarrow, he took it over to the patio, and moved it into the new hole. He shoveled in dirt and she tamped it down, then she dragged over the hose.

"Thirsty?" she asked. He nodded, so she handed him the hose and went into the house. She turned off the music, and returned with a tray laden with two glasses and a tall pitcher. Michael buried the end of the hose into the base of the plant, and they sat down across from each other in two Adirondack chairs, drinking iced tea.

"Thank you, Michael. You just saved my whole morning."

"Always a pleasure to be of service. Is there anything else around here you need help with?"

"No." She spoke quickly and too loudly. She sipped tea. "No, thank you. Besides, you must have something more entertaining to do besides digging around in the dirt."

He made a face and looked at his watch. "Well, sometime today I'm supposed to be going over to my sister Angie's house. She's painting her den.

Whenever Angie decorates, she makes it a family affair. It wouldn't be so bad, but she jumps into these things without knowing what the hell she's doing, and then everyone starts giving advice, and by dinner there's at least one major meltdown." He shook his head and brushed loose dirt from his jeans. "It gets ugly."

"How can painting one room be so complicated?"

"Well, she wants to do stripes and something called a faux finish. She explained it in detail to me the other night, but I have no idea what she's talking about, and neither does anyone else."

"But that's easy, really. My dad was a painter. I worked with him every summer for years." She stopped and poured more tea. "I'd be happy to help."

"Really?" He sat up. "That would be fantastic. You have no idea. You wouldn't mind?"

"Hey, you just performed major surgery back here. I owe you."

"You don't owe me," he said quietly. They sat together in silence for a few minutes. She was suddenly aware of how she must look – no make-up, dirty, hair tumbling down the back of her neck. She drained her glass.

"Why don't you call your sister and ask if she minds me coming with you. And ask her if she has a three-foot level or a plumb line. We'll need those. But if she doesn't have them, I do."

"Okay. Sounds good." He followed her through the French doors into a cream-walled dining room. Wood gleamed and two watercolor landscapes hung on one wall. She stepped into the kitchen and handed him a cordless phone.

"Here. I'll wash my face and change real quick, okay?"

"Yeah." He watched her walk down the hall. It felt very quiet in her house, and he looked into a comfortable-looking living room, furnished in dark wood and rich browns and reds, with a brick fireplace, good art on the walls, and lots of plants. He dialed the phone.

Michael's sisters were all sitting in Angela Bellini's large, gleaming kitchen. Like Michael, they had their father's small and graceful frame and their mother's dark hair and piercing blue eyes. Unlike Michael, they also had her quick temper. Marie, the oldest at 43, was an ICU nurse and was used to averting any pending disasters. She was trying not to argue with Angela over plans for the next weekend. Angela had dug in her heels, so when the phone rang, and Angela answered hello, her voice was tight with anger.

"You've already started, haven't you?" Michael asked accusingly. "I bet you haven't even opened up a paint can, and you're fighting about something, right?"

"Michael? No, we're fine. Marie was just being the older sister. But you're right, we haven't started painting yet. We were waiting for you. We couldn't do a thing without you."

"That's a crock of shit, and you know it," Michael laughed. "The three of you will crowd me out in twenty minutes, just like you always do. But I want you to wait. I'm serious. I'm bringing somebody who knows about painting. She says it's easy and you need a three-foot level or a plumb line. Have you got those things?"

"She? Who's she?"

"Ang, concentrate. Ask Neil. A level or a plumb line."

Angela covered the mouthpiece of the phone. "He's bringing somebody. A woman," she whispered to her sisters. She walked over to the open sliding glass doors and shouted outside. "Neil, have we got a level or a plumb line?"

64

"Not here," came an answer, and she spoke back into the phone. "No, we haven't got those things. Who is she, Mike? Anyone we know?"

"She's a professional. Well, kind of. We'll bring the stuff ourselves, in about half an hour. Wait for us."

Angela hung up the phone and turned back to Marie. "Marie, did you hear me? He's bringing somebody."

"I heard you," Marie said calmly. She was reading a decorating magazine, slowly turning pages.

"It's just after eleven. Have you ever known Michael to even be awake at this hour, the day after a concert? He was probably up until five in the morning. You know what he's like."

"He's awake?" Denise narrowed her eyes. She was holding Molly, Angela's little girl. "What woman?"

"He says she knows how to paint." Angela said skeptically.

"Well, now, why would he lie about something like that?" Marie said mildly. She was reading the magazine. "Ang, this says equal parts paint and glaze. What were you saying about water?"

"I saw it on the H&G Network," Angela said. "But about this woman. What about the one from last night?"

Marie looked up from reading. "Her? Well, she seemed nice, but she was my age, Angie."

Denise set Molly down on the floor and leaned in toward her sisters. "I don't know how old she was, but there was something going on there. We're talking real heat. I stepped between them, and it was like walking into an oven."

Angela shrugged as Marie's two sons came in from outside and headed for the refrigerator. "Michael didn't say anything about how old she was," she said.

"How old who is?" asked Steve Tishman, Marie's husband. He had followed his sons into the house, and was helping pour soda for the boys. He gave his wife a quick look. "Who are you talking about?"

Marie sighed. "Michael is bringing someone over. Angie thinks it might be the woman we met last night, except that she's probably our age."

Steve shrugged. "Michael wouldn't care about that. Age, I mean. That stuff isn't important to him."

"Oh, Dad," protested his oldest son. "Uncle Mike only dates hot chicks."

"Hey you," ordered Marie, "don't say things like that, especially around your Uncle Mike. It's rude."

The boys went back outside. Steve leaned against the counter, next to his wife. "That woman last night? Diane? She seemed very nice. And attractive. You really think forty?"

"At least," said Marie.

"Well, she didn't look it," said Denise. "And she never took her eyes off him."

"Denise," Angela argued. "Maybe she has a thing for him. That I could understand. But the woman had teenage daughters with her. Why would he even bother with someone so much older? Remember Monique last year? Such a pretty little thing."

"Come on ladies." Steve looked at them all affectionately. "You have to remember that Mike has been a lover of older women his whole life. He may be tired of pretty little things."

Angela stirred her coffee. "He told me Diane was lovely, and she laughed like an angel."

Marie looked up. "He said that? When?"

"He called me last weekend. I guess it's the same Diane. He had dinner with her." Angela thought for a moment. "He said he had a great time with her."

"He said that?" Marie turned to Steve. "You have to talk to him."

"No, I don't. Leave your brother alone. He stopped needing advice on his love life a long time ago." Steve picked up paint samples off the counter. "Are you going blue or beige?"

"She still hasn't decided," Marie said dryly. "Apparently there's no rush, at least not until the expert arrives."

"Expert?" Steve looked around. "What expert?"

"The mystery woman," Marie explained, "is apparently some kind of paint maven."

"Speaking of experts, how's my husband doing out there?" Angela asked. Her husband was Nick Bellini, and he was an architect. They had purchased a redwood playground set for Molly and Jane the day before, and Nick was outside, sorting out all the pieces.

Steve shook his head. "There's a million parts to this thing and he's got to put each of them in numerical order. We won't be putting anything together 'till Tuesday. How do you live with him, anyway?" he asked Angela. She shrugged and made a face.

Steve sighed. "Maybe this woman can read Japanese?" he asked. "That would really help us out."

"Denise, did he say anything to you about Diane last night?" Angela asked. "Maybe you could talk to him. He listens to you."

"Yes, he does," Denise agreed. "He listens very carefully, and then he does exactly what he wants to do. He's been doing that since he was sixteen. Have you ever known him to change his mind on my account? Or anyone else's?"

"Well it's a good thing I have extra lasagna," Angela said.

Marie snorted. "You made two more trays. How much do you think she's going to eat?"

"I don't think Diane looked like a painter." Steve remarked.

"What does a painter look like anyway?" Angela asked.

"He was touching her." Denise said pointedly.

They were all silent. Michael was always careful of his behavior around women, and made sure he did nothing that could be misinterpreted.

"What kind of touching?" Angela asked slowly.

"You know. Touching. Hands on each other kind of touching." Denise looked smug. "I told you something was going on."

"Well, that's interesting," Marie conceded. "Anybody notice?"

"I don't know." Denise sighed. "I hope not. It wouldn't be good for him if fans thought he was hanging around the mother of a couple of teenagers."

"Is there a husband?" Steve asked.

"I don't know. God, I hope not." Denise looked worried. "That would be bad."

Just then Angela's older daughter Jane came running into the kitchen. "Uncle Mike is here," she shouted. Angela grabbed Molly's hand.

"I'll check her out," she declared firmly.

In their cavernous living room, Angela said to the two girls, "Go outside, both of you, and say hi to Uncle Mike."

The girls started screaming, headed out the door, and ran down the lawn to where Michael had parked his pick-up in the street.

"He's driving that old truck," Angela called out, watching from her picture window, "so I don't think he's worried about making a big impression." She watched as Diane got out of the truck.

"Well, she's got a great haircut," she said loudly enough for her sisters to hear, "and she's not one of those anorexic types he's usually with. She's not wearing those horrible hip-huggers."

"She used to wear those horrible hip-huggers herself," Marie observed wryly, as she got up from the kitchen stool and followed Steve and Denise. They crowded the window, watching Michael and Diane herd the little girls up to the house.

"It's Diane." Denise announced triumphantly.

"She looks familiar," Angela said slowly. "I know her."

"Really? From where?" Denise asked.

"I don't know." Angela frowned.

Angela opened the front door and kissed her brother. She looked at Diane.

"Oh my God," Angela burst out. "Dr. Matthews."

Michael looked at Diane and raised his eyebrows. "Doctor?"

Diane stared at Angela blankly for a second, then her mouth dropped open in recognition. "Dr. Bellini?"

Michael looked from one to the other. "Diane, I guess you know my sister Angela?"

"Yes, of course." Angela exclaimed. "Oh, it is such a small world."

Diane was shaking her head. "Michael, you should have told me your sister taught at Merriweather."

Michael shrugged. "How do you two know each other?"

"I was on the screening committee for her play." Angela explained.

"Play?" Michael looked at Diane in surprise. "You wrote a play?"

"Oh, it's wonderful," Angela gushed. "She wrote it, what, three years ago? In Sam's class, you know, Sam French, his class for writers. He was so impressed he did a reading workshop last year, and this year it's scheduled for when, Diane, October?"

"Yes." Diane felt herself blushing. "They're casting this summer." She looked around. Everyone was staring at her. "It's pretty exciting."

Michael had a half-smile on his lips. "That's fantastic," he said, and at the tone in his voice, all his sisters exchanged looks.

"So how is Rachel?" Angela asked. Angela had taught Diane's oldest daughter speech and diction when Rachel was in Merriweather's drama program.

"Oh, she's great - tending bar in a French restaurant in mid-town, taking a class at the New School, and doing some workshop downtown, a thirty-minute Shakespeare company, where they edit each play down to five characters and one hundred lines." Diane was shaking her head. "I'm dreading her first performance. I know I'll run out of the place screaming."

"Her daughter is a genius," Angela explained. "Seriously. Double major, in French and Drama, and she blew us all away."

"Yes, Rachel packs a punch, all right." Diane looked around. The women were all watching her carefully. She wondered what they were imagining between her and their younger brother. She felt suddenly uncomfortable.

Michael, as if sensing her mood, put his hand lightly on her shoulder. "Angie, where's Nick?"

Angela explained about the playground project in the back yard, and Michael brightened.

"Well, look, why don't I go out back and help? Ang, you don't really need me. Steve, you can use a hand, right?"

Angela fixed her eye on him. "You're related to me, not them. I'm the one who needs the help. Nick is an architect. I'm sure he'll figure it out."

"Nick designs airports," Michael explained to Diane. "I don't see how that qualifies him to put together a swing set."

Diane grinned as Steve shrugged helplessly. "We were hoping you'd bring somebody who could read Japanese," Steve said, "so at least we'd know what the instructions say."

Diane lifted her shoulders. "Sorry, I really can't help you there. I just know paint."

"Thanks for coming to help out," Angela said, smiling. "I've never done this sort of paint job before."

"No problem," Diane said, "It's really very simple. Just lots of prep work." She took the level from Michael. "This is all we need."

Angela took Diane by the arm. "Then let me show you my den," she said, leading Diane away.

Angela had the house built two years ago, a large contemporary on a quiet cul-de-sac. The long living room had become a dining room to accommodate a table for at least twenty-four. The original dining room had become a small, formal sitting area that was never used. Most of the living was done in the kitchen and family room, and in Neil's private domain. The media room, huge, with a plasma screen TV and assorted speakers, receivers, and other appendages.

Angela explained all this as she led Diane back to what Neil had called the office. Square, sunny, and tucked in the back of the house, she had envisioned a quiet haven. So far, all she had were white walls and half-unpacked boxes.

Diane surveyed the space. "What color were you thinking?"

"She hasn't decided yet," Marie informed her. "We're down to two choices, though. We expect a decision any minute now."

71

Angela waved Marie aside. "Here, take a look. What do you think?"

Diane looked at the two samples. "Well, the blue is pretty, but there might be a problem because your base color is very warm, almost cream. No cool tones. The beige would be better, softer, less contrast."

"How do you know this stuff?" Angela asked her.

"My father had his own business in Columbus. Ohio." Diane explained. "Paint, wallpaper, everything. He loved theater too, and he did a lot of work for the local playhouse, scenery and stuff. He learned most of the faux techniques while working on set design. I helped him every summer, from about the time I was thirteen 'till I got married and came out here."

"Is that what got you interested in theater?" Michael asked.

"Yes." She threw him a smile. "Angela, do you know how wide a stripe?"

"I figured about a foot."

Diane shook her head. "Do you have a tape measure? A foot is really not wide enough. You'll want something broader, since the room is large and the colors are so alike in tone."

Marie fished out a tape measure from a pile of tools and brushes in the middle of the floor, and Diane measured and explained to Angela and her sisters. Michael leaned against the doorjamb and watched her happily. She was beautiful, he decided. She had changed with surprising speed from her overalls to faded jeans and a blue-and-white striped tee shirt, and had brushed the dust from her glossy dark hair. Her face looked warm and flushed without make-up. Her eyes flashed as she pointed and explained. He felt the stirrings of desire, faint, familiar.

"Can I go now?" he called.

Marie, Angela and Denise all turned at the same time and said "No." Diane giggled.

"Come on," he pleaded. "There's a million dollars worth of higher education in this room. Can't you figure it out?"

"No, we can't," Angela said shortly. "We need the Princeton touch."

Diane's eyes popped open. "You went to Princeton?"

Michael was shaking his head. "No, I was accepted, but I never went. I wanted Julliard." He shrugged. "I can't see myself as a mathematician at this point, can you?"

"Math? Good Lord." Diane was dumbfounded. "Well, do you think you can figure out what the perimeter of this room is, and how many sixteen inch stripes we can get in here?"

"Sure." He reached for the pencil, and soon scrawled some numbers on the back of the paint sample. "Can I go play with the boys now?" he asked Angela.

His sister rolled her eyes and pushed him out of the room. Diane organized the women, and they were soon measuring and taping off their stripes, Angela carefully checking with the level. The women worked quickly, Diane mixing the glaze and paint, showing them how to work the dry brush. They all chatted non-stop. The sisters were all within ten years of Diane's age, and they found plenty to talk about. At one point, Neil Bellini slipped away from the back yard to check on the women, and returned smiling.

"They're all singing," he reported happily.

Michael was holding a cedar post as Steve was pouring cement around the base. "That's a good sign," he said.

"Yeah. Crosby, Stills and Nash. Apparently Diane is an alto, and they finally have somebody willing to do harmony."

Michael grinned. "Really? Very cool."

Steve Tishman worked his shovel into the cement, then leveled it quickly. "I'm supposed to be pumping you for information," he said to Michael. "You know your sisters. They want all the details." Steve was very fond of his brother-in-law. He and Neil both were. Michael was one of them, despite the fame and money. He attended birthdays, helped clean up after holidays, or, like today, helped put together swing sets. He bought lavish gifts for the families, but always asked before bestowing anything on one of the kids. Steve had been married to Marie for over nineteen years, and had helped the family raise Michael.

Michael looked up. "She's different from anyone I've ever met. Tell them that. It'll keep them buzzing for weeks."

"She's nice," Steve declared. "She was real friendly last night, and it was a zoo back there after the show. And her daughters were very polite. You can tell a lot about a person from their kids, you know."

Nick Bellini looked interested. "And she works at Dickerson? Watch out, Mike. Smart women are killers. Just ask us. We're married to your sisters. We know."

Michael started laughing as Dave Adamson walked into the back yard.

"Mike, got a minute?" he called.

Nick looked over. "Go on, Michael. We've got this." Michael went back into the house and sat at the kitchen table.

Dave was not as good-looking as his brother Joey, but he was still handsome. He sat down across from Michael, holding a large brown envelope.

"I've got everything here for Toronto," he said to Michael. "This looks like it could be very good for us." By 'us', Dave meant the band. "This director is top-notch. I don't know shit about film, but people who do know are impressed. Sammy did good."

"Sammy is a pain in my ass," Michael grumbled, taking the envelope from David and spilling the contents onto the coffee table. There was a fat script, tickets, and stray sheets covered with notes.

Sammy was Sam Adamson, Dave and Joey's younger brother. Sam wanted to put together a deal with Gordon Prescott, a brilliant theatrical director who occasionally turned out independent films. Sam had pitched Michael to score Prescott's next film, wrapping in Toronto, and Prescott had taken the bait. It was now up to Michael to visit the notoriously difficult director and make the sale.

"This is for when, tomorrow?" Michael shook his head. "Shit, Dave, I could have used a couple of days. I'm beat. You know what this fuckin' tour was like."

"It's a tight schedule, Mike. If you go for it, it's got to be done by December. Recording the soundtrack, the whole score, it'll be a bitch. If you want out, say so now." Dave was hunched forward, watching Michael. He had seen Michael with Diane the night before. He wondered if she could be a factor in Michael's reluctance.

"No, I'm in." Michael was putting everything back into the envelope. "I'll read the script on the plane tomorrow." He glanced briefly at Dave. "Don't say anything about this today, okay?"

Dave shrugged. "Sure, if you say so, but why not?"

Michael said slowly. "Diane is here. Remember her from last night? She's helping in the den. I don't want her to know. Not yet."

Dave sat back and nodded thoughtfully. "Sure."

CHAPTER FIVE

They were driving back to Diane's house, darkness closing in, cool air coming in through the open windows. Angela had insisted they stay for dinner, and it had been delicious - lasagna, salad, loaves of home-made garlic bread, and lots of wine. Diane had a wonderful time. His family was smart, opinionated, and argumentative, the kids noisy and cranky after a long day outside. Conversation ranged from film to politics to children and finally theater. Angela and Diane discussed her play as the kids all drifted away from the table, and the evening ended in a lively discussion of recent Broadway shows.

Now, Diane leaned back in Michaels' front seat. "Your sisters are all wonderful."

"Yes, they are." He glanced over at her. "Did you have a good time?"

"God, yes. The whole family is terrific." She had been drinking wine all evening, and felt relaxed and slightly giddy. "You are so lucky to have them."

"Yes, I know. I'm really blessed."

"I'm an only child. I always wanted to be part of a big family. I invented a baby brother when I was little."

"Really? What was his name?"

"Wallace. And he was blond."

"How long did he last?"

"Oh, he's still around," Diane starting to laugh. "Your sisters kept filling my wine glass."

"No, that was me," Michael said seriously. "I figured I'd take advantage of you later tonight.'

"Oh, you don't need wine for that," Diane said, still laughing. She stopped suddenly. "What time is it?"

"Just a little after nine."

77

"Oh." They were silent for a while. Diane turned in her seat. "So, Angela and Neil have the two little ones?"

Michael nodded. "Right."

"And Marie has four kids?" she asked.

"Yeah. You met the boys. They're still young enough to want to hang out. The older girls, well, they're at that age, you know? They're kind of anti-family now. They only show up if there are presents involved."

"Megan and Emily are the same. It's tough. And Denise?"

"She just spoils her nieces and nephews."

"I bet you do, too." He shook his head, and she started to laugh. "No, I bet you buy them stuff and take them places and drive their parents crazy."

"No, I don't, really. I've watched them, raising their kids. It's fuckin' hard. I don't want to make it any tougher, you know?"

"What a nice person you are," Diane said, suddenly serious. "Really. You're very sweet."

He glanced at her. They were silent as he pulled into her driveway. She was suddenly aware of the darkness, how near he was to her, the unspoken something that had hung in the air between them for hours.

"Want to come in? I could make some coffee."

They went into the house together, Diane turning on lights as they walked through the empty living room. She could feel him behind her. *He's waiting,* she thought. *He's waiting for me.*

She turned suddenly. They were face to face, and she could feel the heat from his body, and his eyes were endless, impossibly blue, and he leaned forward very gently and kissed her. She was trembling, and he kissed her again. This time she kissed him back, softly at first, then with a growing hunger, and her arms went around him, his waist, under the thin fabric of his shirt and pulling him toward her. His body was lean and hard, and she opened her mouth, and she could feel the smoothness of his skin against her hands. As his arms went around her, she made a small noise, like a sob, and then his hands were in her hair, and his lips were brushing her neck, soft, down her throat, a trail of kisses that shook her entire body. She brought her hands up, between them, gripping his shoulders and pushing against him abruptly.

"Stop."

He let her go, stepped back, and dropped his arms to his side. She pressed her hands against her forehead.

"I'm sorry," his breathing was strained. "I thought – I'm sorry."

"No. No, don't be sorry." He took a step toward her, hesitant, and she moved away. "I need to think. I can't think if you touch me."

He stepped back again, and she pointed. Her hand was shaking. "Sit. Please, sit down."

He obediently sat down in a wing chair, leaning forward, his elbows resting on his knees, hands clasped. He was watching her face.

"Okay." She brushed back her hair with one hand and took a deep breath. "I'm forty-five years old."

"I'm twenty-six."

"Exactly. Doesn't that bother you?"

He shook his head. "Not at all. I like being twenty-six."

She laughed shakily. "Michael, be serious. Doesn't it bother you that I'm nineteen years older than you?"

He shook his head again. "No. Would it bother you if I was nineteen years older?"

"Please, Michael," she pleaded, "don't try to confuse me with logic. It's not fair."

He laughed. "Okay. From now on, no more logic. I promise."

She took another breath. "I haven't had sex in over six years. Not since before my divorce."

"Whoa." He sat back in the chair. "Six years? Shit, nothing like a little pressure."

"Pressure?" She crossed her arms across her breast, hugging herself. "That's how much you know. The way I feel right now, the only foreplay I need is for you to unbutton your shirt."

His mouth twitched. "Oh."

"Don't you know how sexy you are? You should read some of your fan sites. I mean, I did, and boy, was I floored.' She began pacing up and down in front of him, hands flying around her face as she spoke. "But then I saw you on stage. I mean, my God, you're incredible. You've got all this talent and energy and I don't know what else, and you put it all out there. Shit, Michael, what a turn-on. No wonder all those women want you."

"That's what I do," he said softly. "It's my job. I love it, and I wouldn't trade it for the world. But it's only what I do. It's not who I am."

" I know," she said. She stopped and looked at him, eyes wide and dark. "If that was all this was about, I could just sleep with you and walk away. And believe me, I am so tempted right now. But I know that you are so much more than just that. And this right now, you and I, this is more. At least," she faltered, "at least I think it is. Unless you just want to get laid. Oh, shit." She covered her face with her hands. "That's it, right?" She dropped her hands and looked at him miserably. "You must think I'm a real idiot."

80

"No, that's not it. And I don't think you're an idiot." He spoke quietly, his eyes boring into hers. "I think you're one of the brightest people I've ever met. I love how passionate you are about things, your work, your kids, your whole life. You're funny and kind and I think you have the most beautiful eyes I've ever seen. When you smile, you break my heart. I think you're amazing."

She looked at him, his blue eyes, the dark, straight brow, the angle of his cheekbones. She knew the taste of him now, and desire came over her, filling her chest and throat. "This is happening very fast. I have to decide what I want to do."

He stood up. "Yeah, I know it's happening fast. And for the record, yes, I do want you. If there was a cave nearby, I'd knock you over the head and drag you there by your hair. That's all I've been thinking about." He had been walking toward her, and she had been backing away until her back hit the wall and she could go no further. He put his hands up, one on either side of her face, and leaned in. "I've been watching you all night, and every time you said something, or laughed, or smiled, or ate something, or drank something, I just wanted to touch you."

She had flattened herself against the wall, palms open, bracing herself. Her eyes were looking into his and she felt warm and dizzy, breathless, and there was a deep, heavy ache between her legs.

He whispered, his breath warm and soft on her hair. "I just want to touch you." His lips were on her cheek, soft and dry as he spoke. Her lips parted as she turned her head and found his mouth, and she closed her eyes and moved toward him.

A car door slammed outside in the driveway, and they heard the faint beep of a car alarm being set.

81

Michael straightened and backed away from Diane. Her hands flew to her cheeks and she drew a deep breath.

The front door banged open. Diane whirled, and her daughter Rachel came into the house.

"Hey, Mom." Rachel was tall, very slender, wearing a mini-skirt and a tight shirt with long flowing sleeves. She looked past her mother to Michael.

"Gee, Mom, I would have been happy with just an autograph, but this is good too." She held out her hand. "I'm Rachel. My sisters have been singing your praises all night."

Michael seemed very calm as he shook her hand. "Michael. Hello. I heard all about you as well. My sister is Angela Bellini."

"You're kidding? Dr. Bellini? She is such a nice woman. How is she?"

"Good." Michael answered easily.

"You had dinner with your dad?" Diane asked. Her voice sounded hoarse, and she cleared her throat.

"Yeah. I've been calling you all afternoon, but no answer." Rachel looked at her mother, then back at Michael.

"My fault," Michael said. "I roped her into helping my sister paint."

"Oh, Mom is so good at that," Rachel exclaimed. "She did a mural on my wall, when I was really little, in our old house, remember Mom? Winnie-the-Pooh. I just loved that room. She could make lots of extra money doing that kind of stuff."

"Well," Diane said, giving her daughter a hug, "now that you have a job that pays a living wage, I don't need to make extra money."

"Yeah, yeah." Rachel headed for the kitchen, dropping a handful of belongings in a heap on the coffee table. "Can I get a drink of something?"

"Sure, honey, go ahead." Diane watched her daughter leave the room, and then looked at Michael.

"I have to go," he said. "I've got to fly to Toronto tomorrow."

Diane nodded. "Rach," she called, "I'm walking Michael out, okay?"

They walked out to his truck, and he got in silently, slamming the door. He started the truck and sat, staring ahead. Diane leaned in through the open window.

"Your daughter is a knockout," Michael said.

"Yes, she is. Want me to fix you up?"

He chuckled. "She looks exactly like the last three women I went out with." He glanced at Diane, then looked away. "I think my tastes have changed."

Diane reached in and very carefully pushed a strand of hair from his forehead.

"How long will you be in Toronto?" She asked.

"I think until Wednesday. I may be writing a score for a movie up there."

"Oh, wow. What's the movie?"

"I don't really know. Do you know somebody named Prescott? He's a theater guy, I think."

"Gordon Prescott? I know who he is. He's supposed to be a genius. How exciting for you."

"This is a very exciting time. I've never done anything quite like this." His skin looked very white in the darkness, his eyes lost in the shadows of his face.

"I bet. Imagine, a movie."

"I'm not just talking about the movie," he said quietly.

Diane chewed her lip. "When will I see you?" She asked softly.

"We could have dinner. Thursday night."

Diane shook her head. "No. Megan has an awards thing Thursday. Girls' softball. How about Friday? The girls go with their father on Friday nights."

"Good. That would be good. What time?"

"They usually get picked up around six, so, what? Six-thirty?"

"Okay. I'll call you from Toronto."

"No." She shook her head. "I could use a little time, I think."

He nodded. "If you want to talk or anything, my sisters have my cell phone number. Ask one of them, okay?"

"Okay. I will. Have a good trip." She backed away from the truck as he pulled away. Diane took several deep breaths, then went back into the house.

Rachel was sitting on the couch, drinking orange juice, legs crossed. "Well, he seems very nice," she said conversationally. "He's adorable in person. His eyes are incredible. I wonder if he wears, you know, blue contact lenses."

"He doesn't," Diane replied, sinking into the couch. "All his sisters look just like him. The same blue eyes."

"Met the family, have we?" Rachel tilted her head as she looked at her mother.

Diane met her daughter's look. "Yes. I had dinner with them."

"And you met him, when? Two weeks ago? Not even. Emily told me the story. How cute. Something to tell the grandkids."

Diane leaned forward. "Why are you angry?" she asked gently.

"You just met him, Mom. I saw how the two of you were looking at each other when I came in. What's going on?"

Diane sat back. "Are you and Gary having sex?"

"You know what, Mom? That's none of your damn business," Rachel said hotly.

"Exactly."

Rachel's nostrils flared. "You're old enough to be his mother."

"Yes. He and I were just having that discussion. I don't think he cares all that much." She leaned forward again. "How is the workshop coming?"

Rachel shrugged. "We start performances in three weeks. Can you come out and see me?"

"In 'Slaughtered Shakespeare'? I'm not sure my heart can take it, but I'll try."

"How many tickets? Will you be bringing a date?"

"I'll bring your sisters." Diane chewed her lip. "Rachel, please don't say anything about Michael being here. Emily and Megan don't know."

Rachel shrugged again. "Sure, Mom. Your little secret is safe with me." She stood up and gathered her things, purse, sweater, a woven carry-all. "I just wanted to stop and say hello. I'm sorry if I interrupted something."

Diane stood with her. "No, honey, you didn't interrupt anything. And even if you did, it still would have been fine." She put her arms around her daughter. Rachel's body was tense, rigid.

"Drive safe, and call me, okay?"

Rachel kissed her mother on the cheek. "Okay, Mom. Good night."

Michael left her house with his mind racing. He didn't want to go home. It was too late to go back to Angela's. He reached for his cell phone, scanned through the memory, and hit the button for Mark. Mark Bender, his closest friend from high school.

Mark answered, and Michael could tell he was out somewhere from the noise and music in the background.

"Mark, man it's Michael. Where the hell are you?"

"Fuck, man, we're at Rollie's. Come, drink with us."

"Who's us?" Michael asked. He knew Rollie's, a bar in Hoboken, blocks from Marks apartment. Mark drank there when he knew he wouldn't be able to drive home.

"Well," Mark said slowly, "there's Brianne, and Laura, and a blonde who won't tell me her name. But if the great Mickey Flynn were here, I bet she would."

"Okay, man. But can I crash at your place? I need to be at the airport tomorrow at eight."

"In the morning? Jesus, Mike, I thought the tour was over."

"It is. Toronto is a different thing. I'll tell you later.I'll be there in thirty. Don't leave on me, okay

"Hey, we'll be here."

Michael hung up headed toward Hoboken. He thought about Diane as he drove. God, she was fantastic. Any woman who could hold her own among the Carlucci girls was a rare bird. His sisters were three of the smartest, toughest women he knew, and Diane had stayed right with them. She had even made them laugh. He didn't often compare the other women in his life to his sisters, simply because so few even came close. But Diane had bowled him over.

She was so sexy, dark, flashing eyes, that shy smile that blazed out unexpectedly. And he could not wait to get his hands on that body. She would be great in bed, he could tell. Smart women, he had found, usually were. She hadn't had sex in six years. *What is wrong with the men around here?* He thought. He couldn't believe she told him that. She must trust him. She must also want him. He felt a flicker of heat. He had been aroused all evening, just watching her, imagining.

She was forty-five. That didn't bother him. She certainly didn't look it. Or act it. She had three or four earrings in her left ear, a series of tiny hoops peeking through her hair. She wore a large, onyx ring on her hand, and gold chains around her wrist. She seemed as comfortable in her jeans and sneakers today as she had been in the sleek pant suit she had worn the previous week to dinner. A class act. Maybe that's why her age didn't faze him. He knew her strength, poise and grace were as much a part of her as her skin, earned through years of living. Too many women he had met in the past few years were slick and flashy, but without any substance. Diane was the real thing.

He drove past Rollie's, looking for a place to park his truck. It was a '99 pick-up, bought with the first check from the first CD NinetySeven recorded. He liked driving it because he didn't have to worry about it being stolen, scratched, or broken into. He parked on a side street and walked back to the bar. He felt grubby, his jeans blotched with dirt from working outside at Diane's, and later at his sister's. He had changed into another shirt, pulled from the duffel bag that was always stashed behind the front seat. He tried to scrape the mud off the side of his sneakers, then gave up. Rollie's was a neighborhood bar, low-key and casual, so he wasn't worried about not fitting in.

Mark was at the bar, leaning over a pretty young blonde woman. He saw Michael immediately, and waved him over. Michael took a deep breath. Mark was very drunk, Michael could tell by the silly grin on his friend's face.

"Mike, come 'ere, meet my beautiful friend. She didn't believe me, but I told her you'd be here. She's a big fan, aren't you, my beautiful friend?" Mark was good-looking, tall and muscular, with medium brown hair and brown eyes that were currently red-rimmed and un-focused. He had buried his face into the blonde's hair, but she was not paying attention. She was looking straight at Michael, and he felt a wave of anger as she licked her lips and leaned toward him, completely ignoring his friend behind her.

"Hey," he said, nodding his head briefly.

"Hey yourself," she answered, arching her brows. "I missed the show last night, but I listen to you all the time."

"Thanks. Hey, Mark. Man, how've you been?" Michael walked past the blonde and put his arm around Mark's shoulders.

Mark grinned sloppily. "Mike, glad you could make it." He put his mouth close to Michael's ear. "This one is for you, Mike. I saved her just for you."

"Thanks, Mark," Michael whispered back, "But not tonight, man, okay?"

Mark looked at the bar and picked up a half-empty glass, sipping it sloppily. The blonde had come around behind Michael and slid her arms around his waist. Michael sighed. He should have gone home. He was in no mood for this.

"Mark," he said, trying to ignore the girl as she pressed against him, "let's get out of here. I need to get an early plane tomorrow."

"That's right. You're going to Toronto. What the fuck is in Toronto?" Mark had finished his drink and was signaling the bartender, who was carefully ignoring him.

"A movie, Mark. I may be doing a movie." Michael tried to pull away from the blonde. His body was responding to her. Diane was still fresh in his mind, and this woman's touch was beginning to affect him. He gripped her left wrist and turned to her. "Please, not right now," he said to her softly.

Mark grabbed Michael and swung him back around. "A movie? A fuckin' movie? Jesus, Mike, can I be in your movie?"

Michael tried to maneuver his friend away from the bar. "It's not my movie, Mark. You ready to get home?"

The blonde slid between Michael and Mark. "Don't go yet," she said, smiling. She rubbed herself against him, and he felt an immediate erection. She felt it too.

"See, I knew you'd be happy to meet me," she purred, wrapping her arms around his neck.

Michael pulled her arms away. "Not now," he said again, louder, rudely. He grabbed Mark and pushed him ahead, through the crowd. He could hear her voice, shrill, following him outside. He and Mark started down the sidewalk, and she was right behind them.

"Hey, hey wait." She put herself in front of Michael again. "Your friend here said you were a nice guy. Come on, be nice to me. I'll be nice to you." She was stroking him through the rough denim of his jeans, and he suddenly thought how easy it would be, that she would probably fuck him in the front seat of his truck. He was rock-hard, and she kissed him, her tongue deep in his mouth.

Mark staggered against them, and the blonde shoved him angrily. Mark started yelling, and Michael grabbed him again, pushing him further away.

"Hey, I'm sorry, really," he called to her. "Listen, I'll be back here tomorrow, okay?" He hurried Mark along, praying she would not follow. When he glanced back, she was walking back into Rollie's. Michael sighed thankfully.

He walked them to Mark's apartment. Mark searched his pockets, dragged out a key, and they went up three flights to a sprawling loft studio. Mark worked on Wall Street, and made easily six figures a year. The rent on his apartment, overlooking the river and Manhattan beyond, was four thousand a month. Michael rolled his friend into a crumpled king-sized bed, then stripped, found a towel and took a long, steaming shower. He dried himself off and stretched out on Mark's sofa, looking out at the lights of New York. He was exhausted. He squinted at his watch, pushed a few buttons, and set the alarm. 5 o'clock. Even that would be pushing it. Was Toronto considered international? Would he need to be there even earlier? It didn't matter. As drained as his body was, he was wide awake. After an hour of tossing, he got up, threw his rumpled clothes back on, and drove to the airport. He went through security, checked in, and sat, reading Gordon Prescott's script, and thinking about Diane.

Diane spent the whole of Sunday working outside. It exhausted her, which is what she had hoped for. The large patch of ground where the azalea had been was going to be a rose garden, she had decided. Since the cutting down of the old maple last fall, she finally had an open, sunny spot in her yard. She cleared the smaller brush, transplanted the pachysandra, and worked bags of peat moss and compost into the soil. When Emily and Megan returned from their father's at seven that evening, her muscles hurt and she felt she could fall asleep standing upright.

She had had trouble sleeping the night before. She kept thinking about Michael. There was not a thing about him she did not find desirable. He was bright. He made her laugh. He was thoughtful and sensitive.

90

He was obviously crazy about his family. And when he kissed her, she wanted to tear all his clothes off. She hadn't felt that strong a physical attraction in a long time. She kept feeling his mouth against her skin, and she finally closed her eyes and rubbed her fingers between her legs until she brought herself to a quick, hard climax. Only then could she sleep.

The girls obviously quarreled at their father's, and it came home with them. Diane was not in the mood. She kept hearing them snipe at each other, and it set her teeth on edge. When Sue Griffen called and suggested a walk, she readily agreed, despite her aching legs. She shouted up to the girls where she was going, and walked outside. Sue was coming down the street, Sharon Ingoe beside her. Sharon was short and sturdy, with legs like tree trunks beneath her shorts, her gray hair cut short. She lived down the street from Diane and Sue, and had known them for years.

Sue waited until Diane got in step with them before she elbowed her friend.

"So? Did he call? Did you see him? Tell us. Sharon knows all about it. What happened?"

Diane gave them a sketchy version of the day before. She told them about Rachel. Her two friends listened without a word. When she was finished, they had walked several blocks, and were in the children's playground. Sue stopped at a bench and sat down, looking at Diane in amazement.

"Holy shit. You met his family and everything? And you have another date? I can't believe it." Sue grabbed Sharon's arm as the woman sat beside her. "And he's a doll. I mean it. His face is beautiful. And he's got the body of a little Greek god."

Sharon was puffing. "I know what he looks like. My Jack plays those guys 24/7."

Diane was walking back and forth in front of them.

91

"Diane, sit and speak." Sharon patted the bench beside her. "I need details." She turned at looked at Sue, saying excitedly, "This is just like Danielle Steele."

Sue shook her head. "Not quite. If this was Danielle Steel, he'd be much taller and Diane would be an exiled Bulgarian princess. But it's still pretty good."

"What about Rachel?" Diane looked at her two friends. "She's angry at me for some reason."

Sharon waved her hand. "Of course she is. She's been panting after the guy since she was what, fifteen? I remember the last time they gave a concert here. Rachel drove you crazy. She had Mickey Flynn posters everywhere. And he was just a cute kid then. Now he's older and sexy and paying attention to her mother."

Diane sat down between the two women. "But Rachel has been with Gary for over a year. They seem good together."

Sharon snorted. "So what? Me and Richie are good together, but if George Clooney wandered in and crooked his little finger in my direction, I'd be outta here."

Diane and Sue burst out laughing.

"That's not true," Diane protested. "You'd never leave Richie."

"Wanna bet? Besides, kids never get that their parents have a sex life. She figured you and Kevin did it three times then folded the tent."

"It's uncomfortable." Diane said. "I'm uncomfortable. I don't know what to do. What should I do?"

Sue smacked her friends' arm with her open hand. "Go for it. You're friggin' forty-five years old. How many more guys like him do you think you're going to meet?"

"But I'm happy with my life," Diane said, shaking her head. "You know I am, both of you. I am not looking for a man. So who do I meet? I mean, shit. He's gorgeous. Okay, so maybe not gorgeous, but, well, yummy."

Sharon looked at her suspiciously. "Yummy? Did he kiss you?"

"Yes," Diane said defiantly.

"Any tongue?"

Sue exploded into giggles and Diane blushed. "What is this, high school? Any tongue, my God. We're grown women here."

Sharon nodded seriously. "That's right, and this grown woman wants to know if there was any tongue."

Diane sat straight. "He's a great kisser."

"So, he got you horny, right?" Sharon prodded.

"Okay - yes. Happy?" Diane waved her hand in front of her face to cool her flaming cheeks.

Sharon was nodding. She was very serious. "That's good, Diane, because if nothing else, you really do need some sex." The women all laughed again.

"I know." Diane said ruefully. "I had a hard time sleeping last night. My imagination was getting a little crazy."

"Want my vibrator?" Sharon asked.

"Get out." Sue burst out. "You have a vibrator?"

"Hey, Richie's on the road a lot." Sharon gave Diane a wicked grin. "So, I guess you're a cougar now?"

"Oh, shit, why do women who go out with older men have to have a name like that? When it's the other way around, we don't call the men anything."

"Yes, we do," Sue said. "We call them lucky."

The women were laughing again, and they giggled and jostled the long way home.

93

CHAPTER SIX

Wednesday afternoon, Diane left the Dickerson campus and walked up the steps of Walter Mosley Hall, which housed the drama department of Franklin-Merriweather University. The building was only a few years old, across a beautiful courtyard from the Walter Mosley Theater. Walter Mosley had left several hundred million dollars for construction of the facility because, he said in his will, he had never been happier than when he worked the lights in the old Merriweather auditorium.

Sam French had arranged a meeting. There were sets and costumes to consider. A large cast had to be chosen over the summer. Rehearsals would begin mid-July. They would open in October and run eighteen performances, six weekends, through Thanksgiving. Diane was thrilled and terrified at the thought of seeing her words on a real stage.

The meeting went well. Everyone was excited and enthusiastic, but Diane was impatient for it to be over. Angela Bellini's office was at the end of the hallway, and Diane wanted to see if she was in. As everyone closed notebooks and laptops, Diane said a hasty good-bye and walked quickly from the conference room. Angela's door was second from the end. Diane could not tell if it was open until she was right there, and the door stood ajar. Diane knocked softly, heard a muffled "Come in," and pushed the door open.

Angela was at her desk, typing on her desktop. She glanced up, saw Diane, and smiled in surprise.

"Hi. Hold on just a sec." Angela continued typing and Diane sat down. Angela hit the save button, then swiveled her chair.

"What a surprise. I was wondering if maybe I would see you out this way. I heard Sam's got a bunch of meetings lined up. He's going crazy over this."

Diane nodded. "Yes, he is. I think he's more excited than I am. We were just down the hall. That's why I popped in."

"Well, great. I'm pleased to report I've actually unpacked a few books and bought an easy chair. Big steps for me. And we even got a swing hung up on Sunday, so both projects were very successful."

"Great. It was a lot of fun for me. Your family is terrific. You're lucky."

"Yes, we are. Very lucky. I'm just sorry you couldn't meet Dad. He left for Miami, a lawyers' conference. He's retired, but on some advisory board. He likes keeping busy." Angela crossed her legs. "Mike still in Toronto?"

"I think so, which is the other reason I stopped by. He said you could give me his cell number. Would you mind?" Diane kept her voice light, but her throat felt dry and tight.

"Sure." Angela reached for her cell phone and hit a few buttons. She jotted down the number on a post-it. Diane took it and slipped it into her purse. "So, you haven't heard from him?" Angela asked.

Diane looked at her levelly. "No. I asked him not to call."

"But now you've changed your mind?"

"Yes."

Angela looked thoughtfully out the window for a moment, then turned to Diane. "He's an old soul, Michael. My mother used to call him her little wise man. He has a remarkable capacity for being quiet. I know that sounds trite, but it's not. It's almost a Zen thing. When he's listening, or thinking, or trying to decide something, he becomes completely still. You

95

can barely see him breathing. He kind of turns inside himself. Even as a kid, he'd be racing around like a maniac one minute, then the next he'd be just sitting." Angela took a long breath, deciding. "Our mother died when he was eight. He never really knew her as a healthy woman. She got breast cancer when he was just three. There were surgeries and chemotherapy and trips to Mexico. Then it went to her liver. She died at home, and it was long and hard and very sad. That may have had something to do with it, his being that way, but I think he's just always had an inner strength, or maybe an inner peace, that he could draw on. He was always special, not just smart and cute, but a rare person. We all love him very much." She looked down at her desk. "We're all very protective of him." Angela carefully lined up a stack of papers. "We worry about him quite a bit."

"Are you worried about something specific? Diane asked carefully.

"Of course we are," Angela said patiently, looking up at Diane. "We all know why we love Michael. He's a remarkable man. He's a great brother. I've never met anybody quite like him. But someone like you, Diane, you're so different from the women who are usually around him, we're just wondering what the attraction could be, that's all."

"I see." Diane chewed her lip thoughtfully. "Has it ever occurred to you that I've never met anyone quite like him either, and maybe that's the attraction?"

Angela looked faintly surprised. "No, actually."

Diane stood up. "Michael and I have just met. Why don't we see what happens before we continue this discussion, okay?"

Angela nodded. "Good idea. Thank you."

Now Diane looked surprised. "For what?"

Angela shrugged. "Well, I'm not quite so worried now."

Diane smiled and left.

Diane spent all evening trying to decide what would be the best time to call Michael. She finally settled on 9:30, giving her a little over an hour to work before calling. She settled at her desk, proofreading her final exam questions, when the phone rang and it was Michael.

"Look, I'm sorry to call, I know you told me not to, but I just talked to Angie and she said you stopped by and got my number, so I figured you'd changed you mind and here I am. Is that okay?" He said it in a breathless rush, sounding very young.

"Yes, of course." Diane grinned happily. "So tell me all about Gordon Prescott."

Prescott was a maniac and a genius, he told her. There had been meetings, screenings, dailies and more meetings, with the producer, the man who would do the orchestration, the second choice to do the orchestration, the assistant director, all of the actors. It was madness. She sat, curled into the corner of the couch, Jasper on her lap. When they finally hung up, it was too late for her to do any work, but she didn't care. She spent Friday in a panic. Michael was picking her up at six-thirty. What if Kevin was late picking up the girls? She needed to shower and get ready. She didn't know what to wear. She felt fifteen.

"I'm a total mess," she said miserably to Marianne Thomas. "I can't believe I am being so pathetic."

Marianne looked at Diane. "Yes, I agree, you are being pathetic. But at least he's single. Remember Quinn Harris?"

"Oh, God," Diane said quickly. "Quinn." Quinn Harris had breezed onto the Franklin-Merriweather campus two years before, a visiting professor from London. He was England's most sought-after theatrical director, married to a talented and flamboyant English actress. He had been invited by Franklin-Merriweather to teach a Master class. Because Diane's play had just been embraced by Sam French, she had been invited to the cocktail party welcoming Quinn Harris. There had been an instant attraction. Quinn Harris was not conventionally handsome. Tall, slight, a few years older than Diane, he was soft-spoken man of intellect and quiet charm. He was as close to her ideal man as she could have imagined. They went out several times, and she found in him a kindred spirit. But he was married. She would not sleep with him. She had stopped seeing him.

"I always admired you for how you handled that whole thing," Marianne said, spearing a piece of chicken. The two women were having lunch. "A lot of women would not have cared about the wife."

Diane sighed and pushed around her pasta salad with her fork. "He would have broken my heart."

"He's divorced now," Marianne said.

"Yes, well, he told me the marriage was over." Diane shrugged. "What did you expect? They were both sleeping around like crazy."

"I don't know about that. He never went after anyone else after you froze him out, and believe me, plenty were trying."

Diane smiled. "Yes, he was something else." She took a deep breath. "Michael is something else too."

"So, are you perfect for each other? Are we talking happily ever after?"

"No, actually, we're not. Perfect for each other I mean. He hates traveling."

"Oh, no." Marianne stared at Diane. "But that's what you do best."

"I know. And he hates cities. And he wants to retire to Montana so he can live miles away from everybody."

"Well, don't take that too seriously. Didn't we all want that, at that age? I wanted to herd sheep in Wyoming, if I remember correctly. But I was young and stupid. I outgrew it." Marianne waved her hand. "So will he."

"He's apparently bought about five hundred acres somewhere outside Butte. He wants to ride horses and watch the sun set."

"Oh, how boring." Marianne looked at Diane closely. "This could seriously dampen the entire happily-ever-after aspect of this relationship."

Diane laughed. "I haven't looked that far ahead. I think he's a lot of fun, and I have the major hots for his body. Does that count as a relationship?"

"Close enough." Marianne looked fondly at her friend. "You look happy. Your whole face is lit up. You deserve somebody wonderful. So where are you going?"

"Dinner again. Last time, we went to Marco's."

"Well, at least he knows good food. So call Kevin, and tell him to get the girls at five. Shave all the critical places and not too much perfume. Some men are allergic."

"Thank you for the advice."

Marianne looked smug. "You're welcome. Make sure you have condoms. And make sure he feeds you first."

Diane buried her face in her hands and laughed out loud.

Kevin picked up the girls at five. A little after six, Diane called Sharon.

"Listen, Sharon, here's what I've got. Black pantsuit. Makes me look thin. The red jersey dress clings in the right spots, but it's sleeveless. Is it too cool for sleeveless? Or there's the old standby, that African print, you know the one. What do you think? Which one looks best?"

Sharon snorted. "Who the hell cares what they look like? Which one is the easiest to take off?"

Diane hung up and put on the red dress. She brushed her hair carefully. She put on one of her favorite CD's, classical and calming. Jasper sat on her bed, watching her put on earrings and make-up. She felt nervous. The condoms she had bought were in her top drawer, and she pushed them aside as she searched for pantyhose. When the doorbell rang, she was still barefoot.

She ran to open the door. Michael was wearing a beautifully pressed white button down shirt, sleeves carefully folded up, a narrow, red tie, jeans, and loafers.

"You look very neato. I'm glad to see you got something out of that expensive prep school you went to." she said.

He grinned. "I'm traveling incognito."

"Shouldn't you have a cashmere sweater draped around your shoulders?" she teased, as he came into the living room."

"It's in the car," he said seriously, "with my double-breasted navy blazer."

Diane laughed. "I've got to get shoes and stockings. I'll be right back."

"Okay."

Diane went back into the bedroom. The top of her closet was packed with shoeboxes. Diane knew the exact pair she wanted, the Nine West pumps, but as she tried to dislodge the box, she pulled too hard and a dozen boxes came spilling out of the closet. She covered her head with her hands, and let out an involuntary cry as the shoes tumbled down. She ducked for a moment as they all fell to the floor, then she looked down in dismay. There were shoes everywhere.

Michael burst into the room. "Are you okay? What happened?" He looked around and said, in a different tone, "What happened?"

"My shoes tried to commit suicide. They all jumped." She turned to him. "I'm sorry. I'll be ready in a sec."

She got down on her knees and began to pile the shoes together. Michael got down next to her. "Let me help you. Here." He put two shoes in a box.

Diane looked at him and shook her head. "No. These are two different shoes."

Michael sat, legs crossed Indian-style, and looked around him. "But they're all the same."

"No, they're different. See, this has a rounded toe. This one is squared off."

He picked up two more shoes. "They're all black. You have, what, ten pair of black shoes?"

Diane grabbed the shoes from his hand. "You're mocking me. I can tell."

"No." He picked up an empty box and handed it to her, controlling his laughter. "I would never do that. I grew up with three women. If nothing else, I learned that the relationship between a woman and her shoes is a sacred thing."

She looked at Michael. There was a half-smile on his face. His dark hair curled around his ear. His lashes were perfectly straight and very long. She touched his cheek and he turned to her. She kissed him very carefully, catching his lower lip in her teeth and pulling gently.

"I think I've made a decision," she said in a whisper.

"Yeah?" He was very close.

"Yeah."

"So," he said, his voice rough, "what do you want to do?"

"Everything." She kissed him, slow, teasing kisses, her hands on either side of his face. His arms went around her, drawing her to the floor. Her hair fell around his face and she kissed his cheek, neck, the hollow at the base of his throat. She pulled off his tie, and began to unbutton his shirt, her tongue hot against his smooth flesh. Her fingertips brushed him gently, thumbs against his nipples, and she heard an intake of breath, and felt him strain his body against the floor.

"Shit," she muttered. "Wait." She reached back and grabbed a condom out of her top drawer. She held it up before him, then pushed it into his palm. She pulled his shirttail from the waist of his jeans and unsnapped them in a flick of her thumb, pulling down the zipper. He lifted his hips as she eased them down and tossed them aside, then bent to take him into her mouth. He made a sound, soft, and he moved uncontrollably as she closed her lips around him, one hand running lightly across the tight muscles of his abdomen, the other stroking him, following the rise and fall of her mouth. His hips moved, imperceptibly at first, matching her rhythm, and he grew harder.

Diane flicked her tongue, delighted with the smell of him, inhaling deeply as she felt her own desire grow. He filled her mouth, not just the feel of his flesh, but the taste of him, sweet, and he made another sound, a low groan, and his legs moved, his hips rising faster. His hand grabbed her hair.

"Wait," he gasped. "Wait."

She lifted her head, hitched up her dress, and swung one leg over, straddling him. He sat up and pulled her to him, and his hands came up her legs, under her dress, pulling it over her head. His breath was ragged, and he pulled away her bra as she pressed herself against him, feeling him through the thin fabric of her panties. Her breasts felt tender, and when he put his mouth to her nipple, she whimpered. His hands were on her hips, holding her as she rubbed herself against him, feeling a rise, a swell of pleasure.

She had wrapped her legs around him and he moved, lifting her, then laid her down beneath him. She was gasping, eyes closed, her arms outstretched, fingers gripping the carpet, and he slid his hands under her panties, pulling them down, kissing hungrily her ankle, then the tender spot inside her knee, and the soft flesh of her thighs. She arched her back as she felt his tongue, and her eyes flew open.

"Oh, God," she whispered, and she tried to push her hips upward, but he held her down.

"Patience," he said softly, and she felt him again, tongue moving slowly, slowly, and each sweet touch brought from her a sound, deep and breathless. The blood pounded in her ears as she strained against him, and she could feel her climax building. She could hear her voice, pleading, please, please, and she came in a violent wave that took her breath as her body heaved away from him.

Her head was thrown back, and when she opened her eyes, his face was above her, and he kissed her cheeks, and then her mouth, deeply, and she could taste herself on his lips, and the salt of her tears. He was between her legs, and she rubbed his erection, hard against her belly. She reached down and guided him, and he entered her gently, her flesh still throbbing, and she lifted her body to meet his. Her legs curled around him, her hands running down his back, pressing him deeper. He was moving slowly, deliberately, looking into her eyes, and she felt too open, too vulnerable, but she could not look away from him. She felt his body quicken, and at the same time she felt something of the same begin in her again and she wrapped her legs tighter, pushing herself harder into him.

"Don't stop," she whispered. "Please, don't stop." His eyes darkened and his jaw clenched, she could feel all the muscles begin to strain, but he did not stop. He rose himself above her, watching her as she arched against him, and she came again, crying out, and as she pulled down his head, searching for his mouth, he came with a shudder, his own cry muffled.

He lay still against her. He was lightly built, almost delicate, all wiry muscle and lean flesh. When he tried to move, she tightened her arms, her legs, keeping him close.

"No," she whispered. "Not yet." He lifted his head and smiled at her, his body loose now and damp with sweat. The house was quiet, music playing softly from the living room, her breathing finally slowed. He lifted himself off her and rolled on his back, eyes closed, breathing deep.

Diane felt stunned. Every inch of her skin felt new and exquisitely tender. She stared at the ceiling, wishing she could find words, something to say to him, something clever and smart, so he would not know how shaken she was.

Michael rolled to his side, facing her, head propped on his hand. With one finger he outlined the line of her lips, swollen and red, and she bit his fingertip very softly, then kissed it. He brushed the damp hair from her face.

"What is that music?" he asked quietly.

She listened. "Vaughn Williams. It's called 'A Lark Ascending'."

"Pretty. Do you like classical music?"

"Sometimes. I like this. It helps me relax."

He was watching her. "You needed to relax tonight?"

Diane let out a slow breath. "I told you. I haven't done this in a while." She turned her head to look at him. "I was afraid I'd do something stupid."

"We did just fine."

She lay there, wanting to touch him again, just to feel the smoothness of his skin against her. She lifted her hand and he caught it, kissing her palm. She rolled to face him and kissed him again, without passion. He pulled her close, wrapping his leg around her. She lifted the thin silver chain that was around his neck.

"This is very beautiful."

"It was my mother's," he explained. "She bought it in Rome, along with a crucifix. She had it blessed by the Pope. I have the cross at home."

Diane heard a soft thump as Jasper leapt off the bed. He walked over and sat on the floor where their heads lay, almost touching, and began to purr.

"You have a cat," Michael said.

"Yes. This is Jasper."

"Was he watching?"

"Probably. Now he'll run out and report to all his cat friends."

"Tough room."

"Oh, I don't know," she said lightly. "I bet when you leave, all the cats in the neighborhood will be lined up outside, applauding."

He laughed softly and kissed the corner of her mouth.

"Are you hungry?" Diane asked.

"Yes. Where would you like to go?"

"I have food here." She sat up. "I'll be right back. Don't go anywhere." She walked across the hall and into the bathroom. She stared at herself in the mirror. Her cheeks were still flushed and blotchy, eyes faintly red. She sat down and urinated, the flesh between her legs achy and sore. She had the smell of him everywhere. She splashed cold water on her face and smoothed back her hair.

The bedroom was empty. She picked up her dress and pulled it over her naked body. He was in the kitchen. She watched him taking out eggs and cheese from the refrigerator. She crossed her arms over her breasts.

"If you can cook," she said seriously, "I may have to propose."

He threw her a smile. "I can make a great marinade for cooking anything out on a grill, and I make mashed potatoes that will take a year off your life from too much butter and cream. I also make perfect omelets. Cheese? Or would you prefer mushroom? You have a great kitchen. You must be serious about food."

"Yes, we're pretty serious about food around here. I have some ham. We could run a few slices under the broiler."

"Fantastic. Is that sourdough from Jimmy's up there? Great bread, just great."

He was standing in front of her stove, barefoot, jeans riding low, his shirt still open. She came up behind him and put her arms around his waist, looking over his shoulder. His movements were quick and efficient. He was cracking eggs into a large bowl, one-handed. She watched him for a minute, enjoying the feel of her hands on his skin, the play of the muscles in his back against her breasts.

"I'll set the table," she said. He nodded, and gave her a quick kiss before she stepped away from him.

She carried dishes into the dining room, set out cloth napkins from the sideboard. The table was a long oak farm table, the wood golden and softly gleaming. In the center of the table were a cluster of candles, each on a different candlestick, brass, copper, pewter. Diane collected them, one from each of the dozen countries she had visited. She lit them carefully, and the room bloomed with soft light. She went to change the music, a jazz station, and then closed the drapes of her living room window against the darkness.

The meal was wonderful. She ate slowly, listening to him as he spoke, laughing with him. After they cleared the table, she brought a bowl of grapes into the living room, and they drank cold white wine and sat on opposite ends of the coach, facing each other, backs propped against the arms of the couch, feet and legs intertwined. She talked about her marriage, the girls. He talked about the movie, about being a celebrity. She refilled the wine glasses and lit more candles. He watched her as she moved about the room, his body relaxed, and his eyes bright and intense.

"Would you like to go sailing tomorrow?" he asked her as she settled back into her corner.

"Sailing? You have a boat?"

"Yeah, a small one. It's fantastic - like flying."

"I bet. I'd love to go with you. Where?"

"We'll go to my place. Mendham."

"There's a lake in Mendham? I never knew that." She was surprised. She had been there often, antiquing. It was a small, wealthy community surrounded by woods and horse farms.

"Well, there's a lake where I live." He looked sheepish.

"You own a lake?" She asked carefully.

"Well, kind of. My neighbors and I do. There are four of us."

"Wow. Your own personal lake." She ate a fistful of grapes slowly.

"I didn't make any money until the second CD," Michael explained. "My Dad took one look at the check I got when it went platinum and told me it was time to move out of his house. I was twenty-one. A friend of his, a judge, was selling his place. My father and I drove out to Mendham and bought it. The house was a mess, so I knocked it down. Nick found an architect for me. We'd been to Japan on the first tour, and the buildings blew me away. So I had a house built, and a dock, and bought a boat 'cause I always wanted to sail."

"Who takes care of everything while you're on the road?"

"I have a guy, named Fred Chu. He was an old client of my father's. Immigration problems, I think. He looks after the house, feeds Max, and organizes all the other guys."

She raised an eyebrow. "Other guys?"

"Well, there's a guy for the yard, a guy who cleans the house, a guy who looks after the cars, a pool guy, and a boat guy." She had started to laugh, and he was shaking his head, laughing with her.

"I know, it sounds ridiculous. I mean, it's just me and the dog, right?"

"Man, being a rich celebrity really sucks, Michael."

"Oh, you know it." He put down his wine glass and began to crawl to her side of the couch. She spread her legs and he lay between them and kissed her, hard. She sank deeper into the couch, wrapping her legs around him, her arms creeping around his neck.

"Would you like to stay here tonight?" She asked.

"Yes. Absolutely. Although the original plan was to wine you and dine you, then take you to my place."

"You had a plan?"

"Of course. Waiting at home are three bottles of champagne and a closet full of rubbers."

"A whole closet full? Your recuperative powers must be impressive."

"Very. Someday I'll write a song about it."

"Wow. So, do you mind going to plan B?"

"Not at all. In fact," he said, the corner of his mouth curling into a smile, "I happen to have a toothbrush in my glove compartment."

She kissed his neck. "Really?"

"Yeah. I'm something of an optimist." His hands were back beneath her dress. He was kissing her as she began to move her hips against him."

"It would seem," he said softly, "that you aren't wearing anything under your dress."

"That's right," she said. "I'm something of an optimist too."

She began pulling his shirt away, tugging at his jeans, and she stopped and looked at him. "I do have a bed, you know," she told him.

"I know," he replied, kicking his jeans to the floor. "Don't worry, we'll get to it."

And they began again.

In the morning, they left the house early. There was a beautifully restored Volkswagen convertible bug sitting in Diane's driveway. She stared at it, delighted.

"This is yours?" she asked. "It's perfect. Can I drive?"

They put the top down, she slid behind the wheel and Michael found his cell phone in the back seat and began to check messages. They stopped for breakfast at a diner, then went back up Rt. 24, through Morristown, and on to Mendham. Michael talked on his cell phone, and Diane drove happily, the wind whipping her hair. He directed her off the main road, winding through quiet country, until she turned up a narrow drive, gently rising, with a grove of massive pines offering only a glimpse of a house set far back from the road.

Michael's house was long and low. She stopped the car before a tall, red, double doors and they got out.

"Your house is beautiful, Michael."

"Thanks. I really love it."

They walked into a low-ceilinged foyer that opened to a large, lofty space, glass walls opening to a pool and a stretch of blue water beyond. Diane caught her breath. It was beautiful, the room, with its stark, elegant furnishings, and the view, bright and glittering.

Max came bounding from somewhere, and Michael yelled loudly, "Fred, it's me." He looked at Diane. "Want the tour?" She nodded.

Beyond the living room was a dining area, equally quiet and gracious. The kitchen was a gleaming space of stainless steel and black, with a small, round gentleman Michael introduced as Fred, who bowed over Diane's hand and welcomed her. There were guest rooms and a large media room, and on the other side of the house, a small office, a vast studio, and Michael's bedroom, walled on two sides with glass, looking out over the lake and lush trees.

Michael led her back to the kitchen. "Fred, can we have lunch? Around one. Out on the dock?" He asked.

Fred smiled and nodded. "Very good cold crab. Salad. Good bread. White wine."

"Fantastic. Thank you." Michael led Diane out past the pool, down a beautifully manicured lawn to a small dock that stretched out into the water, with two weathered Adirondack chairs facing the water.

Diane had never been in a sailboat before, and he was patient, explaining what everything was and what it was used for. They practiced a few moves with the sail down, the boat simply rocking in the water. When they really got underway, Diane felt confident. They sailed around in small circles within the sight of his house. She was dressed in jeans and sneakers, and had worn a heavy sweatshirt on his advice. The wind was high and cold out on the water, but she found it exhilarating. They brought the boat back in and had lunch, sitting at a small table Fred had set up at the edge of the dock.

When they went out again, he took her past a curve of land and there was the rest of the lake, huge and glistening. They spent the next few hours racing across the water, Diane sailing the little boat by herself while Michael sat back and watched her. She caught him looking at her intently at one point, but when she questioned him, he just smiled.

"You look happy," he yelled as an explanation.

They returned to the house and went into the village for dinner, to a loud, lively place in the center of town, where their casual clothes and Diane's tousled hair did not matter. The staff was young and friendly, and they all knew Michael. Their waiter brought him a mug of beer without being asked. A waitress came over to chat, a young girl who Michael knew by name, and cast puzzled looks in Diane's direction. Afterwards, they drove back to his house, and made love on his huge bed, the windows open to the cool night air, the room flooded with moonlight and the scent of water.

They had breakfast the next morning outside on his terrace, looking out over the lake. Fred served them Eggs Benedict. Diane stared down at her plate and shook her head.

"This is incredible. Do you get this kind of thing every morning?"

"Nope." Michael poured coffee. "Fred must like you. I usually get half a grapefruit and stale Raisin Bran."

"You do not. This coffee is delicious, and fresh squeezed orange juice. God, I could get used to this." She spoke lightly, just chattering, stirring cream into her coffee cup, and she glanced at him and found him staring at her.

"What?" She glanced behind her. "What is it?"

He shook himself and looked down at his plate. "What should we do today?"

"I need to go home. I have work to do in my yard. I'm putting in a rose garden. Remember that azalea you helped me with? Well, that used to be under this huge tree that finally died, and last year I had it taken down and hauled away, so I finally have a sunny spot. I've always wanted roses. I've been planning and plotting all winter. I need to finish some heavy-duty soil turning today."

"Okay. I'll help you." He drank orange juice.

Diane put down her fork and stared at her half-eaten breakfast. "Thank you, but no, really. I want to do this by myself."

Michael ate thoughtfully, watching her face. She was still staring at her food.

"It's just that my Dad, he had this big self-reliance theory," she said, looking up at him. "He always said that if you relied too much on others, you would forget your own strength. So I like to do things alone."

"That must have been tough on Kevin when it came to raising the girls," Michael observed dryly.

"No. I know when to share." She picked her fork back up. "Kevin always was right in there, pitching in, and I always let him. It was important for them to have two good parents. He's still a great dad. It made me squirm a few times, but I got over it."

"Then why don't we have dinner tonight?"

Diane put her fork down and sat back again. "Please don't take this the wrong way, but I don't want Emily and Megan to know about this, about us. Not yet, anyway." She drank the coffee, trying to find words. Michael leaned forward, curious.

"A couple of years ago, I met someone who could have been, well, special, but he was married, so I backed away and that was that. But the girls had met him, and they loved him. He was just such a gentleman, you know, very old-world. He was from England. When I told the girls he wouldn't be back around, they were upset. I think Rachel had a little crush on him." She looked at Michael. He was cradling his steaming coffee, looking at her intently.

"I already know all three of them have a huge crush on you. Rachel was angry the other night. She's been madly in love with you since she was fifteen, and she walks in, and there you are with me. Not so good. And the other girls, I don't know." She shrugged and smiled ruefully. "You're not just some dopey guy Mom is going out with, you know? There are certain, well, extra problems here."

Michael nodded. "Yes, you're right. So when can I see you again?"

"Not next week. Next week is finals week, and I have to be at Dickerson every day. I'm sorry, but that's the way it is. My students need all the attention I can give them." Diane leaned forward, grabbing his arm and giving it a shake. "Please understand, if I have something that needs to be done, I don't allow any distractions. I have to stay focused. And I could not concentrate on some poor freshman worried about a final grade if I thought I would be seeing you. Please, Michael, Friday night. Okay?

Michael blew out through his mouth and looked out over the lake. "Are you always this tough?"

"Yes. This is how I live my life. This is what has worked for me for a long time now. I am not blowing you off, believe me. "

Michael grinned. "Yes, I know. Okay, how about this. I have a program on my computer inside. We'll plan out your garden, I'll take you home, and I'll call tomorrow."

"You have a landscaping program? Really? Oh, that is so great. Yes, let's go."

They spent an hour on his computer, Diane pointing and trying to explain as Michael patiently clicked and double-clicked. He printed out her design, and drove her home. He kissed her very hard, then backed out of her driveway. She stood there for a long time, watching where his car had turned down the road, before she went into the house.

CHAPTER SEVEN

Finals week was the worst Diane could remember. She had been a full-time professor for six years, and had thought she had learned to weather the storm, but this year was horrific. The students were complaining non-stop, with one junior in particular who left e-mail messages that ran pages long. Emily and Megan were usually respectful of the pressure Diane was under and left her alone, but Emily had been asked to the senior prom by a young man, and wanted to spend the entire weekend down the Jersey shore with a group of seniors. Diane had said no. The battle was on. Megan, usually quiet and easy-going, wanted to spend a semester in France the following spring. Diane could not afford it. Kevin was balking. Megan was raging.

Diane was tired, ill-tempered and running out of patience with everyone and everything. She had finals to grade, evaluations to write up, and Rachel was still acting cool towards her. Diane could not wait for the week to be over. She could not wait to see Michael.

By Thursday, she was pretty much at her wits' end. Then, Kevin called to say he was picking the girls up early, right after school on Friday. They were all going down to Long Beach Island to open up the shore house. She thanked him coolly, hung up the phone, and called Michael, telling him to meet her at four on Friday.

She got caught in a meeting Friday afternoon, then hit traffic. When she got home a sleek, silver car was parked in front of her house. A DeLorean. She walked around to the back of the house, and Michael was stretched out on a lounge chair, eyes closed. The faint jangle of the brass bell on her garden gate had not roused him. He seemed totally relaxed, dressed in jeans and a denim shirt. She watched him for a moment, still and quiet in the cool afternoon.

"Hey, is that your car out front?" she called, walking toward him.

He lifted his head and grinned. "Yeah - isn't it fantastic?"

"It was my dream car for years." He stood up and put both arms around her. She leaned against him with a sigh.

"This has been the worse week of my life. I'm so tired and miserable. I hate everybody." She pulled back her head to look at him, kissing him hard. "Except you. You are the only person I can stand to be with right now."

"Lucky for me. So, tell me what you need. A cold drink? Hot shower? Food? Sleep? Sex?"

"Yes. I need all that." She kissed him again, slower this time, and her body began to burn. She stepped away from him. "A drink first, I think. We'll go from there."

He followed her into the house, declined her offer of a vodka martini, and opened a beer. She was wound up, talking nervously as she mixed her drink. She had kicked off her shoes and was pacing around the living room while he sat and watched her silently, letting her ramble. She finished her drink quickly.

"Look, I need a shower. And I really need to eat. Do you feel like a steak? Kevin used to say that stress made me carnivorous."

"Sure. I'll call Longacre's and get a table for what, an hour?"

"Shit, it's almost six. I can't believe it's this late. We'll never get a table on a Friday night, not now."

"I'll call," he said soothingly. "We'll get a table. Shower. Change. Go."

She looked at him suspiciously. "Do you have an uncle at Longacre's too?"

He chuckled and shook his head. "No. But I'll use the name Mickey Flynn. That usually gets me what I want."

She tilted her head at him. "I bet it does. Do you do that often?"

He shrugged. "Not so much anymore. There's not a lot I want that badly."

"But tonight you want a table at Longacre's?"

"No. Tonight I want to make you happy."

"Oh." She chewed her lip. "You've already done that. I've had the week from hell, and I just kept thinking if I made it to Friday, I'd be with you and then everything would be all right again. You can't believe how glad I am to see you." She took a deep breath. "I need to shower now." She turned and walked down the hall.

She felt better after she stood under the steaming water, and some of the tension left her. She grabbed a towel and wrapped herself in it, and looked out of the bathroom, still dripping.

"Did you call? How much time do we have?"

He appeared in the hallway, and began walking toward her.

"We're in at seven. How long for you to get dressed?" he asked.

"In a pinch, ten minutes. Why?"

He was looking at her, her damp hair piled on top of her head, water glistening on her shoulders. "Perfect. Ten minutes to get dressed, ten minutes to get there. That means we've got about half an hour to spare."

"Half an hour?"

"Yeah." He reached for her, pulling off the towel. "That's just about enough time."

After dinner they walked up and down the streets of Milton, looking in shop windows, talking. Michael was stopped for an autograph by a bunch of teenage boys. He was friendly and gracious, answered their questions, but declined their offer to buy him coffee.

"Does this happen to you a lot?" she asked after the boys had moved on.

"No. I'm lucky. The only people who recognize me are the fans. It's not like I'm an actor, where thousands of people see my face on television or whatever. And here, the fans are cool. I'm the hometown kid. They tend to give me some space." He thought a moment about the woman at Rollie's, and felt a pang of guilt.

Diane had been watching him, and saw a flicker across his face. "What?" she asked.

He told her about the blonde, how she had come on to him so strongly. He told her about standing in the middle of Hoboken, with a stranger's arms around him, and how he thought about taking her into his truck for a quick release, knowing that all that the woman wanted anyway was to be able to tell her friends that she had fucked Mickey Flynn.

They found a café, still open, with a few tables on the sidewalk. Michael had another beer and Diane sipped white wine.

"So," Diane asked finally, "why didn't you?"

He shrugged. "I wasn't in the mood for generic sex," he said.

Diane raised an eyebrow. "Generic sex? As opposed to name brand sex? Did you just make that up?"

"No." He looked embarrassed. "I had just left you. I wanted you. I didn't want a substitute."

Diane felt herself grinning happily. "Oh."

He was silent for a minute. "Are you done with school?"

Diane shook her head. "No. I still have to post grades, evaluations, and finish reports, just paperwork. All my finals are done, thank God. I'll have to put in a few mornings next week to clean things up. Then I can work on my rose garden."

"Ah, yes, that impressive rectangle of dirt I was looking at this afternoon," Michael said, teasing.

She looked at him sternly. "It takes a lot of work to get good dirt. I can now actually begin to plant things. I can even set down the pavers, because the ground is perfectly even. Of course, it's supposed to rain tomorrow. I'm going to have the biggest mud puddle in the state."

"And the most beautifully prepared." He stood up. "Are you ready to head home?"

"Yes. Do you have a toothbrush in this car as well?"

"As a matter of fact, I do."

"So, would you care to stay at my place again?"

"I would love to stay at your place again."

"I have to finish grading exams tomorrow."

"Can I watch the Mets?"

"Sure. Then I could cook you dinner."

"That sounds great." He took her hand as they walked. "Do you want to sail again Sunday? Or we could go down to New Hope. I like walking around down there."

"New Hope? Really?"

"They have a couple of great places for old toys and collectables. My niece's birthday is coming up. She'll be fourteen. She likes all that retro stuff."

"That would be fun. But I've got to be home by six."

"Yes, Cinderella."

She spent Monday and Tuesday in her office. Michael called Tuesday night, just after nine.

"I'm ten minutes away. Can I see you?"

"Michael, the girls are here."

"So, they're upstairs, right? I'll sneak in the back door."

"Michael, I don't know."

"I miss you. Just for ten minutes, I swear."

"Ten?"

He chuckled. "Absolutely"

She lowered her voice. "I miss you, too."

"So, fifteen minutes. Twenty tops. Please?"

"Yes. Come around back."

She stared at the phone in her hand. He was coming over. Desire moved through her like a slow pulse, pounding in her chest, deep in her gut. She stood at the foot of the stairs. Both the upstairs doors were closed. She could hear the television faintly. She went to the French doors and opened them, walking out onto the patio. She sat in the darkness. She did not hear his car. She did not hear the bell at the back yard gate. He was suddenly there, walking out of the darkness, and she led him back into her bedroom, locking the door behind them. They fumbled with their clothes in the darkness, falling together onto the bed.

"Is this our first quickie?" She whispered finally, feeling the red tide of pleasure wash through.

"I guess. How was it?"

"Pretty amazing."

"Yeah. The best ninety seconds of the day."

She covered her mouth to stifle her giggle. "Don't make me laugh," she whispered furiously.

"I'm sorry," he whispered back.

"I have to work tomorrow. Are you busy Thursday?"

"I have to go to Kennedy Airport. Seth and I are picking up a guy, David Go. He's from Ireland. He's orchestrating the movie."

"Then I won't see you?"

"No."

"Can you come here for lunch Friday?"

"Sure. What time?"

"Well, the girls are out by eight. You could come right after that."

He smiled in the darkness. "That's more like breakfast."

"So, come for breakfast, stay till lunch."

"And what will we do in all the time in between?"

"I was going to clean the bathroom and go to the dry cleaners."

"Sounds fun. But if I think of another plan, you won't be upset, will you?"

"No. Not at all. You have to go."

"I know." He sighed and got off the bed.

"The girls will be gone in three weeks," Diane told him. "They'll be with their father all summer."

"Really?" He looked down at her. "You'll miss them."

She got up and reached for her robe, hanging in the closet. "Yes, I will. But hopefully you'll be around more. That will make it easier." She knotted the belt.

He put his arms around her. "You mean I won't have to park my car around the block and sneak in for a nibble?"

She giggled softly. "No. Shh. Let me see what's going on." She went out and walked into the living room. The sound of the television was still coming down from Emily's room. She waved to Michael, and he followed her back outside.

"Listen, if your neighbors call the cops about the stranger sneaking through their yards, you'll come and bail me out, right?"

"Promise." She grinned. "Thanks for stopping by."

"Anytime. See you Friday."

"Okay. Good night."

Marianne Thomas stopped by her office the next morning. "Hi. I'm glad I got a chance to see you. Have you got everything you need for next year?" Marianne asked.

"You mean the grad class? Yes, I think so. When do you leave for Greece?"

"July." She watched as Diane packed some potted plants into a box. "You never told me about the musician. The one who wants to live in Montana? How is that going?"

"Very well, thanks." Diane glanced over. "Why?"

"Just curious. Are you still seeing him? Usually by the second or third date you find out he's married or a kleptomaniac or worships pygmies or something equally bizarre."

"We've seen a lot of each other. So far, very good."

"Really? How nice for you. How old is he?"

"Twenty-six."

"Really? And in a band of some sort?"

"Yes, Marianne. He's actually kind of famous."

"Then bring him to the picnic next week. You'll have the entire faculty in an uproar. Is he really outrageous? Blue hair, lots of tattoos, that sort of thing?"

Diane laughed. "Sorry. Truthfully, I have more tattoos and piercings than he does. And he dresses like an Ivy League grad student. If you're looking for shock value, you're going to be disappointed."

"Does he at least drive a fancy sports car?"

"Yes. A DeLorean."

Marianne sighed. "Well, that's something. Invite him. I'm sure he'll be a fascinating addition."

"I'll ask. Thank you."

"Wait. Does he have a posse?"

Diane rolled her eyes. "Good-bye, Marianne."

On Thursday, Diane answered her front door and found a pick-up truck in her driveway and a large man in khakis and a tee shirt on her front step, holding a clipboard and a potted rose bush.

"I have a bunch of stuff here for Diane Matthews. Is that you?"

Diane looked past him. There were three men in work clothes standing by the truck. "What kind of stuff?"

"Forty-two slate blocks, nine rose bushes, two flats of – "

"Wait a minute." Diane took the clipboard from his hands and looked at it. Underneath the order sheet was a print-out of the rose garden plan she had made on Michael's computer.

"Where did you get this?" She asked.

"I do Mike Carlucci's place. He asked me to get the stuff and bring it over. Now my guys would be happy to set everything in for you, especially those slates, they're heavy. But Mike said we just deliver, nothin' else, unless you ask." He looked down at her. "Mike's a good guy. I'm Ed, by the way. You can call him and check it out."

She touched the rose bush. The tag said Lagerfeld. The bush was a healthy green with tiny, tight buds. She walked out of the house and peered into the back of the truck. It was filled with everything she needed, including bags of bone meal, compost, and edging blocks. Ed had followed her.

"We could unload right here on the side yard, but I'd let us haul this stuff in the back for you, I'm tellin' you, it's heavy," Ed advised.

Diane nodded. "Sure, that would be great. Follow me." She took him to the back yard and showed him her prepared ground. Ed nodded approvingly.

"You did a good job. And you'll get plenty of sun. This little slope here, good drainage. Nothin' should die. But if it does, call Mike. Our stuff is guaranteed."

He walked off, shouting to his men, and Diane watched as they unloaded flats, bags of stone, slate blocks, pavers, a small stone bench. There was even a shining silver wish ball for the center of the garden. He had remembered everything.

When they were done, she went inside and called Michael.

"Hey," she said, "a man just filled my back yard with half a million bucks worth of roses."

"Half a million bucks worth? Really? Dammit, he charged me a full million."

"Thank you very much, Michael," she said softly. "I'm not very good at taking things from people."

"I noticed. I hope I didn't step on your toes."

"No. Not at all. I can't believe you went to so much trouble."

"No trouble."

"I'll see you tomorrow?"

"Yes.

She hung up and spun around the room, laughing with delight, and danced back into her yard.

The next morning Emily was cheerful and Megan was pouting. Emily was going to the prom, and down to the shore. One of the parents was going down with the group, and Diane had relented. Emily had been beaming for three days. Megan was still fighting with her father over the trip to France. Diane was staying out of it, but her daughter's mood spilled over onto everything.

Megan was staring into the back yard, chewing a bagel. "I thought you didn't have the money for all that stuff," she grumbled, looking at the rose bushes and bags of compost. "I thought you could only do a little at a time."

"I got my state tax refund," Diane lied calmly. "I had forgotten all about it."

"Do we have to help you with all that?" Emily asked. "You know I hate all that gardening stuff."

"No. It will be my project. It will give me something besides work to do while you girls are gone all summer."

"Maybe you should find a boyfriend," Megan suggested.

Diane turned and stared at her. "What?"

Megan shrugged. "Well, you should think about it. You're still pretty."

"Thank you, sweetie," Diane said, hiding a smile.

"How about Dale Watson's father?" Emily suggested.

"Bill Watson?" Bill Watson was about fifty, thinning hair, very shy and painfully thin. Diane looked from one girl to the other. "Is that the kind of boyfriend I should get?"

"Well, he's nice," Emily offered. "And tall."

"Besides, Mom," Megan pointed out, "you're not so lucky with guys."

Diane chewed her lip to keep from smiling. Michael would be there in twenty minutes. "Tell you what. You girls work on saving some money this summer. I'll work on my rose garden. We'll leave the whole boyfriend thing to fate, okay?"

Emily shrugged. "You're not getting any younger, Mom. You don't want to end up one of those ladies with a bunch of cats," she said.

"Like Mrs. Winship," Megan added.

Diane looked up at the clock. "Isn't it time for you girls to go?"

"Yeah, yeah." Emily swung her backpack over her shoulder. "What are you doing today?"

"What? What do you mean?" Diane asked, flustered.

"You look nice. Are you going somewhere?"

"No. I'm just hanging around here all morning."

"Okay. Bye." Emily slouched out. Megan kissed Diane quickly and followed her. Diane listened as the front screen door slammed shut, then leaned back against the kitchen counter in relief.

"Bill Watson," she said aloud. "Oh, my God."

She heard the front door swing open. He was early. She looked out of the kitchen and Sharon Ingoe was smiling at her.

"Hey, talking to yourself so early in the morning?" Sharon said cheerfully. "About what?" She tossed a file folder on the counter. "Here's that stuff for Megan's project you needed."

"Thanks," Diane said as she poured coffee. "My daughters think I should get a boyfriend. They have placed Bill Watson's name up for consideration."

Sharon made a face. "Boy, are they way off base.

Diane shook her head. "No, they're right on base. He's exactly the kind of guy I should be dating. He's my age, nice, stable, divorced with kids, so he knows that whole trip. He's got a good job, we're both from the same community, and we know the same people. He's pretty much perfect for me."

126

Sharon leaned her hip against the counter. "What the hell are you talking about? I thought you were dating Michael the Cute."

Diane stirred her coffee thoughtfully. "I'm forty-five, divorced, with three kids. I should feel lucky to get a guy like Bill Watson. What am I doing with a twenty-six year old poster boy who goes on tour for a living?"

"I thought you liked Michael."

"I do. God, yes, he's incredible. But he is so far removed from the kind of man I thought I'd be with at this point in my life. If you were single right now, what kind of man would you want?"

Sharon pursed her lips. "I'd want a man I don't have to explain Paulie's ADHD to. Somebody who understands why I'm at a soccer game instead of making dinner. Somebody who knows why I'm miserable about putting my mother in a nursing home."

"Exactly. Bill Watson. Does Michael even come close to any of that?"

"Listen, you've been going out with one form of Bill Watson or another for the past few years. Without much success, I might add. The only man who's managed to float your boat since your divorce was that English guy, and he wasn't very Bill Watson-like. What's so wrong with a guy who's incredible?"

"I don't know. I'm just a little overwhelmed right now."

"By a poster boy? Well, that's understandable."

"He should be here any minute."

"Oh?"

Diane blushed. "I'm making him breakfast."

"Uh huh." Sharon's eyes danced over the rim of her coffee cup. "Is that what you're calling it these days?"

Diane was smiling. "We are kind of in that can't-keep-our-hands-off-each-other phase," she admitted.

"I am so jealous. Really. He's how old?"

"Oh, stop it. He had all the stuff I need for my roses sent over. A guy delivered everything yesterday. Can you believe it?"

Sharon looked into the back yard. "Now, there's class for you. Most men send a dozen long-stemmed roses after that first big night. He sends a whole garden."

"I know. I'm so lucky."

"Hey, so is he," Sharon said stoutly, "and don't forget it." She was still looking into the back yard. "Is that him?"

Michael had come around and was standing in the patio, looking at the pile of slate, roses and bagged compost. He smiled as the two women came out, kissing Diane and nodding to Sharon.

"Hello. I'm Michael." He held out his hand.

Sharon shook it warmly. "Nice to see meet you. I'm Sharon. I was on my way out."

Michael held up his hands. "Wait. Don't leave on my account. Want to have breakfast with us?"

Sharon grinned at Diane. "Isn't he sweet?" She turned back to Michael. "No, thank you," she told him as she headed for the back gate. Once behind Michael's back, she turned around to her friend and mouthed, 'He's so cute', before leaving them alone.

Diane kissed him. "See. All the stuff is here. Everything is going to be beautiful," she declared.

"Will you please let me help you with this?" he pleaded. "At least today? I mean it. You've already proven what a great hole-digger you are. We'll get some things in the ground, okay?"

"Okay. Thank you. That's what we can do this morning."

"Now, about tonight. Do you like to dance? Ever hear of the 1896 Club?"

"I love the 1896. We were just there, in March - for my birthday. All the girls."

"The girls? Emily and Megan?"

"No. Sue and Sharon and Carol and Clair and Ginny. The girls."

"Oh," he chuckled. "Well, how about tonight with the boys? Seth wants to take David there. Some people we know are playing. Great music. Even some Motown."

"I'd love to go."

"Good. So what's for breakfast?"

"Blueberry pancakes, sausage, coffee, juice. How does that sound?"

"That sounds good."

"But I thought," she said slowly, sliding her hands under his shirt, "we could do something else first."

He smiled. "Something else sounds good too."

She heard his truck drive up, and came out the door to meet him. He was wearing a cowboy hat made of finely braided straw, with a thin band and a small blue feather. She met him in the middle of her walk and kissed him warmly.

"Are you in disguise?" She asked politely.

"Yes, as a matter of fact," he explained as they walked to the truck. "The 1896 is the kind of place where I'll get recognized. I'm not in the mood. I figure in a club famous for R&B, they'll leave the jerk in the cowboy hat alone." He started the truck. "What do you think?"

She was looking at his feet. "Boots too?"

"Hell, yeah. Hand made by a guy outside Austin. They're beautiful, really. And they add an extra two inches."

129

"Michael," she said wickedly, "you don't need an extra two inches."

He turned bright red. "Thanks. But I was actually referring to adding two inches to my height."

"Oh. Well. My mistake." She was grinning at him. "Couldn't you find a big silver belt buckle? Maybe in the shape of a cow's head?'

"Ha. Ha. Keep it up. I'm tough."

"Isn't this a little early for the 1896?"

"Yes, but I figured we'd eat first. Are you hungry?"

"Of course. Are you going to wear the hat in the restaurant too?"

"I can't believe you don't like my hat. I'm crushed. Really. The girl who sold it to me told me it made me look sexy.'

"Michael, if you looked any sexier, we'd never get out of bed."

He reached for her hand and squeezed it. "You look great, by the way."

She smiled. She was wearing a denim skirt and a red sleeveless tee shirt, with an oversized black linen shirt as a jacket. "Thank you. If I had known we were playing dress-up, I'd have worn my fringed leather jacket."

"You have a fringed leather jacket?"

"Since high school. It's older than you are."

"Oh."

The 1896 Club was an old mansion that had been built in the twenties. The address was 1896 Main Street, and since the mid-seventies it had been a known primarily for the blues bands that came through on their way to the Big Apple. The owner, Bobby St. John, was an aging hippie who was on a first name basis with some world class musicians. NinetySeven had played there often, before they made it big.

It was almost nine by the time Michael and Diane got there, and there was already a small crowd gathered on the front porch. Michael was ignored as he made his way to the front table, and as he paid their way in he asked if Bobby was around. The bouncer had been leaning up against the wall. He was big, over six feet tall, heavy and brutish. At Michael's question, he walked over and stood beside him, looming. He glared at Michael.

"Bobby who?"

Michael looked up at him. "Bobby who signs your paycheck," he said patiently.

"How the fuck do you know Bobby?"

Michael looked at Diane. Her eyes were big and dark. He carefully put his wallet into his back pocket. He looked back up.

"I know Bobby," he said calmly. "I've played here before. Is he upstairs?"

The bouncer shrugged and took another step toward Michael. The people in line behind them were watching. Michael took Diane's arm.

"Excuse me," he said quietly. The bouncer glared, looked around at everyone, and stepped aside. Michael and Diane went inside.

The place was crowded, but most of the people were milling around. Michael made for a table off in a corner. As they sat down, he looked around.

"This is a good spot. Too close to the speakers and you'll loose your hearing for a week. What do you want to drink?"

Diane was looking at him, still wide-eyed. "What was that all about?"

Michael shrugged. "It was about him being the size of Duluth and me being a small guy he thinks he can intimidate. What are you drinking?"

"But that was shitty. Why did he do that?"

131

"Because," Michael said patiently. "He can do that. He's big and tough and he can be as shitty as he wants to be, because he figures I can't stop him. And he's right. Drink?"

"But," she began, then stopped.

"But what?" he asked.

"Does it bother you?"

"Yeah, it bothers me. But I figure I've made more money so far this year than he'll make in his lifetime. A month ago I had lunch with Mick Jagger. I'm spending my Friday night with a lovely, gracious woman instead of standing guard at a nightclub. Now. What do you want to drink?"

"Just club soda."

Michael stood up and turned as a short, stocky man with a long white pony-tail grabbed him from behind, growling, picking him up off the ground.

Michael grinned. "Hello, Bobby."

Bobby St. John dropped Michael and gave him a loud kiss on the cheek. "When Jackie said some douche-bag in a cowboy hat was giving him a hard time, I figured it was you."

"Jackie needs a leash," Michael said mildly. "Behave yourself, Bobby, this is Diane. And this is Bobby St. John."

Bobby looked at Diane carefully. "You've been here before," he declared.

Diane nodded. "Yes. A couple of months ago."

"I remember. A bunch of women. A tall blonde got Will Richenbach to play 'Happy Birthday'."

Diane smiled. "Yes. You have a very good memory. It was my birthday, actually."

Bobby pursed his lips. "I remember good-looking women. The blonde was hot.

"Carol. I'll tell her you said so."

132

Bobby squinted at Michael. "What's with the hat?"

Michael sighed. "Please sit, Bobby. I don't want to deal with any more shit tonight."

Bobby sat down heavily and signaled the waitress. "Sure, Mike. Jackie is just an asshole. Hey, Seth and the Irishman are upstairs doin' lines with the boys. Why don't we go up?"

Michael shook his head. "No, thanks. We're here to listen."

Bobby shrugged. "Sure." To the waitress. "A shot and a beer for me and Tex, whatever the lady wants, and no tab, okay?" The girl took the order and left. Bobby leaned toward Michael. "Just one number, towards the end? Jonelle would love it. She sounds great. Been clean for almost a year."

Michael shook his head again. "Seth will sing with her."

Bobby shrugged his shoulders, resigned. The drinks arrived. Michael and Bobby took their shots together, talking. Diane watched them, and the crowd around them. No one even glanced in their direction. Suddenly, there was a murmur and Seth Bascomb came up to the table, followed by a very short, balding man. Both were grinning.

Seth grabbed a few chairs from the next table and sat down. He smiled at Diane and introduced David Go, who was clearly stoned and obviously enjoying himself very much. Bobby left after a few minutes, and then the band started playing.

They played old R&B covers, Motown, reggae. She and Michael danced. He was loose and graceful. She was having a wonderful time. For the third number, the guitar player who had been singing stepped aside and tiny black woman got up and sang, an old Staple Singers hit, in a deep, sexy voice.

133

"She's great," Diane said into Michael's ear. He nodded, smiling, pulling her closer. Over his shoulder, she could see Seth. He had been dancing with a tall redhead, then had switched to a heavy-set black woman. Seth was the center of attention on the dance floor, grinning and happily putting on a show. No one had even glanced at Michael.

The music slowed, and she and Michael moved together closely. He was slightly taller now, and she had to tilt her head to look into his eyes, very blue and serious under the rim of his hat.

"You're making me crazy, you know," he said into her ear, his hands on her hips. He kissed her hair softly. "Let's get some air."

They went out onto the front porch. The air was slightly chilled, and the street was quiet. People were smoking and talking, and they found an empty space on the steps to sit.

"Having fun?" he asked, slipping his arm around her shoulders.

"I always have fun with you. You're a good dancer. The band is great. Do you know them well?"

"Yeah. Jonelle has an amazing voice. We were kinda close. She got pretty fucked up for a while. Seth is tight with the percussionist. They spend too much time stoned. They'll never be more than a cover band, but they're a great cover band. Lots of fun."

"Have you played with them before?"

"Yes. They're talented. It's fun to play with different people. And they're really into blues. I love playing blues."

"So play with them."

He shrugged. "We'll see."

"Seth is having fun."

"Seth is always on. I don't know how he does it."

"Hey."

"What?"

"Your hat really is sexy."

"God, we need a room. Now."

"Listen. About next week," she looked sheepishly at him. "You've been invited to a picnic. The chairman of my Department, Marianne Thomas, who is also a good friend, asked me to ask you to her annual year-end extravaganza. I told her about us, and she wants to meet you. I also think she's hoping to shock the rest of her guests, but I warned her that you're very normal."

"Normal? Shit, that's deadly. Sure, I'd love to come. Can I wear my hat?"

"No, you may not. Maybe the boots."

"I have something to ask you, too. My father wants to meet you. Lunch at the Country Club was his suggestion."

"Really? Oh, my. The Club. I'd love to meet your father. Any day will be fine."

"Fantastic. I'll let you know. Stand up - the set's over. We'll get trampled."

She stood up quickly and leaned against the railing as people surged out the door and onto the sidewalk. Diane was watching them when she heard someone say Michael's name. She turned and saw Jonelle, the singer from the band, wrap her arms around Michael's neck and give him a slow, deliberate kiss in his lips.

"Michael, baby, you look fine," Jonelle cooed. Michael smiled.

"Hello Jonelle. You all sound great."

"Yeah, we're doin' good." She was leaning against his side, one arm around his shoulders. She was petite, pretty, with close-cropped hair and dark, honey-colored skin. Diane watched her with interest. She could tell by the way Jonelle acted, her careless

familiarity with Michael, the intimate smile, that they
had been lovers.

"What's with the hat, baby?" Jonelle teased, her
hand rubbing Michael's chest. You goin' to the dark
side?"

Michael chuckled and shook his head. Jonelle
turned deliberately to Diane.

"Seth said you had a new lady," she said flatly,
looking Diane up and down.

"Yes. This is Diane."

Jonelle turned back to Michael, ignoring Diane.
"You gonna play later, baby? We used to play good
together."

Michael smiled faintly. "Maybe," he said, a slight
edge to his voice.

Jonelle took her arm away. "So, ask the new
girlfriend. Maybe we could do a request." She looked
at Diane again. "You got a request?" she asked.

Michael looked over to Diane. She smiled
innocently. "How about 'The Man That Got Away'?"

Michael's mouth twitched. Jonelle cocked her
head. "Two points for you, honey." To Michael, "That
would be good, right baby?"

He nodded, grinning. "Sure. But no intro, okay?"

"Sure, baby. But lose the hat. Ain't nothin' so sad
as a rich white boy in a cowboy hat playing blues,
okay?" She turned on her heel and left. Diane looked
at Michael with her eyebrows raised.

"Oh, man, I'm going to be in trouble for this, I can
tell," Michael said, laughing and taking her hand.
"Come on, let's get back. I need another drink."

Seth and David were at the table, Seth in deep
conversation with the redhead he had been dancing with
earlier. David was smiling and drinking heavily,
watching the people around him. When Diane sat next
to him, he immediately brightened and launched into a

discussion of American blues. Diane sipped club soda and tried to hear through his thick, slurred accent as Michael watched, grinning. Then the band started up again, and they were back on the dance floor, now more crowded than ever.

Seth sang with the band a couple of times, to great applause. Finally, Jonelle waved the crowd quiet and invited her 'good friend' up to join them. Michael took off his hat and set it on Diane's head with a long kiss. He went on stage and sat at the upright piano. The crowd was noisy and restless, but after he hit a few chords, they were silent, listening.

Michael played alone, the rest of the band members silent, and Jonelle sat beside him on the piano bench, her voice soft and sexy. When they were done, and the crowd was screaming, she whispered in his ear and he nodded, and they began another number, familiar to Diane, an old love song. This time, the bass player started in, and the drummer hit the snare. When they were done, Michael stood up and walked off-stage, grabbing Diane's hand as he hurried out.

"Can you drive?" he asked her as they walked toward the truck. She nodded, got behind the wheel and watched him as he took off his hat and sank down into the seat.

"You okay?" she asked, pulling away from the curb.

"Yeah. Just tired. That last beer and shot didn't help."

"You could do that all night, couldn't you? Just sit behind a piano and play for somebody like Jonelle."

"Easily. I'd love it. If the band ever breaks up, that's what I'd probably do, get a nice steady gig someplace, work weekends, no hassles."

"What about writing music?"

"I'd always do that. But I write for myself. If somebody else plays it, or hears it, then I'll get paid. But the fun is in the writing. I can't wait to start this movie thing. I've got so many ideas. David is really sharp. He's going to be a big help."

"You're pretty amazing, aren't you? I'm used to smart people, and talented people. I work with them. But you are something special."

"Shucks. Now I'm embarrassed."

"Cut it out. You know how good you are."

He looked at her, curious. "Do you think I'm arrogant?"

"No, not at all. You're very comfortable with who you are. You're one of the most self-assured people I've ever met. I mean, that guy tonight? Jackie? Most men I know would have had to make a point, somehow."

"I did make a point. Bobby will fire him."

"Really?"

"Not because he pulled that shit on me, but because he pulled that shit, period. When people pay money to listen to good music and have a nice time, they shouldn't have to put up with that kind of asshole."

She glanced over at him. His eyes were closed, his face looked very young and peaceful. He opened one eye.

"What?"

She grinned. "So, you and Jonelle were kinda close?"

He closed his eye and sighed. "You picked up on that?"

"Oh, yeah."

"I met her when I was just eighteen. She felt there were certain, ah, gaps in my education."

"I see. So is there anything in particular I should have thanked her for?"

He chuckled. "Maybe. When I started my senior year in high school, the prettiest girl in the whole class, hell she was head cheerleader, asked me over to her house to watch 'General Hospital' after school. She made a pass. I was shocked. She had never so much as looked at me before, but her sister had seen us playing over the summer, and I guess she thought it would be cool to screw a guy in a band. She didn't want anyone to know. Not only was I the shortest guy around, but I'd skipped third grade, so I was younger than everybody else. It really sucked. But two or three afternoons a week, we'd be at it. Unfortunately, she lacked imagination, and any time I suggested anything other than the missionary position, she freaked. When I met Jonelle, my technique was rather limited. Jonelle, on the other hand, had been hopping in and out of bed for years. Twenty going on forty-five, you know? She gave me a rather advanced tutorial."

"Remind me to send her flowers."

He yawned. "I'd like to think I'd have eventually improved on my own. There's a Marriott just ahead. Pull in. We'll get a room."

"Are you serious?"

"Yeah. It'll take us at least forty minutes to get home. It'll be fun. Besides, you've been getting me hot and bothered all night."

She turned the truck into the parking lot. "I thought you were tired."

"Not that tired."

She shut off the truck and turned in her seat to face him. "And you can't wait?"

"I've been waiting all night." He got out and walked around to the other side of truck, opening her door and pulling her out.

139

"You're being ridiculous," she scolded, walking past him. He grabbed her and pulled her back to him, pressing her against the truck. He kissed her very slowly, one hand sliding up her skirt, the other against her breast. He kissed her again, more deeply, and her arms went around him, and she opened her legs as his hand crept further up her thigh. Abruptly, he pulled back, and she leaned back against the side of the truck, blood pounding, her lips swollen.

"So, you want to drive home or what?"

She licked her lips. Her skin felt on fire. She couldn't catch her breath. "You son of a bitch."

He grinned. "It's the hat."

CHAPTER EIGHT

They passed into the summer together. After Emily and Megan moved down with their father, they were together almost every day and night. Michael was working on the score for the movie. The band had decided to take on the project. Michael had been hooked when he saw the first rough takes of the film. Gordon Prescott was filming a version of the Canterbury Tales, with a script based on the original stories. His pilgrims were a group of people taking a bus trip to Atlantic City on the Canterbury Bus Line. During the course of the trip, various tales would be told, all in flashback. It was a fascinating idea, and beautifully acted. For Michael, it was a chance to develop distinct themes for each of the characters. And so it had been agreed. Michael would do the writing. Seth and Joey would produce the soundtrack. The band would record at least three original numbers, and Prescott would get other bands to contribute to the soundtrack.

They spent most of their time at Michael's house. He would work all morning in his studio. David Go, the elfin Irishman who had been tapped to do the orchestration of the score, had moved into one of Michael's guestrooms. Seth Bascomb had moved into another. Seth owned five different homes, but none in New Jersey, so he always stayed at Michael's.

Diane started spending mornings on the sailboat. She had spent enough time with Michael that she felt confident enough to go out on her own. She would go over to Merriweather in the afternoons to prepare for her new class. A graduate level class, an analysis of three works by Arthur Miller, required at great deal of research. This was the kind of work she had not done since her doctorate days, and she enjoyed it thoroughly.

She was invited to Marie's for the Fourth of July. Marie and Steve had a beautiful 100 year old Victorian in Madison, with high ceilings and beautiful woodwork. Out back there was a large yard and a patio and pool. When she and Michael arrived, the place was already crowded with family, Marie's friends and co-workers, as well as Steve's family. Steve was a director for a major pharmaceutical house, and he had invited his whole department.

They mingled with the crowd. Diane had been accepted warmly by his family. Marie waved happily at them, and a few minutes later, Angela came running up to them, her face flushed with the heat.

"I have some hot news for you, Diane." Angela said, giving Michael a quick kiss on the cheek "Guess who's back in the States and planning on returning to Merriweather?"

"Not a clue," Diane said, taking a sip of cold white wine.

"Quinn Harris." Angela said excitedly. "He's bringing his Coward revival, the one that did so well last season in London, to the St. James for a limited run, sometime in the spring. Sam told me all about it. So Quinn asked about taking on another class here, this fall. Isn't that great? That would be such a coup for Sam, getting him back. We got a lot of attention last time, remember? And with your play going on while he's here could mean some impressive coverage, don't you think?"

Diane had to take a deep breath. Quinn Harris, back at Merriweather.

"That's great. For Sam I mean," Diane said. "Quinn is quite a catch."

"Who's Quinn Harris?" Michael asked.

Angela told him. "He's a very famous director in England, and he was here a few years ago as a visiting Professor. It was very exciting for us drama types."

Michael had been watching Diane's face. "Did you know him?" he asked casually.

Diane met his eyes. "Yes. Usually I wouldn't be hanging around the Merriweather drama department, but Sam had just decided to workshop my play, so I did get to know him." She smiled briefly, then caught sight of Marie. "Your sister looks like she could use some help." She gulped more wine and moved away from Michael.

Her heart was pounding. Quinn was returning. She never imagined she would see him again. She could hear voices around her, but they seemed to be at a great distance, and her hands and lips turned icy cold. Quinn.

She had been invited to a cocktail party to welcome Quinn Harris to campus, and she had not wanted to go. But Sam French had insisted, and from the moment she saw Quinn, she could not take her eyes from him. He caught her staring at him, and when she did not turn away, he made his way slowly across the room until it was just the two of them, standing in a quiet corner, talking for a few minutes that made all the difference in the world to both of them. They met the next day for coffee, early in the morning, and by dinner that evening she had fallen, so swiftly and surely that she could not even remember how she had felt about her life before she met him. That evening he told her about his wife. He would leave her, he said. They would be together. They were meant to be together. And she had believed him. But in the end she had said no. He was married. She said no, and her heart had broken.

Diane reached over to take a basket of grilled chicken from Marie's hands, setting it on the table. Now Quinn was divorced and coming back. She had not thought about him in months, certainly not since Michael. Now, knowing she would see him again caused a powerful reaction, totally unexpected and unwelcome. Diane had no desire to face him again. She did not want any old wounds reopened.

Michael had come up behind her and put his arms around her waist, pulling her away from the table and against him.

"My sister has hired scores of people to help her with this stuff," he said into her ear. "You're supposed to be a guest, remember?"

Diane smiled and leaned back against him. "Sorry. It's automatic."

"Yeah, well you're depriving people of their gainful employment."

She rubbed her hands against his arms. "Sorry."

Diane could feel the question hanging in the air before he asked it. "What about this Quinn Harris?"

Diane chewed her lip. "Did you ever meet somebody, and in like, three minutes you're thinking, wow, this is who I've been waiting for my whole life?"

Michael stepped back away from her. When Diane turned around, his face was blank.

Diane continued. "Well, that's how I felt when I met Quinn. But he was married. So nothing really happened. Then he went back to England." She reached out to touch his face, tracing the line of his jaw, running her fingertips over his lips. "It was a long time ago. Things are different now."

"There was something in your face, when Angela was talking about him," Michael said.

"It was a long time ago," Diane repeated. "I'm hungry. And I need to cool off."

He kissed her. "Okay."

By the second week of July, Sam French began casting for 'Mothers and Old Boyfriends'. Diane began spending time at Merriweather in the mornings. She was enthralled by the whole process. They were casting ten male and eight female roles, and because the Merriweather program had been so well received for a number of years, the caliber of people auditioning was high, many known theater and television actors from Manhattan.

In ten days, they had a cast, and they began to read through her script. It was then that her real work began. She and Sam discussed which lines were working, which sounded hollow, where the laughs were. Diane was not a good collaborator, but she knew Sam was thinking only of the best for her play, and she made extensive notes on his suggestions, as well as suggestions from the cast. It was difficult for her to see characters that she created and felt belonged to her become absorbed by the actors, and the line between the character and the person portraying the character became blurred.

Michael listened to her, nodding in sympathy as she tried to articulate her frustration. They were sitting in her back yard, and she was pacing her patio, trying to explain. He grabbed her, pulled her into his lap, and kissed her soundly.

"I know exactly how you feel. There were times I'd write a song, spend all this time on, it, agonizing over each note, and the band would hear it, and they'd be, like, 'that's the best song you've ever written, man', and I'd be thinking how fuckin' great I was, then Seth would say, 'hey, maybe we should do this', and Phil would say, 'let's change this chord', and in fifteen minutes, the best thing I ever wrote would be completely different. It sucks. I know how hard it is to turn this over to somebody else. But unless you want to act all the roles yourself, you've got to allow for a little, well, freedom of interpretation."

"I know. I guess the whole time I was writing, I never thought it would be actually performed, so what's been in my head for all this time is hard to shake loose." Diane kissed him right behind the ear, then began taking small bites on his neck

"Your neighbors are watching," Michael murmured as she slid her hand under his shirt.

"Are they holding up scorecards?" She asked. "I think we deserve at least a 9.2."

"I think we deserve even more, but we either have to wait 'till it gets darker, or maybe go inside." His hands were moving up the inside of her thighs.

She stood up, grabbed his hand, and led him into the house.

"You don't text."

"Neither do you."

"Yes, I do. I text the girls all the time, especially now that they're down the shore."

"Who would I text? All the people I need are right here."

"You don't Tweet, either."

Michael laughed. "Seth is in charge of all that. He's the maven of all Social Media."

"And you don't have a Facebook page."

"My life isn't that interesting. What would I put on a Facebook page?"

She shrugged. "I don't know. Isn't yours the generation that must be in constant contact with everyone and everything?"

"Maybe. I'm an old-fashioned guy at heart. I don't even like talking on the phone all that much. My cell is five years old. I'm not even sure I can text."

"Your fans must be disappointed in you."

"If they knew I was spending the morning naked in bed with you, some of them would be very disappointed."

"True. Do you think if people found out about us, it could hurt your career?"

"Are you kidding? You sexy older women are very in right now. I'd be the envy of all my fans."

"Ah. Is that why you keep coming around?"

His hand, which had been resting lightly on her stomach, suddenly moved.

"That's one reason. Here's another."

They fell into a pattern as the summer wore on. The nights they spent at Diane's, they would cook out on the grill, often asking Sue Griffen and her husband Pete to join them. Michael and Pete were both Mets fans, and after dinner, Diane and Sue would take a walk around the neighborhood and the two men would watch the ball game together. Sometimes, Sharon and her husband Richie would come by and the four of them would go out to Richie's favorite pub. Richie played darts, and he began coaching Michael, who was a quick study and became fairly proficient. Sometimes, all three couples would meet at one home or another for drinks. Michael liked her friends. They liked him as well.

At Michael's, there were a string of guests that came and went even if Michael was not at home. Mark Bender would come by to sail into the middle of the lake, then spend the day fishing. Theresa Milano, Michael's first childhood love, would drive in on days off, swim laps for an hour, then fall asleep on Michael's shady, perfectly mown lawn. His family came by often, to sail or to fish, often staying for dinner and far into the night.

Members of the band dropped in and out, checking on the progress of Michael's work. They were starting to lay down tracks for the singles on the soundtrack. The Martone brothers did not want to spend any more time away from home, so the band decided to do as much work in Michael's studio as possible. The band worked quickly together.

She started making dinner at Michael's, two or three nights a week. She would stop by the store on her way back from Merriweather, and come back to his house with bags of groceries. Fred Chu, a Buddhist and vegetarian, never accepted her invitation to join them. He cooked and ate his own meals in the apartment he lived in over Michael's three-car garage. Diane loved to cook, and Michael would often wander out of his studio to watch her. Seth and David Go would join them. For Diane, it was like cooking for a new kind of family.

She was careful they didn't spend a full week together. She found reasons to spend a night alone. She would drive down to the shore to see her daughters, staying at a motel. She would start cleaning her house, pulling closets apart, calling Michael late in the afternoon saying she was going to stay there and finish up. She would catch the bus to Manhattan and spend the night at Rachel's.

For the first time in a long time, Diane felt she was slightly out of control. Her feelings for Michael were a complete surprise to her. Her physical desire for him was intense. She would find herself, in the middle of the day, doing something as ordinary as washing dishes or watering plants, when a sudden wave would come over her, beginning as a throb deep in her belly and moving up, a physical jolt, leaving her breathless and wanting.

But she knew, and not just from the many nights that she slept peacefully beside him without passion, that it was not just his touch that held her to him. He had a boundless energy and enthusiasm about everything that she found a complete delight. They could talk about any subject. They laughed a great deal together. When she was with him, the world was in sharper focus. When they were apart, she found countless things to remember to tell him, to ask him about. Her solitude was no longer a comfort to her. It was just time spent waiting to see him again.

She thought that she was in love with him. She would turn to Jasper and say the words aloud, trying on the sound of them. "I think I love Michael." Her voice was always in a whisper when she said it. The cat would blink wisely in response. She would take a deep breath and go on with her day. But the thought was always there, crowding out the quiet and carefully planned life that she imagined she would be living. "I think I love him," she would say to herself, driving out to his house. She sometimes reasoned that Michael was so irresistible to her because she had married relatively young. She had missed the sexual adventures of other women her age. She had slept with only a few other men before meeting Kevin, her high school sweetheart and a couple of brief college flings. She had loved Kevin deeply when they married. She was twenty-one, just out of college, and he, being five years older, had not wanted to wait. She continued to love him for many years into their marriage, and had remained faithful to him, despite the attention other men may have paid to her.

She wondered if she was just another sexually frustrated middle-aged woman responding to the attention of a younger man, but she dismissed the idea, because she realized that the spark that had been there from the very beginning, the thing that had drawn her to him from the very first day, was still going strong. He made her happy. From the moment she met him, it was not just passion he stirred in her. It was more. It was joy. And she had no idea what to do next.

If she was away more than a day, Michael would drive over to her house, unannounced. She was always there, waiting for him. Sometimes, he would come around the back of her house, and see her in the yard, tending her roses. He would wait outside the gate, not wanting the brass bell to give him away, and watch her as she weeded or raked. Her movements were quick and graceful, her concentration complete. She did not realize he was there, watching her, until he would call to her, or push open the gate. Sometimes he would walk into the house, and she would be in the kitchen, music blaring, dancing alone in front of the stove, and again he would watch her until he could resist no longer, and he would join her, and they would dance together in her tiny kitchen.

He hated them being apart. Gordon Prescott was bearing down on him, a huge, suffocating cloud that blotted out everything else. Michael spoke to him sometimes four or five times a day. FedEx delivered revised tapes several times a week. Prescott wanted him in Toronto. He wanted to know at every moment what Michael was doing, and Michael, used to the freedom of writing alone, under no restraints, was in agony. Diane was the one cool, soothing presence in his life. The nights she was not with him he spent awake, in his studio, with David Go, or Seth. Without her there, the movie pressed down upon him relentlessly. Her presence forced him to live a normal life.

They went into Manhattan together. Diane went to see Shakespeare in the Park. Michael followed gamely. He was not passionate about theater the way she was, and he did not like New York, but her excitement was contagious. They had dinner with Rachel. Rachel's boyfriend, Gary, was a third year law student, clerking at a large firm on Madison Avenue. He was also a huge music fan, and he and Michael would get into long, rambling discussions of obscure bands, European bands, and techno-music. Gary was twenty-five. Rachel and Diane slipped back into their old relationship, much to Diane's relief.

By the first week of August, Michael and David Go began to try to figure out what Toronto would be like for them. David thought they would need six weeks to record the score, at least. The tracks for NinetySeven were almost complete. Joey and Seth would produce the rest of the soundtrack, so Michael would not be needed for any further recording. Gordon Prescott did not believe in time off. Michael knew it would be a grueling time, not only physically, but he would be away from Diane. *Thank God it's only Toronto,* he thought. He could fly back easily enough, for a day at a time. And she could fly up to see him on the weekends.

"What are you doing?"

Diane was in his bedroom, on her mat. "It's called the Gate Pose."

"Yoga? I didn't know you did yoga."

"Hey, a girl is entitled to a few secrets, you know?"

"Sure. Okay, what's that one?"

"Downward Facing Dog."

"Really? It looks like Take Me From Behind."

She collapsed on the mat in a fit of giggles. "Michael, I was trying to focus."

"Me too. I gotta tell you, that is a very good look for you."

She wiped her neck and chest with a towel that she threw into the colorful tote bag she carried back and forth to his house.

"You're taking home your towel? Why?"

She threw him a look. "I don't want one of your minions doing my laundry."

"Minions? I don't have minions."

"Of course you do. You have a person for everything around here."

"No."

"No? Then who does your laundry?"

He grinned. "I take it downstairs, knock on the secret panel, give the password, a blind, one-eyed gypsy takes it, and the next day, it reappears in the closet. Isn't that how everybody does it?"

She had rolled up her mat, and now swatted him playfully with it. "You are impossible."

He grabbed her. "Maybe. But since you're all hot and sweaty anyway, want to try that Downward Dog thing again?"

"Tomorrow night I'll be staying at my place," she told him, stretching her legs out in front of her. They were out on the terrace of Michael's house, sipping wine, watching the sun set over the lake. Diane had cooked dinner for them. "Sharon's got the girls together. We're all hitting the town."

"Ah. The mythical Girls Night Out. What is it you all do together, anyway?"

"Well, we're currently plotting to take over the world by manipulating the stock market to resurrect all the tech stocks, which we've been secretly buying up all year long. Then we'll sacrifice a couple of chickens, and drink and dance naked around a statue of Simone de Beauvoir."

Michael raised his eyebrows and nodded. "That's what I would have guessed."

Diane smiled. "We'll go to Maxwell's, probably. We can walk there, so we can all drink, and we'll probably dance, but with our clothes on."

"What a disappointment."

"Then we'll sit around and drink some more and talk about our kids and our jobs and complain about men."

"Complain about men?"

"Oh, yeah. It's inevitable."

"God. You all are going to crucify me, right?"

"No." Diane patted his hand. "You're the new guy. I promise we'll be very kind to you."

"Gee thanks. I like your friend Sharon, but I would not want to be on her bad side."

"Don't worry. She likes you too. She thinks you're cute. And besides, you told her you could get her Lyle Lovett's autograph."

"Oh, I did, didn't I? I'd better not forget. I'll call him this week."

"You'd better, 'cause you're right about Sharon. You don't want to get on her bad side."

There were five of them, sitting at an outside table at Maxwell's, waiting for the band to start playing again. They had met at Sharon's and walked the six blocks, and were all feeling no pain. Ginny Smith, the youngest of the group at 36, was pouring margaritas from a pitcher. Carol Coopersmith, divorced and always on the look-out, had been flirting with the waiter. Sharon had a fight with Richie before leaving and was feeling feisty. Sue and Diane had been giggling all night.

They had spent the first part of the evening catching up, comparing vacations, the kids, and the heat. When the band had started playing, they all got up on the dance floor. Maxwell's was a popular spot with all ages, and they were not the oldest people dancing. During the seven or eight songs that played, Diane was asked to dance by three different men. She declined the offers. When the set had ended, and they were back at the table, Diane gulped another drink.

"Okay," she announced loudly, "I have been coming here for years without incident, and tonight I get hit on three different times." She looked around the table. "I need somebody to explain this to me."

Carol Coopersmith leaned forward. She was very attractive, sleek blonde hair, tall and thin, brilliant blue eyes. She pointed a perfectly manicured finger.

"I have a theory," she said. "It's because you're in love."

Diane blinked as all four women looked at her. "What?"

Carol nodded. "You know how, in nature, when a female is ready to mate, she sends out something, a phoneme or something-"

"Pheromone," Sue corrected.

"Thank you. So anyway, the female sends out this pheromone thing and every male in the neighborhood knows she's ready for sex and comes a-calling. Well, I think it happens to us. When a woman is in love, and knows she's going to go home and have great sex, she sends out her own little pheromone and every guy in the room smells it, and figures he might be able to get a first crack. That's why women who aren't dating

154

never get approached. But women in a hot relationship are like magnets." Carol shrugged and took a drink. "And that's my theory."

Diane looked around the table. Sue and Sharon were grinning. Ginny raised an eyebrow.

"Are you?" Ginny asked.

"Am I what?" Diane sputtered.

"Going home and having great sex?" Ginny kept a straight face, but Sue was starting to giggle.

"Of course she is," Carol announced. "We all know who she's been seeing. How could she not? Besides, what do you think they do together? Play chess?"

Diane was annoyed. "Now, wait a minute, what's that supposed to mean?"

Carol shrugged innocently. "Listen, Diane, I say more power to you. If you can keep somebody like him waiting up for you, that's great. But don't try to tell us there's actually something going on aside from sex. He's what, not even thirty? What else could you have in common with him?"

"WHAT?" Diane leaned across the table as Sue reached over and took hold of her arm. Diane glared at Carol.

"Listen. Michael and I have tons in common. We both love Aretha and hate Prince, we both like Spanish films, we both read Eastern philosophy, and we hate pro football. We have a great time together, and I can't believe you would think that."

Carol blushed and looked closely at Diane. "Well, I guess I stand corrected. I didn't think you actually, well, dated."

Sharon had been looking at Carol critically. "What did you think, Carol? That she had him stashed in a motel room somewhere and just dropped in for servicing?"

155

The women all laughed as Diane rolled her eyes. "God, Carol. I mean, yeah, he's younger, but so what? Would this be a big deal if he were twenty years older? No."

Ginny waved a pretzel in the air. "If he were twenty years older, we probably wouldn't be so interested in the sex part," she said.

Sharon burst out laughing, burying her face in her hands. Sue looked at Ginny and patted her hand. "Well, Carol might still be interested," she told Ginny soothingly.

"It's just that dating is so different at our age," Carol said. "Diane knows what I mean. In your twenties, you've got all the time in the world to date around, and you can spend time with a guy who may or may not be the one." She shrugged. "In your forties, especially with kids, you don't have time to fuck around, unless you want to just fuck around, you know? Come on, Diane," she waved her glass. "Tell them. You know by the third or fourth date if a guy is going to be a wash-out. You can't afford to waste time on a maybe. So, if you stick with a guy for any length of time, it's either sex, or it must be pretty serious." She tilted her head and leaned back in her chair. "So tell us, Diane," she asked, smiling, "is it serious?"

Diane scrunched up her nose, making a face, and stared into her drink.

Sue explained. "Diane is having a hard time reconciling her two selves, the staid professor and respected mother by day, crazed groupie by night."

"I am not a crazed groupie," Diane said stoutly. "I'm the keyboard player's hunny bunny."

Ginny frowned. "Do musicians in rock bands have hunny bunnies?"

Sharon shuddered. "No. And that sound you hear is Jim Morrison rolling over in his grave. I can't believe you still haven't figured this out," she said to Diane disapprovingly. "Jesus Christ, why are you so wishy-washy about this? Why don't you just admit that you're crazy about him?"

"Okay," Diane said happily. "I am crazy about him."

"Oh good," Ginny chirped. "Can we get shots now?"

"Yes. We need to celebrate." Sharon said as she looked around for the waiter.

"And is he crazy about you?" Carol asked.

"Shit, yes," Sharon answered. "You should see them together. He's a doll. He laughs at all her jokes."

Diane looked at Sharon haughtily. "I happen to be a very funny person."

"Not that funny, sweets. And he stares at her."

Diane looked at her in surprise. "He does?"

Sue nodded in agreement. "Yep, he sure does. But you stare at him too, so it's okay."

"I do?"

Sharon was emphatic. "Oh, yeah, all the time. Face it kiddo, you're in love."

"Wait." Diane felt panicked. "God, that's what this is, right?" She chewed her lip as a shot glass of tequila was set down in front of her. "I don't know. Maybe. Do you think? Maybe I'm in love?"

"It's an age-old question," Carol said sadly. "Is the sex great because you're in love, or are you in love 'cause the sex is so great?"

"I think the pheromones have spoken." Ginny said, reaching for the salt shaker.

"Let's just drink up in a hurry. The band is about to start again."

It was after two in the morning when they left Maxwell's. They walked back slowly, laughing and singing. They dropped off Ginny first, then backtracked toward the street where Sue and Diane lived. As they approached Diane's house, she could see Michael's truck in the driveway.

"He's here," she said happily. "He drove down to see me."

Sue squinted. "Does he have a key to your house?"

"Yep." Diane nodded. "He sure does."

Sharon looked at her sideways. "Do you have a key to his place?"

Diane shook her head. "I don't need a key. He has an electric pad thingy to get in. I know the code, but Fred is always there. Fred lets me in."

Carol had her arm around Sue's shoulder. "Who is Fred?"

"The butler," Sue said carefully. "Michael has a butler."

"Ooooh, really?" Carol made a face.

"Yep." Diane giggled. "I think I'm a little drunk," she whispered loudly.

"Me too," said Sue, "but we're almost home."

They went up Diane's walk. Diane fumbled in her purse for her keys, and Sue leaned against the doorbell. Diane made shushing noises, giggling as she tried to fit the key into the lock. She was leaning her head against the door, fumbling with the lock, when the door opened and Diane stumbled forward. Michael caught her, straightening her up.

She broke into a wide smile. "Honey, I'm home," she sing-songed.

Michael stood, shirtless, jeans low on his hips, squinting at the women. He had obviously been asleep.

He looked at Diane, then at her friends, and smiled groggily.

"So, I guess you had a good time."

Diane walked around, stood behind him, and put her arms around his waist, head on his shoulder. "We were celebrating," she told him.

He chuckled. "Celebrating what?"

"My rhizomes," Diane said distinctly. Sharon and Sue began to laugh. Carol held out her hand. "Hi, Michael. It's a real pleasure to meet you. I'm Carol."

Michael shook her hand, then looked over at Sue. "Okay, what do I do? I've never seen her this drunk before," he said.

"Well," Sue explained, "luckily, the situation is not dangerous, only embarrassing."

"Am I embarrassing you?" Diane asked him in a loud whisper.

"Of course not," he said with a smile. He looked sideways at her. "You're adorable."

Sharon sighed. "See," she said to Carol, "I told you. Good night, Michael."

"Good night. Hey, wait, should I walk you home? Sharon, are you going to be okay?"

"Thanks, we'll be good," Sharon told him. "Carol is crashing at my place, so we'll get Sue home and stagger the rest of the way together."

"Unless," Carol purred, "it's too much trouble, Sharon. I'd hate to impose. Maybe Michael could drop me home?"

Sharon snorted in disgust. "Forget it, babe. That ain't workin' here." Sharon waved. "G'night Diane. Sleep tight."

Michael closed the door and turned around to face Diane. She stood, leaning forward against him, still smiling.

"I had a good time," she told him, "but I think I need to go to bed now."

"I think so too. Can you find the bathroom? Can you get undressed?"

Diane nodded, determined. "Of course I can." She straightened up, turned around, and marched down the hallway. Michael shook his head, went into the kitchen and poured a large glass of orange juice. Passing back through the living room, he locked the door, turned out the lights, and waited until Diane came out of the bathroom. She had changed into a tee shirt, and grinned when she saw him.

"Here you are again," she exclaimed happily. Michael went into the bathroom and came out with a bottle of aspirin. She was sitting on the bed, and he spilled out two tablets into his hand.

"Take these," he said, trying to sound stern, "and drink all the juice."

She did as he said; handing him the glass, then fell back onto the bed. He picked up her feet and pulled the sheet over her, turned off the light, stripped out of his jeans and got into the other side of the bed. She immediately curled to face him.

"I hope I'm not hung over tomorrow," she whispered.

"Me too. The juice should help, and the aspirin. You'll be fine."

"I had a lot of fun. I have really great friends."

"Yes, you do." He could feel her body, pressed against him, starting to relax. He lowered his voice a little.

"You friend Carol seems nice, too."

"She's a bitch, sometimes," Diane told him sleepily. "She thought the only reason we were together was because of sex. She didn't think we could have anything else in common. Sharon yelled at her."

"Sharon did?"

"Um huh."

"And you said?"

"I said we had tons in common."

"That's true."

"Um huh. Then Sharon said I was in love," she murmured.

He held his breath. "And you said?"

"I said maybe," she breathed, as she fell asleep, and he lay next to her, staring into the darkness.

She awoke once, near dawn, and went into the bathroom for more aspirin. When she climbed into bed, he opened one eye.

"Drink more juice," he said.

She nodded as she slid back to sleep, "I did." When she awoke again, the sun was shining weakly and she was alone. She looked at the clock. It was after ten. She lay still, her head barely throbbing. Good. She got up and went into the bathroom. She stood under the shower until the last of the headache was gone. She stepped out of the shower, dried herself off, and put on gym shorts and a tee shirt. As she went into the hall, Michael called from the kitchen.

"Get back in bed. It's too wet to sit outside. It rained all morning while you were still asleep. I'll be right in."

She climbed back into the bed, plumping the pillows behind her. Michael appeared with a tray, laden with coffee cups, muffins, and the morning paper.

"Oh, God, look at this." Diane watched as he set the tray in the center of the bed. She grabbed a mug and sipped coffee gratefully. "This is so delicious. And I need this so badly, you have no idea. And muffins? You went out to the bakery in the rain? You are an angel. Really."

161

He carefully got into bed beside her. "So, how are you? How's the head?"

She reached for a muffin. "So far, so good. I think you saved my life last night with the juice. I feel almost normal. Thank you so much." She broke apart a muffin and glanced up to find him watching her.

"You were celebrating rhizomes?" He asked.

She laughed softly. "We were sure as hell celebrating something," she said ruefully. "God knows what I said last night. Half I don't remember, and the other half was a crock of shit. But I did have a good time, I remember that." She chewed her muffin and sipped more coffee. When she glanced at him again, he was very still, gazing at her thoughtfully.

He leaned forward. "Do you remember what you said to me last night? About being in love?"

The blood rushed to her face. She could not look at him. She nodded. "Yes," she whispered. "I remember. Oh, Michael, I wish I were sure."

"I have never felt more positive about anything in my whole life."

She looked at him then. "What?"

"I'm in love with you."

She caught her breath.

"I'm in love with you," he said again. "I think I have been from that very first day. There hasn't been a moment in months that I haven't thought about you, wanted to be with you. You are the sweetest, truest, best thing I have ever found, and I can't imagine what my life would be like without you."

"Oh," she whispered, as she broke into a smile. She felt a rush of happiness. She stared down into her coffee, then back up at Michael. He had a half smile on his face.

"I'm overwhelmed." She put the mug back on the tray. She was still smiling, feeling young and silly and happy. "Michael, I just – oh, my." She reached out and grabbed him, pulling him toward her, kissing him, small, excited kisses on his lips and face. She was half laughing, and he took her by the shoulders, kissing her deeply.

She stopped laughing. "I don't know, Michael. I think I am in love with you. But I'm not sure." She stroked his cheek. "Is that going to be enough for you?"

"Are you kidding? It's fine, it's great." His eyes were bright. "I'll take it." He kissed her again, and she sank into the pillows.

"I need to celebrate again," she whispered.

"Again?"

"Long story. Move the tray. Kiss me again."

He did.

The next week she stopped by her house and there was a message from Sharon for her to call.

"I need new toes," Sharon complained. "Let's get a pedicure and have lunch. I haven't seen you in days."

Diane looked at her feet. "Good idea. Actually, I think I need a total tune up. How about TonyO's?"

"Wow, aren't we fancy schmancy? Can we get something for tomorrow on short notice?"

Diane flipped through the phone book. "It's summertime and everyone is off somewhere else. I'll call. I'll let you know."

When Sharon walked into Antonio's Day Spa the next morning, Diane was waiting for her. Sharon looked at her closely as they sat down, plunging their feet into foaming water.

"Did you get your eyebrows done?" Sharon asked.

"Yes. And a bikini wax, mud treatment and a facial. I feel like I've been here since dawn."

"Since when do you spring for all the extra treatments?" Sharon spoke cautiously. She knew that Diane, while financially comfortable, did not have a lot of extra money. And everything at Antonio's was very expensive.

Diane looked guilty. "Well, with the girls gone and Michael feeding me, I felt I could splurge."

Sharon nodded her head slowly. "Sure. But since when have you been getting facials? And mud? What the hell is that about?"

Diane took in a deep breath. "A couple of nights ago, Michael and I went to the movies, and afterwards, I went to the bathroom, and you know how those lines are, so I was in there for a while, and when I came out, this incredible girl was talking to Michael. Sharon, she was gorgeous, legs up to her neck, boobs out to there, swinging all this long hair around. I just looked at her and felt, well, old and run-down. So I figured I'd treat myself to a little sprucing up."

"Shit." Sharon said angrily. "You look fantastic, Diane."

Diane looked at her friend. "I know I do. I think I look great for my age. But I'm still forty-five, you know? My boobs sag, I've got those great little lines around my eyes, my jaw line is soft and puffy, not to mention the gray hair."

Sharon snorted. "Now wait. Your hair always looks terrific. I haven't seen gray on your head in a long time."

Diane made a face. "I'm not talking about the hair on my head," she said wryly.

Sharon sighed. "Oh, that gray hair. Yeah, that really sucks."

Diane shrugged her shoulders. "I've never been very self conscious about my appearance before, but now it seems important, you know?"

Sharon was watching her friend's face. "What does Michael say about all this? I mean, I don't know him all that well, but he seems very, I don't know, unimpressed by the physical. Or material. He's really down-to-earth, isn't he?"

Diane chewed her lip. "He is. He would never say anything. He tells me I'm beautiful and sexy and gorgeous, no matter how I really look."

Sharon sighed. "So, what gives?"

Diane watched as bright coral polish went on to her toes. "He told me he was in love with me."

"But that's great!" Sharon exclaimed.

"I know it is. It's better than great. I've been walking around with this huge ridiculous grin on my face, feeling like a silly fifteen-year-old. And then I saw him with this woman and it just, I don't know. It made me feel perfectly awful. I wanted to scratch her eyes out."

"Jealous? My goodness. So you must be in love with him after all."

"I don't know, Sharon."

Sharon looked at her closely. "What's holding you back?"

"Well, for one thing, I just spent a small fortune trying to make myself look ten years younger because of him."

"No, Diane, you did that because of you. He doesn't care, remember?"

"I'm suddenly feeling very insecure about things. Does that make any sense?

Sharon raised her eyebrows. "You? Insecure? Jesus, Diane. That's ridiculous."

Diane shook her head miserably. "I know. It's becoming serious and I'm a little freaked."

"That's understandable. I can't imagine what it would be like to fall in love at our age, with all we know and have been through. It's got to be huge."

"It is. And I feel I've got more at stake than he does, but that's not very fair, is it?"

"Maybe not fair, but true. You've got kids to think about, and he may be a smart guy, but he's clueless when it comes to all that."

"Exactly."

"Still, I think the two of you are great together."

"I do too. I just wish I were ten years younger."

"Hey, don't we all?"

When she got back to Michael's, David Go was sitting in the kitchen, watching Fred take apart three large, cooked lobsters. David reminded her of a garden gnome, small, bald, and ugly. He was charming and funny, and, according to Michael, very talented.

He grinned up at her. "Hello, love. You and Michael will be feasting tonight. Look at the size of those blighters."

"Fred, I said I'd cook tonight," Diane admonished.

Fred shrugged. "You will make him fat. Too much carbohydrate. Too much dessert. You very good cook, I can tell. You treat food with much respect. But he needs protein tonight. He worked all day. Mr. Prescott called four times."

Diane looked at David. "Oh, no. How bad?"

David shrugged. "Prescott is a fucking maniac. But Michael's tough. Go on in, we're done. He's floating around in there somewhere. I'm off to Manhattan. I'll be back tomorrow sometime."

"Have fun. Are you sure I can go back there?" Diane never interrupted Michael when he was working.

"Yes. Have him play for you what we did today. He's bloody brilliant, our Michael. Really. I've been doing this a long time. He'll win awards, if Prescott doesn't kill him."

She walked back towards the studio. Music was playing, a woman's voice, very sweet and Celtic. She looked into the studio, a long, windowless cave-like space that always intimidated her. It was empty. She took another few steps into his office and looked in.

Michael's office was covered on two walls with floor-to-ceiling bookcases, crammed with books, papers, his awards, and souvenirs of his travels. There was also a television and stereo equipment on the shelves, a few videos, and CDs. One wall was solid glass, overlooking the front expanse of yard. The last wall was filled with his desk, a long, cluttered work table filled with two computers and various printers, fax machines and a copy machine. There was a battered leather sofa by the window, and a large leather swivel chair in front of the desk

He was there, barefoot, dressed in shorts and a polo shirt, listening very carefully to the music playing. She could see the concentration on his face, the complete stillness of his body. She did not interrupt him, but listened with him as the song ended. He sensed her, turned, and broke into a smile.

"Hi. You're back."

She crossed over to him and kissed him lightly. "Yes. David says you're to play something for me. He says you're bloody brilliant."

"Listen to this girl. Prescott wants her for the ballad. What do you think?"

"I like her. She's got a great quality to her voice."

Another song started up."Yes, she does," Michael said. "She's well trained. I never had voice lessons. I just open my mouth and hope for the best. But she's got great control."

167

Diane sat down and began to spin around on the swivel chair. Michael reached over to pick up a stack of papers, a fax from Prescott, frowning. He glanced at her.

"I like your toes," he said, smiling quickly.

"Thanks. They're supposed to make me look devastatingly sexy."

He chuckled, still reading. "You're already sexy," he murmured, flipping a page.

"As sexy as that blonde the other night?"

He was frowning again. "What blonde?"

Diane stopped spinning and was watching him as he read, eyes moving, looking displeased.

"At the movies."

He was shaking his head at something, then glanced up at her again. "You mean Janice?"

"Janice? She told you her name?"

Something in her voice made him look back up. "Yes. Her name was Janice."

"Did she come on to you?"

He put down the papers. "She invited me for a drink."

Diane sat up straighter. "What did you say to her?"

Annoyance flickered in his voice. "What do you think I said? I said sure, and we drove to her place, had a couple of drinks, then I fucked her and drove back to the theater, just in time for you to come out of the bathroom."

Her eyes narrowed. "Are you pissed off at me now?"

Michael took in a deep breath. "What are you doing? What is this all about?"

"I'm not doing anything."

"Yes, you are." He was angry. She could hear the hard edge in his voice. She had heard it before, but

168

never directed toward her, and braced herself against him.

"You're trying to pick a fight," he continued. "I had never met that woman before, and will never see her again, and you're trying to make something out of it. If anyone has a reason to be jealous, it's me, not you."

She stared at him. "What have you got to be jealous about?"

"Your old boyfriend is coming back, isn't he? In a couple of weeks?"

"Who are you talking about?" she asked, angrily.

"The Englishman. Harris."

Diane clamped her jaw. "He has nothing to do with this."

"And what the hell has Janice to do with anything? I didn't spend three minutes with her and decide I wanted to spend the rest of my fucking life with her, as you apparently did with Harris. It's funny, we've been together every day for weeks and you can't figure out if you're in love with me or not, but you made up your mind about him quick enough."

"I told you that was a long time ago."

"Not so long, Diane. Only two years ago. Were you in love with him?"

She chewed her lip. "Yes."

"Did you fuck him?"

"No."

"Did you want to?"

"Yes." She looked at him, her eyes blazing. "Yes, I wanted to. I wanted to go off to London and marry him. I fantasized about bringing up the girls in England. I used to imagine terrible things happening to his wife so we could be together." The words were coming faster now. "I thought that if I could spend the rest of my life with him, I'd never ask for another thing.

When I made up my mind not to see him anymore, I spent two days in my room crying. If I saw him on campus, I'd have to run in the other direction because it hurt so much. After he left, I actually bought a ticket to London so I could fly after him. When I cancelled the ticket, I was drunk for a night and a day. Is that what you want to hear, Michael? How much I wanted Quinn Harris?"

"Do you still want him?" Michael's voice was quiet, his face pale.

"I'm with you, Michael," she said softly.

"That doesn't answer my question."

"No," she said tiredly. "I guess it doesn't." She stood up and walked across the room, staring out the window.

"Quinn was like a dream come true," she said softly. "He was kind and thoughtful and charming and brilliant, really brilliant. It wasn't just who he was that I fell in love with, but what he represented, the kind of life I could have had with him. It was the kind of life I had always thought I wanted. Until I met you. Now I don't know what I want."

She turned and looked at him, taking a deep breath. "I never imagined I could be happy with somebody like you. Not just the age thing, but everything about you is just so different from what I've been planning for the rest of my life. Do I still want Quinn? How can I? What I feel when I'm with you is so far removed from anything I imagined with Quinn. It's like wanting to walk and then learning to fly. It's overwhelming. It makes everything in my head so much harder to figure out." She hugged herself tightly. "I don't know if I love you, Michael, but I know I can't lose you. I couldn't stand it. When I saw you with Janice the other night and thought that maybe you might want somebody younger, I felt so awful, God, this huge empty feeling in the pit of my stomach." She spun around, spreading her arms wide, laughing shakily. "I just spent about three hundred dollars to look younger and sexier so you won't leave me."

He was watching her. "I'm not going to leave you, Diane," he said carefully. "You know, my father never found another woman after my mother died. He said that she had been his great love, and he wanted no other. I believe in that. I believe that you can find one person to love forever. And I love you."

"I know." She nodded and hugged herself again. She chewed her lip. "Do you think we have a future, Michael?"

He pushed his hands into his front pockets and leaned back against his desk. "Why wouldn't we?"

"I think about it, that's all. When you're my age, I'll be retired. I'll probably be a grandmother. You could still have a great career going, I mean, look at people like McCartney and Jagger, they're in their sixties. When you're in your sixties I'll be in a walker, going to the MTV Awards hooked up to oxygen. Do you ever think about that stuff?"

He chuckled and shook his head. "No, I don't."

"What about kids? Because if you want any, you're with the wrong woman."

"I haven't thought about that either. My dad has plenty of grandchildren, I have lots of cousins to carry on the family name. If I wanted children badly enough, we would find a way. It's not a deal breaker."

"What if I got sick? My dad died of cancer, and there's heart disease on Mom's side. Genetically, I'm doomed. You were eight when your mother died, Michael. Would you want to go through something like that again?"

He stopped smiling. "No. I can't think of anything more excruciating than watching – no." He took a step toward her, then stopped. "Something could happen to me too, you know? I could get sick as well, get into an accident, hell, Diane, it's all a crapshoot, isn't it? I love you, and if you get old and feeble and toothless, I'll still love you. And if I'm crippled or senile, I hope –" He stopped. They looked at each other across the room.

"This is a very strange conversation we're having, isn't it?" Diane asked softly.

He shrugged. "We've talked about everything in the past few months, religion, music, books, skin diving, everything except what we want from each other. Why do you think that is?"

"Because, generally we're happy with each other? If it ain't broke, don't fix it, right?"

"So does this mean we're broke?"

"No." She crossed over to him and put her arms around his neck, feeling the strong, familiar strength of his body. "I think we're fine. I think we just needed to set a few things straight. Please don't worry about Quinn."

His hands were in her hair, pushing the soft curls away from her face. "And I don't want you running off spending money on trying to look younger every time I talk to somebody under thirty, okay? Although, you do look great. You've got a glow, or something."

"Mud treatment."

"Really? Okay, that's gross. But you look great." He grinned. "Are you glowing all over?"

"Maybe we could get naked later and see."

"Okay," he said softly. His eyes were still troubled, and she traced the outline of his lips with her finger.

"Michael, don't you trust me enough to know that I would never hurt you?"

"I know that you would never deliberately look around for somebody else. But this is different. How do you know what you'll feel when you see him again?"

"I don't know. And maybe you're right. Maybe I'll have this irresistible urge to spend the rest of my Sundays in front of a quiet fire, reading the London Times, instead of sailing off with you into another glorious day. But I wouldn't bet on it, okay? I think you're stuck with me."

"Yeah?"

"Yeah."

"I can live with that." He kissed her, and she kissed him back, deeply, her arms tightening.

"When you kiss me like that," he murmured, "things start to happen."

Diane pulled away from him, smiling. "Sorry, didn't mean to start anything. Not just this second, anyway. Now, do you feel like lobster?"

"You tell me." He slid his hands down her back and pressed her against him. "Is this what a lobster feels like?"

She giggled, easing her hands into the waistband of his shorts. He kissed her again, hard, no longer playful and teasing.

"Wait," she whispered, "wait, the door. What if David –"

"I don't care," he said, reaching behind her to pull the zipper of her dress down her back. The dress slid to the floor, followed by her bra, and he pulled her forward, sinking back onto the couch, pushing away her panties as she straddled him. He brought his hand between her legs, a feather's touch, and she kissed him, soft, light kisses, as he stroked her.

He took her breast into his mouth, and she froze, sensation becoming too intense, and she waited, because she knew what his hands could do, knew how his mouth could make her feel. He was always slow, patient, coaxing her along until her orgasm broke like a pounding wave, and she gripped his shoulders as his fingers slid into her, wet and waiting. His tongue teased her, and his hand moved faster, flat against her now, and she threw her head back as the spasms took her, unable to breathe, mouth open in a noiseless scream. Then she sagged against him, a roar in her ears, and the ragged sound of her own breath.

She opened her eyes at last and she realized it was his body that was trembling now, not hers. His eyes were wide and blue, and his hands gripped her thighs.

"It's just that I love you so much," he said, as though picking up a thread of conversation they had just dropped a moment ago. "I love you, and I need you." His voice was low and hoarse. "Prescott, and the movie, it's making me crazy, and you are keeping me grounded. I need that, more than I ever knew."

"What happens when the movie is done?" She swallowed hard. "Will you need me then?"

He shook his head hard. "I didn't mean it like that." He looked away from her, finding words. "This house - I've lived here for almost four years now, and it's never been home. Even when Gretchen lived with me, it was just a place to eat and sleep. I never felt it was mine. Until you. You're here now, and at last I have a place to belong. Wherever you are, that's where I belong. That's what I need. That's what you give me."

He moved beneath her, and as she rose on her knees, he slid forward, pulling down his down, and when she lowered herself down, he was hard and slick, and he filled her, as he filled all her lost and empty places.

"When we make love," he whispered, "it's where I'm supposed to be. With you."

She moved against him, and a flicker of pleasure took her. He saw the change in her face, and took his hands away from her, forcing them down on the cool leather.

"Go on. Do what you want." She moved again, rubbing herself against him, and his eyes glittered as he watched her. "Just tell me when. I want us to come together." He pushed his hands against the couch as she rose and fell, and he clenched his jaw. "Don't close your eyes," he told her, and she pressed her forehead against his.

"I'm here, Michael, for as long as you want me." She did not recognize her own voice. "You know that. I'm right here." She felt the heat exploding. "Now. Now."

He gripped her around the waist and plunged and they both felt the white-hot flash, Diane crying out, Michael again finding home.

CHAPTER NINE

Mark Bender called to ask Michael if he could come out for the weekend. "It's too fucking hot in Hoboken, man. I need green."

Sure," Michael laughed. "Come on out. It's green here."

Mark left Manhattan early Friday and drove straight out to Mendham. Fred showed him to a guest room, and he quickly changed and headed out to the pool. Michael was alone, drinking beer, looking out over the lake.

"So - where is everybody?" Mark asked, sitting down, sipping beer.

Michael took a deep breath. "Seth is in Atlanta. I don't know why. David is up in Toronto, getting musicians lined up. Diane is down at the shore." He glanced over at his friend. "Glad you're here, man. I don't know what I'd do all by myself."

Mark looked at Michael closely. He was thinner, looking tired. "How's the movie thing coming?"

Michael brightened. "Great. I'll have to play some stuff for you. Different, you know? Really different from anything I've done before. The director is driving me fucking crazy, but it's cool. So far I can deal."

"So, what's with Diane?" Mark asked. He was fascinated by his friends' relationship with Diane. They were the same age, and had until now been attracted to the same type of woman. Diane had come out of left field, as far as Mark was concerned. Not just her age, but her interests, background and attitude. Mark was the first to agree she was a sexy, attractive woman. But beyond that, he was mystified.

Michael shrugged. He knew that Mark didn't understand his feelings for Diane, but that didn't affect the friendship. "She's with her girls," he explained.

"They're staying with their father down in Beach Haven. He's got a house. She drove down yesterday, just for the night, to spend some time with them."

"So, how come you're not with her?" Mark asked.

Michael took a long drink. "She hasn't told them we're seeing each other. It's some kind of, I don't know, code or something."

"What the fuck are you talking about?" Mark shook his head. "What kind of code?"

"I don't know. She doesn't want them to know, because I'm a fucking rock star and both of her girls have a crush on me, or some such shit. And she doesn't want them to get too attached, because we haven't been together very long, and what if we break up tomorrow, then the girls would be all upset. I don't know, I've been drinking all afternoon. But I think that covers most of it."

"Oh, man," Mark pulled a bag of pot out of his pocket and began to roll a joint. "How do you feel about that? Sounds pretty fucked up."

Michael shook his head, watching Mark carefully tamp down the marijuana. "No. She's got a point. Her oldest daughter got kinda pissed off when she found out about us, you know?"

"Yeah?" Mark ran his tongue down the edge of the paper, and sealed the joint shut. "Did the oldest daughter have a crush too?"

Michael shrugged.

Mark flicked his lighter and drew on the joint. "So, is she hot?"

"Who?"

"The daughter, man. You could do, like, a threesome, you know? How fucking cool would that be?"

Michael passed his hand over his eyes. "Mark, you are so twisted. I can't believe it. I wouldn't sleep with her daughter. Shit." He started laughing. "Yeah, I can see me suggesting that. Diane would fucking kill me. She'd pick up a chair and beat me to a pulp."

Mark took another hit. "Want some?"

Michael made a face. "You know better."

Mark leaned his head back. "Can we go sailing later? I love sailing when I'm high."

Michael took another swig of beer. "Sure. Then we'll eat. How about the pub?"

Mark nodded, and smoked the joint in silence. He carefully tamped it out, and got to his feet. "Let's go, man. I want to sail."

They spent the next hour on the water, then came in and went into town to eat. Mark was a good distraction for Michael. They talked about their high school days together, about the upcoming reunion.

"Next year," Mark said excitedly. "It'll be great. You and I were two of the biggest geeks, man, and look at us now. You're like a star, and I'm going to make a million fucking dollars this year. Don't you want to see Warren Estes face when he sees us?"

"Warren Estes? Shit, I haven't thought about him in years. He was such an asshole."

"I know, man. I hope he's selling fucking insurance somewhere, married to some fat bitch." Mark was trying to roll another joint as Michael drove home. "I want to see that redhead, you know, the cheerleader. Shit, she had the most perfect set of tits in all of Fabian's. You know who I mean?"

Michael chuckled. "Yeah. I know who you mean."

Mark lit the joint and took a long drag. "Every guy in the whole school tried to get in her pants. I know she was fucking somebody, I mean, I know it. I could just never figure out who."

Michael looked sideways at his friend. "That was me, man."

Mark stared. "What? You? You're kidding me. You have to be. She was a fuckin' foot taller than you, Mike."

"Just about. It was after I joined the band - of course. She didn't know I was alive before that. But that whole senior year, it was amazing. Denise followed me around every weekend, chasing girls away, trying to protect my innocence. But during the week, I'd be over at her house." Michael shook his head, remembering.

"Fuck you, man. I can't believe you never told me. Shit." Mark stared out the window. "So, tell me now. Was that the best sex ever? I mean, it had to be. She was so fuckin' hot. I know, you've had more women than any five regular guys, but she was the best, right?"

Michael drove, watching the road, turning up toward the house. "No, man. The best is right now," he said shortly. He looked sharply at his friend. "And I'm not going to tell you all about it, okay?"

Mark threw up his hands and shrugged. "Okay."

They went into the house. Mark headed for the kitchen, grabbed a couple of beers, and met Michael back out by the pool. Michael had not turned on the lights, and the only light was from the quarter moon. He took the beer from Mark and watched as Mark pulled off his clothes and dove naked into the pool. Seconds later, Max jumped in after him.

"If your dog tries to bite my dick, I'm gonna be really pissed off," Mark called, swimming lazily.

Michael laughed. "Max ignores anything under an inch long, man, you're safe."

Mark pulled himself out of the pool and padded to the table, took a long drink of his beer, then slumped down into a chair. "So, you'll see Diane tomorrow night? Do you want me to leave?"

Michael shook his head. "No, she'll probably spend tomorrow night at her place. I won't see her 'till Sunday. Stay. I have to work tomorrow, but you can hang. Seth should be back, though. You two can go trolling for women."

"Yeah?" Mark looked encouraged. "That would be cool." They sat in silence for a few minutes. "So, why won't you see Diane?"

Michael shrugged. "She likes to spend time alone, that's all. It's no big deal." He looked at Mark. "This is kind weird for her, I think. She wasn't exactly expecting somebody like me to suddenly appear in her life. She just has to re-group sometimes."

"She sounds like a very complicated woman," Mark said, shuddering.

"She is. That's the great thing, you know? We've been together almost three months. And I've never been bored. Not once. She's fantastic."

Max hauled himself out of the pool and stood in front of Mark as he shook himself. Water flew everywhere. Mark cursed. Michael just laughed.

Michael drove over to Diane's late Sunday afternoon. It was hot, the air heavy with rain, the sun behind clouds. Her car was in the driveway. He walked into the house without knocking. She had given him a key at the start of the summer, but he rarely used it. She was always home when he came by.

Music was blasting, as usual. The Supremes. He smiled as he followed a series of thumps back to the den.

She was rearranging furniture, trying to push the loveseat against the wall. Michael stepped in and picked up an end, sliding it effortlessly in place. She grinned at him.

"You have perfect timing, as usual." She came over and put her arms around his waist, kissing him.

"What happened to you?" he asked, frowning. There was a long scrape down her cheek, and a gauze bandage on her elbow.

Diane shrugged and looked embarrassed. "I fell. Megan wanted me to go roller-blading, and I stupidly said I'd try. I'm the world's biggest klutz. I should have known better. I totally wiped out on my very first attempt." She twisted her arm and looked at her elbow. "This isn't so bad. My thigh is all tore up." She turned to show him. Her upper leg was red and raw.

"God - does it hurt?"

"Just a little. The worst part was having an ER nurse pick gravel out of my butt."

Michael chuckled. "That, I would have liked to see. How are the girls?"

"Great. Help me here, okay?" They maneuvered the television back into the corner. Diane looked around. "Better, don't you think? More room?"

"Yeah. I wish you'd let me help you with this kind of stuff."

"You just did. Thank you." She put her arms around him again. "So how was your weekend?"

"Good. Mark was over."

"And how is Mark?"

"He thinks you're a complicated woman."

Diane shook her head. "Nothing against your friends, but Mark would think a bendable Barbie was complicated." She kissed him, slowly. Michael brought his hands up from her hips, across her back, and she winced.

"What? Your back too?" He turned her around and lifted her tee shirt. The left side of her back was badly scraped . "That has to hurt," he said.

"Only if I touch it," she said ruefully.

"Well, that shoots the hell out of my next suggestion," Michael said with a chuckle.

"Hmm, we'll see. Beer?"

"No. Thanks." He followed her into the kitchen. "Mark was drunk or high all weekend. Un-fucking-believable. I drank so much beer I'm going to feel buzzed for the next three days."

"And every other word out of your mouth for at least a week will be 'fuck'"

He laughed. " He does say that a lot. Can I help?"

"Sure." She was husking corn, and handed him two ears. "I've got crabs in the cooler in the garage, still kicking, so they'll be great, and corn and tomatoes and half a peach pie from a farm stand down there. How does that sound?"

"Wow, you mean I'll get to eat and everything?"

"Of course. You think I'd just have you move furniture then send you home?"

"Here." He handed her the corn, then shook the silky fibers into the garbage.

"So, what did you say to Mark?" She poured iced tea and handed him a glass.

"Say to Mark about what?"

"About me being complicated?"

"Oh, I knew you weren't going to let me off the hook about that one. Let's see." He took a long drink of tea and looked deliberately thoughtful. "I told him I didn't understand a thing you said or did, but you gave the best blow job I'd ever gotten, so I didn't care."

Diane rolled her eyes and went past him into the living room. She sat down gingerly on the edge of the coffee table and Michael sat across from her on the couch, his feet propped on the table next to her. "So tell me," she said softly. "Tell me everything that you did while I was gone."

He told her, watching her face. Her hair was wild around her, thick and curling from the humidity. Her face was tan, lips pale with no make-up. Her eyes, as she listened, got wider, dancing as she smiled. She leaned forward, and he could smell the clean lemon of her shampoo. He had stopped talking, he suddenly realized, and was staring, listening to the hum of air conditioning. The music changed. The Temptations.

"Don't you listen to anything recorded after 1982?" he asked her.

She tilted her head to the side, thinking. "I don't think so. What are you staring at?"

"You look gorgeous."

She chewed her lip, glancing downward, and he could see her starting to blush.

"I look like a gypsy," she said, bringing her hands to her hair and trying to pat down the curls.

"Okay. You look like a gorgeous gypsy."

She smiled, grabbed his hand and pulled him off the couch. He followed her into the bedroom.

"What about your back?" he asked as he pulled off his clothes.

"You can't touch. At all." She pushed him onto the bed, and climbed on top of him. "I mean it." Her hair fell around his face as she kissed him. He tried to bring his hands to her face, but she caught them and pushed them back against the bed, holding his wrists on either side of his face.

"Close your eyes," she suggested, "and try to relax." He gave himself over. He could feel her, her mouth, her hands, the thick fall of her hair. He kept his eyes closed, his hands buried into the bedclothes. He heard thunder, loud and very close. She stroked him, licked him, and kissed him until he thought he would burst. Her voice was in his ear, a warm whisper. Is this good? How about this? Do you like it? Tell me what you want. Then he felt her, her weight on his hips, sliding onto him slowly, rocking, and he opened his eyes and saw her watching him, a smile on her lips as she led him, faster, until he rose against her as thunder rattled the windows and rain pounded against the roof. She slid off him and snuggled against his shoulder. He was breathing heavily, damp with sweat.

"I think the earth really moved," he said at last.

She giggled. "It could have been the thunder."

"Oh - okay. Well, still." He turned his head to look at her. "How about you? Do you mind when you don't come?"

Diane kissed him quickly. "Sometimes it's not about the big orgasm, you know? Sometimes it's just about being close." She traced his lower lip with her finger. "I just wanted you inside me, that's all."

He exhaled slowly. "That is such a chick thing."

She giggled again. "Oh, d'ya think?"

"Yeah. I'm pretty sure, in the entire history of mankind, no guy has every said to his buddy, 'well, I didn't come, but that's okay, I just wanted to be close.'"

Diane blew into his skin, making a loud raspberry noise. "You men are pigs. Seriously."

"I know we are." He got up on one elbow and looked at her back. "Man, your ass looks horrible," he said, startled.

"Oh, I don't know," she said, turning to look. "A little cellulite, maybe, but not that bad."

"You know what I mean." There was a large scrape, looking red and ugly against her pale skin. "Are you supposed to be putting something on that?"

"Yes. The doctor gave me salve and gauze and stuff."

"In the bathroom?" he asked, rolling from the bed and walking naked across the floor. He returned with a white plastic bag, sat back next to her, and spilled the contents on to the bed.

"Here, let's try this first," he suggested, examining a tube.

"Michael, you don't have to do this," she said, feeling embarrassed.

"Who else is going to do it? You can't reach. Besides, you just fulfilled one of my long-standing fantasies."

"Oh? You've always wanted to make love to a woman with rocks in her butt?"

He chuckled and applied the salve gently. "No. During a thunderstorm. It's very tricky timing. Now, I can check another one off my list. Want some on your back?"

"That would be good. Any other fantasies I can help you with?"

"Maybe. Since you don't have a sister, are you close to your friend Carol?"

"Forget it. Next please?"

"How do you feel about handcuffs?"

"Oh, very cute. Ouch, not so hard."

"Shit, I'm sorry. Is that better?"

"Yes. It takes the sting out. Thank you."

"Sure." He wiped his fingers with gauze. "All done."

"I really appreciate it. You're always doing the nicest things for me."

"I love you, remember?"

"I know. And I'm grateful every day."

"Are you hungry?"

"No, not really."

"Will the crabs keep?"

"For a while."

185

"Then let's just stay here. When the rain stops, we'll get out of bed."

"Good plan."

He stretched out on his back, and she curled against him, and they fell asleep with the sound of the rain on the roof.

Marianne Thomas gave Diane a call. Classes were starting, and Marianne had come back from her annual pilgrimage to Crete. They agreed to meet for lunch.

Marianne could not believe how lovely Diane looked. Her hair was long, glossy and curling. Her face was tanned, her eyes bright and happy. Marianne clucked her tongue as Diane sat down.

"I take it you're still with that beautiful boy?" Marianne asked, arching a plucked eyebrow.

Diane made a face. "He's not a boy, Marianne."

"No, but he is beautiful. What happened to your face?"

"I fell. I tried to go roller-blading with Megan."

"God, why would you want to do that?"

Diane shrugged. "I don't know. Maybe I'm having a midlife crisis."

"I would think," Marianne said carefully, "that having frequent sex with a man roughly half your age would ward off any impending midlife crisis."

Diane examined the menu. "So, tell me. Tell me about Greece. Did everyone remember you again this year? It must be like a family reunion by now. You've been going back to the same place since before I knew you. What, eight years?"

"Yes, as a matter of fact. It has been eight years. They even fixed me up this time, with a lovely English woman, who was as desperate about the dearth of Greek lesbians as I was." Marianne shook out her napkin. "She left me feeling pretty much the way you look"

"How do I look?" Diane looked over the top of the menu.

"Cherished."

Diane took a gulp of the wine the waiter placed in front of her. Marianne sipped hers, watching her friend.

"Are you in love with this man?" Marianne asked suddenly.

Diane set down the menu slowly. "I've been asking myself that question a lot lately. The girls are home next week. I won't be able to see him every day, once I'm back to work. The play is going to take up so much time, I had no idea. I feel like a junkie about to be taken off drugs. Is that because I need him? Love him? I don't know. I think I do. He says he's in love with me."

"He says?"

"Yes."

"Do you believe him?"

"Oh, yes."

"Have you been living with him?" Marianne asked.

"No. Not exactly. I've been going home everyday, usually on my way to school, to feed the cat, get mail. Change clothes. All I've got at his place is a toothbrush. I do stuff at the house. I can't call my mother from his place, it just feels too weird. She never forgave me divorcing Kevin, and I can just imagine what she'd think of all this. But we haven't been apart more than a couple of nights in a row all summer."

"How cozy."

"I know. And it's all about to change. And Quinn Harris is coming back and teaching another class this fall. It's a done deal. Sam told me."

Marianne took another sip. "This is all so interesting. Maybe I shouldn't go away next year. It seems I've missed an awful lot."

"I've been living in a very artificial world all summer. I mean, he has a boat, we sail. We have lunch served by the pool. We run into The City whenever I want. There's all this great sex at the drop of a hat. That's not how I usually run my life, you know that. I don't know how I'm supposed to fit him into my real world."

"Well, this can't be the real world for him, either, can it? I mean, isn't he usually doing something other than catering to your every whim? Doesn't he tour or record or make videos or something?"

"Yes. Right now he's working on a score for a movie. He'll probably be going up to Toronto in the next few weeks. For a month or so, he thinks."

"So, you won't be able to see him all the time anyway, right?"

Diane shrugged. "We haven't really figured that out. He says he'll fly back. I could go up on weekends"

"There, see, aren't you glad I'm back? I've solved all your problems for you in half a drink."

Diane shook her head. "I don't know what to do about Quinn. Until I met Michael, I kept hoping he would divorce his wife, come back here and sweep me off my feet. Apparently he has divorced her, and he's on his way back. Now what do I do?"

"My dear woman," Marianne said severely, "You've already been swept. Don't get greedy."

"You know how I felt about Quinn," Diane said. "He was everything I ever wanted."

"What's Michael?"

"Michael is more," Diane said softly. "He's wonderful, but let's face it, he's almost twenty years younger than I am. How much longer can this possibly last?"

"Have you asked him?"

Diane stared down at the linen tablecloth. "He says there's no reason we can't have a future together. He just hasn't exactly figured out what it would be like, and neither have I."

"Well maybe it's time you did, especially if he's going off to Toronto. How would you feel if he got lonely up there and latched on to somebody else?"

Diane gaped at her friend. "Michael? He would never do that."

"How the hell do you know? You're sitting here, trying to decide if you should make a run at some man you met two years ago, just in case the whole Michael thing takes a dive. How do you know he's not thinking the same thing about some cute little Canadian groupie he met up there?"

"He would never walk away from what we've had for the past three months," Diane said indignantly. "He's in love with me."

"And you aren't in love with him. How long do you think he's going to be happy with that?"

"Shit," Diane said softly.

"Amen to that." Marianne signaled the waiter, who came and took their order. They sat quietly for a few more minutes. Diane chewed her lip thoughtfully.

"So I guess it's time to fish or cut bait, huh?" Diane asked at last.

"It might not be a bad thing, you know. Wouldn't you like to know where this is going?"

Diane shook her head. "No. And this is so unlike me. You know how I am about stuff. Although the phrase 'control freak' rarely comes up in conversation with my close friends, I like knowing exactly where things are going, and how, and why. I think I love him.

I really do. I feel like a kid with my head in the clouds. But what if I'm not? Does that mean it will all end? I don't want this to end." She ran her fingers up and down the stem of her glass. "He's in my head all the time. He crowds out so much. Maybe it's a good thing he'll be gone, because I don't know how I could concentrate on anything with him right there. I feel like it's him and then everything else. But the everything else is my life. It's my job and my house, picking up the girls after school, doing laundry. I don't know how I'd say no to him because of something I had to do for Emily. I'd hate it."

"Don't you think you're not giving him enough credit?" Marianne leaned forward, covering Diane's hand with her own. "He's not a selfish person, is he? Surely he would understand your choices."

Diane sighed. "It's not about him. He's very generous. Of course he'd understand. He makes no demands on me, Marianne, even when I know that maybe he doesn't understand what I'm doing, or why. He never questions me, never tries to talk me out of anything. It's me. I'm projecting, I guess. Isn't that the current psycho-babble? He doesn't ask things of me, but I feel the need to change for him. For his happiness, or comfort. It's scary. It's confusing. I don't know how to get my mind around it."

The waiter appeared, setting their plates in front of them. Diane cut her burger in half and began eating, slowly and carefully. Marianne watched her.

Diane put her burger down suddenly. "So - how can I even be thinking about Quinn? God, I am such an awful person."

"No, you're not. You're one of the best people I know." Marianne speared a tomato and chewed thoughtfully. "Quinn isn't quite so scary or confusing.

Maybe that's why. He would be a much simpler choice."

Diane looked at her burger. "When I'm under stress, I tend to eat lots of red meat," she said.

"Yes," Marianne agreed, "I've noticed that about you. You'd better buy lots of steak."

Diane nodded glumly, and finished her lunch in silence.

She drove out to Michael's that afternoon. The sky had become cloudy, rain threatened, but she found him out by the pool. Seth was there, a beautiful, leggy redhead beside him. Stephanie had become a regular visitor. As far as Diane could tell, she had no job of any kind, other than making Seth happy, and she seemed to do that fairly well. The table was littered with glasses, wedges of lemon, and a half-empty bottle of tequila. Diane took in the scene with mild alarm. Michael did not drink often, not to this extent, and never so early in the day.

Michael was sitting at the table, wearing shorts, his Hawaiian-style shirt unbuttoned, and his feet bare. His hair had grown longer during the summer, his skin was smooth and brown. Seth saw her first, and shouted a greeting. She liked Seth a lot. He was smart and very talented, took very few things outside his music seriously, and was a great friend to Michael.

"Sit down, my sweet," Seth yelled at her as she came out of the house. "We have decided to go to Bermuda. Stephanie says there are pink beaches in Bermuda, and I want pink beaches. Lochinvar here is coming with us."

Diane came up behind Michael and kissed the top of his head. "Lochinvar hates to go anywhere. How did you manage this?"

"Come with me," Michael said, grabbing her hand. "We'll only be three or four days." His eyes were slightly unfocused, his speech loose and happy.

Diane shook her head. "I cannot go to Bermuda. Sorry."

"Why not?" Michael kissed her hand.

"For one thing, I just spent eight hundred bucks on the car and I can't afford to go."

"That's bullshit," Michael said happily. "I'll pay for everything. No, don't get all huffy. I know you don't like me paying for shit, but this would be different." He drew her head in closely and whispered loudly, "Once we get there, I fully intend to exploit you sexually."

Diane laughed. "Oh? Well, then, that's different." She wrapped her arms around his neck and rubbed her cheek against his. "Would costumes be involved?"

Seth and Stephanie were smiling, but Michael looked thoughtful.

"Well," he said finally, "Maybe just that French maid thing. I like you in black."

Seth threw back his head and howled. Michael turned to him in mock anger.

"Oh, yeah, like you never played 'The Pirate and the Princess.'"

Seth was laughing, pounding the table with his palm. "I can't believe you, man, you are one fucked up dude," he sputtered. "Pirate. Oh man." Seth took a breath and sat up straighter. He looked at Stephanie seriously. "Maybe we'll try that tonight?" He asked, and then burst into laughter again. Diane was laughing with him.

"How long have you guys been out here?" She finally asked. "I'm going to have to play catch-up, I think." She sat down and poured a shot, then sprinkled salt on her hand. "And why did we decide on this little trip anyway?" she asked, licking the salt and downing the shot. She grabbed the lemon wedge, sucking it as Seth answered.

"Because London is going to be so fucking cold," he shouted, pointing an unsteady finger at her. "London is always so fucking cold. I need a major dose of sunshine before London. I hate the fucking rain." He turned to Stephanie, nuzzling her neck. "Will you keep me warm and dry in London?" he asked, and she giggled.

Diane licked the taste of lemon from her lips and turned to look at Michael. "London?"

Seth stopped laughing. Michael was looking closely at the backs of his hands.

Michael cleared his throat. "London. Prescott called this morning. His daughter starts school in a few weeks, so he's doing all his post-production work there instead of Toronto. We'll do all the sessions for the soundtrack as well as all the scoring in London. He's got the studio. He wants us there Tuesday."

"London?" Diane repeated. Michael did not look at her. She turned to Seth. His eyes were large and round, sober now.

Diane reached over and took Michael's hand, pulling him out of the chair. She led him back to the house and to the end of the terrace, where the sliding doors to his bedroom were open. She pushed him into the room, and carefully shut the doors. She reached and pulled the pale gray drapes closed. His room was very quiet.

She took a deep breath and turned around. He was sitting on the edge of his bed, leaning forward, his head in his hands.

"How long, do you think?" Diane asked softly.

He shrugged. "Prescott is a ball-buster. You know what he's been like." He lifted his head and looked at her. "The print that he sent me, the one I've been working on for three fucking weeks, he now says has to be re-cut. Again. That means new music to be written. David left this morning, right after Prescott called, to get everything set up that he's going to need, lining up musicians, all the shit that I know nothing about. Toronto was going to suck, but at least it was close, at least the same fucking continent. I could have come down for a night or a day. Not now." He shook his head. "I hate this. I am going to miss you more than you can imagine."

Diane was shaking her head. "I can't believe this, I mean, Marianne and I were just talking about this, how things were going to be so different. Once the girls were back, and school started, it was going to be hard, you know, not being able to see you whenever I wanted. This makes it easier for me, really." She was watching Michael's face, seeing his expression soften and change.

"I wasn't even sure how I was going to tell the girls about us, you know? I've been going crazy about this, how I was going to get up to Toronto, the whole thing was going to be such a mess. So I guess this kind of solves everything, doesn't it?"

"Yes," he said, very quietly. "I guess it does."

He stood up and reached to hold her, but she stepped back from him. He watched her as she took a deep, ragged breath, dragging her hands through her hair, closing her eyes tightly. He covered his face with his hands, exhaled slowly, and when he pulled them away seconds later, she was calm, her breath slow, hands falling away. When she looked at him, her eyes were shiny with tears.

She did not want him to go. Suddenly faced with the long and dark days and nights that stretched out ahead of her, she wanted to ask him to stay with her.

But she knew that this movie was more than just a new and different project for him. This was something that could help define him as a musician, as a composer. This was something that would take him from being a just another guy in a band and put him someplace else, not necessarily better, but someplace different. She knew he wanted it. She knew how badly he wanted more.

"I'm going to miss you, too," she said simply. "Terribly." She tried to smile. "Is this where we pledge undying loyalty and devotion?"

His eyes were very big. "Do you think we need to? You know I love you."

"Yes. "

"Forever, Diane. I will love you forever."

She looked at him. "Michael, think about what you're saying. You and I will never grow old together. You know that. There is no forever with us."

"Of course there is," he said softly. "We aren't like everybody else, you and I. You know that. We'll have a different kind of forever."

She moved then, and they fell back onto his bed, fierce, hungry, and she was aware of every hard line of muscle, each inch of familiar flesh. She tore at his clothes, her mouth closing on him, her hands stroking, coaxing, bringing him to the edge then pulling back, until he was gasping, breathless, and she straddled him and rode him, her hair falling around his face. His hands were on her breasts, then down around her waist, pulling her, arching deep inside her, and she wanted to brand him somehow, to make sure he would remember this day, above all the other days; because this was the day she did not try to stop him from leaving her. She climaxed, and he came an instant later, and she fell forward, panting, tears coming, and he held her until the sobbing had stopped and she lay quiet and still in his arms.

And then he was gone, and the girls came back, and the rhythm of her life began again, almost, but not quite, as it had been before she had met him.

CHAPTER TEN

Emily was in her senior year. She had worked during the summer as a waitress and she had saved some money. For her car, she announced. After all, she was getting her license in March, and she didn't think she'd be happy sharing the Subaru, she wanted to use the money she made for her own car.

Diane sighed. "What about insurance? How are you going to pay for that?"

Emily shrugged. "Just add me to your policy," she said.

Diane raised her eyebrows. "What makes you think I can afford to add you? Do you have any idea how much that's going to cost?" Emily sighed and went upstairs without answering. Diane felt a headache coming on.

Megan decided not to go to France after all. She had met a boy while at the shore, Stan, a year older, a junior at a neighboring high school. She was in love, and didn't want to leave him next spring. Diane was relieved that it was no longer an issue, and did not mention to her daughter the possibility that Stan would be only a memory by next year.

Diane had one less class to teach that fall. Marianne had taken away her freshman comp class, to free time for the graduate class that she would begin in January. Rehearsals for her play were every day. Her part of the process was technically over, but she still was there two or three evenings a week, just to watch.

It was during one of those evenings, early in September, that Quinn Harris slipped into the back row of the auditorium and sat through a rehearsal. Diane did not notice him. The cast was getting through a complicated, funny scene in Act 1, and, when Sam called it a night, Quinn rose from his seat, clapping his hands.

Diane was surprised and happy to see him. He greeted her warmly, giving her a hug and a dry kiss on her cheek. He congratulated the cast, who were slightly star-struck in his presence. He and Sam began an immediate discussion of the scene. Diane listened, fascinated. Quinn had an intimate knowledge of all things theatrical. His passion for his work was one of the things she had loved about him

She watched him closely. He had not changed. He was a tall, slightly stoop-shouldered man, well-made and graceful. He was around fifty, with thinning hair and surprising green eyes. He had a nervous energy and seemed constantly in motion, his hands moving through the air as he spoke, his foot moving back and forth. He was shy, quiet with strangers, but dynamic and charming when talking about his craft, or among friends.

She was grateful for the small flurry of butterflies in her stomach. She was afraid she would react badly on seeing him again, afraid that all the old feelings would come back in a painful rush. She had worried about it, a small, constant nag that had been following her since classes had started. Now there was just a shimmer of nervousness, no icy palms, no rush of blood to her temples. She took a long slow breath. She really was over him.

He turned to Diane. "I would love to talk to you about this, both of you. Can you get away for a drink? Sam?" Sam was agreeable. Diane accepted gratefully. She was feeling anxious about the way the play was going, and knew that Quinn would give a sound, honest opinion.

They went down to the campus pub, drank coffee, and talked about her play until the place closed. He had

198

gotten a copy of the play from Sam a week before, and had read it carefully. He thought it was wonderful. He was pleased to see that Sam was keeping the actors light and fresh. It was a positive discussion, and as they left the pub, Diane was grateful for his input.

Sam said good-night, and Quinn walked her to her car. His hands were in his pants pockets, shoulders hunched.

"Would you like to have dinner, say, tomorrow night?" he asked, as she knew he would. When she hesitated, he hurried on. "Or the night after, or lunch, if that would be better."

"No, tomorrow would be fine. I've got a late class. I could meet you somewhere."

"Alright. Wonderful. Name the place."

"Where are you staying?"

"I'm in Manhattan, actually. I've got a flat up on West 82nd."

"Oh." She thought a minute. "Do you drive in?"

"Oh, good Lord, no. Train. Drops you right at the end of the lane here. Do you really think I'm idiot enough to try to drive through the Lincoln Tunnel?"

She smiled. "No, of course not. There's a great place, about three blocks from here. O'Briens. Ask for directions at the station. Around six thirty?"

"Lovely." He kissed her again, on her forehead. "Good night."

She got home late, too late for any work. She did not go on her computer, although Michael e-mailed her almost every day. He sent her bits and pieces of his life, the weather, Prescott's tantrum, Seth's adventures. She returned in kind, the girls, the play, her students. They did not say they missed one another. They did not talk about seeing each other again.

She had thrown herself into work, reworking her current classes, fine-tuning the graduate class to begin that spring. Emily had basketball practice almost every night. Megan became involved in the high school play, and was at her own rehearsals every night. Diane was pulled in too many directions, and she knew she had spread herself too thinly, but it filled the hours that had once been filled with Michael. She missed him unbearably. There were nights that her body ached for him. There were countless things each day, small, funny, moments that she would file in the back of her head so she could tell him, until she remembered he was not around. Every time it happened, it hurt her cruelly. She kept waiting for the feeling to dull. So far, it had not.

She met Quinn the following night with no expectations. She was lonely, and he was going to be pleasant company. He was waiting for her in the bar, ordered her a vodka martini without her having to remind him what she drank, and placed his hand on her arm as they walked to their table. He was impeccably dressed in a suit and tie. He was drinking scotch, neat, and immediately asked about her daughters, remembering their names, ages, and even the fact that Rachel had wanted to be in the theater. Diane answered his questions, flattered, smiling. *What a lovely man,* she kept thinking.

"So tell me," she finally said. " 'Present Laughter' is coming this spring? This is so great, Quinn. I'd heard it got raves on the West End."

"Well, we're casting now. Derek Shore is coming over, reprising his role. He was just knighted, did you know? Thank God we signed his contract before that whole affair. Sir Derek would have come at quite a premium, apparently. We've found a few girls, all lovely, we'll decide next week. We're opening in February. It's a limited run, so I'm not concerned about all that Tony Award madness that everyone seems to be so frantic about. We've got a young set designer, really brilliant. Should be quite a good time."

"That all sounds wonderful, Quinn. Is your daughter here with you?" Diane asked. Quinn's only child was in her twenties, and often traveled with him.

"No," he said shortly. "She's madly in love with a soap opera star and won't leave London."

"And you've divorced your wife?" she asked casually.

"Yes. It was a long time coming, actually." He was tapping his finger on the arm of his chair. "I really wish I had done it sooner."

Diane straightened her silverware. "I never thought you would do it. Get a divorce."

Quinn studied her. "I told you I would. I told you I was in love with you."

"Yes, I know you did, but after – I mean, I broke things off and then you went back to England and I didn't hear from you again, and I thought – I just didn't think you would. That's all."

"Yes. Well, the first piece of advice I received from my solicitor was to not give my wife any ammunition. If she thought for a moment there was someone else, she would have fought like a tiger. As it was, she dragged her heels for as long as she could." He leaned forward. "I won't be so presumptuous to ask you to pick up where we left off two years ago, but would you consider starting over? I could tempt you with flowers and bad poetry to start."

"Oh." Diane sat back in her chair and felt the blood drain from her face. "Oh, Quinn. I've met someone. Rather recently, in fact. It was quite unexpected. I'm still getting used to the whole idea, actually. He's younger, and a musician. But he's – " She licked her lips and felt a sting of tears behind her eyes. "He's unlike anyone I've ever met. And he's in love with me."

"Well." Quinn frowned for a moment, then shrugged. "Does he mind you having dinner with a man who once had designs on your body?"

"He's in London now, scoring a movie. He's been gone a few weeks. But even if he were here, he wouldn't mind."

"A movie?" The waiter served salads, and Quinn ordered another scotch. "Who's he working with?"

"Gordon Prescott." Diane ate some salad. "Michael says he's a lunatic."

"Good Lord. Yes, in fact, Gordon is a lunatic. Your musician must be very talented. Gordon only works with the best. Unfortunately, he has a tendency to chew his people up, suck them dry, then spit them back out. Very few people work with him a second time. He's brilliant, of course, but brutal." He was watching her. "You do seem very happy. And you look splendid. He's a lucky man."

"Thank you for saying that. But I'm the one who feels lucky."

He sighed. "Well, here's the thing. There's a dinner in a couple of weeks, welcoming Derek the Great to New York. It's a black tie thing, at the Pierre, very posh. I was rather hoping you'd come with me. I'm in need of a date, apparently, and you can make decent small-talk, know the right fork to use, that sort of thing." Diane smiled. "The food will probably be dreadful," he went on, "but you'll get to meet some very notorious theater people."

Diane thought a moment. "That would probably be a great evening. I'd love to come with you."

"Excellent. I'll call you, and let you know everything, times and so forth." He held up his half-empty glass. "Here's to being friends then, I suppose."

"Yes." She touched his glass with hers. "That would be good. Friends."

Rachel came to a rehearsal one night the following week, and she and Diane went out to dinner afterwards. As Rachel praised her mother, Diane looked at her skeptically.

"Thank you, my darling daughter, but I know your taste. You have little patience for comedy, unless of course it's combined with blazing satire or in protest of some massive government plot to subvert the masses. You probably think my play is trite."

"Mom." Rachel's hair was still long, and she wore it in a braid over one shoulder. She had attracted several looks as they entered the restaurant, her legs endless under a short skirt. Now she took a sip of her water. "Mom, not everything I like is avant-garde. I love some of the old stuff. In fact, I'm dying to see your old lover-boy, Harris, and his Coward thing. Next spring, I hear. Have you seen him?"

Diane nodded." Yes. I'm going with him to a dinner for Sir Derek Shore."

"You're going on a date with him?" Rachel set down her glass, hard, spilling water. "Mom, what happened to Michael?"

Diane looked at Rachel, puzzled. "Nothing happened to Michael. He's having a miserable time. We e-mail just about every day." Diane narrowed her eyes. "When did you become my watchdog, anyway?"

Rachel shrugged. "I kind of got to like Michael, Mom, you know that. I just remember back when Quinn was in the picture. You were ga-ga over him."

Diane looked at her daughter. "No, I wasn't ga-ga. That was you."

Rachel looked at her severely. "No shit, you were ga-ga, okay? I was waiting for the two you to live happily ever after so he could cast me in his next play."

"Rachel!" Diane exclaimed. "What a thing to say."

"So you two are, what, just friends now? Invite him to see me."

Diane stared. "See you? When?"

"Saturday, Mom? You said you were coming." The company that Rachel was involved in, the 13th Street Chorus, was finished with Shakespeare and working through George Bernard Shaw. They were doing three abridged versions of his work in one show, and Diane had said she would try to go.

"Oh, come on," Rachel urged her. "It's the least you can do. It's not like I'm asking you to sleep with him to advance my career."

"God, Rachel."

Rachel rolled her eyes. "He wanted to, didn't he?"

Diane looked at her daughter, undecided, then nodded. "Yes. How do you know I didn't?"

Rachel sighed. "He was married then, wasn't he? And you did raise me. I know you wouldn't fool around with a married man. Not even Quinn Harris."

Diane's mouth dropped open. "I can't believe it. I actually made a moral impression here. My mission as a mother has been successful."

"Don't get sloppy on me, Mom." Rachel shrugged. "But yeah, you were a good mother."

"Tell your sister, Emily, for me, would you please? She hates me so much right now."

"What is it this time?"

Diane shrugged. "The same thing it's been for weeks."

Rachel looked thoughtful. "The car thing? Dad says he's going to take care of all that, didn't you know?"

Diane was surprised. "No. I didn't know. Then why is she so angry at me?"

Rachel shrugged. "Who knows? With her it could be anything."

"You're right." She shook her head. "So, on another subject, how do you like your new half-sister?" Kevin's wife had delivered a baby girl two weeks before. Rachel launched into a story about her father and his second round of diaper changing. Diane half-listened, her mind wandering. She was worried about Emily. She thought about Quinn. Mostly, she missed Michael.

Indian summer returned on the Saturday night that Quinn and Diane went to see Rachel's show. Quinn met her in the seedy little theater, where they sat on folding chairs and the air conditioning did not work. But the house was full. The little troupe was developing something of a reputation. They whizzed through three of G.B.Shaw's finest in a little over ninety minutes. Quinn and Diane laughed along with the rest of the audience. The writing was very good. Rachel was in all three bits, playing a man each time, her bad makeup and ill-fitting wig, along with a shabby costume that did nothing to disguise her lovely figure, all part of the gag.

Afterwards, Quinn took the whole cast to a corner bar and bought them round after round. Rachel's cast-mates were all young and obviously impressed with Quinn Harris. This was Quinn in his element, telling stories of his own early days, dissecting scenes and speeches with people as passionate about theater as he was. Rachel and her crowd were enthralled. Diane was charmed.

The impromptu party broke up after one in the morning, and since Diane did not want to take the train home so late, she stayed with Rachel. Her daughter had a studio that once sat in the shadow of the Twin Towers. She had been there a little over a year, and loved living in Chinatown. The next morning, they had breakfast together, and Diane didn't get home until Sunday afternoon. Megan had called to say she and Emily were staying at their father's another night, and wouldn't be back until Monday after school. Diane went outside and spent the warm afternoon raking leaves. Then she went inside and sat alone, waiting for Michael to come home.

Diane had the perfect dress for the Pierre Hotel. She had found it in a vintage clothing shop, black satin, strapless. She tried it on at a whim, with Sue Griffen egging her on, and it had fit perfectly, sewn-in bones lifting her breasts beneath the shimmering fabric. Sue insisted she buy it, saying that, someday, she would need a dress like that. It hung in the closet for two years, but she took it out Saturday night. Quinn sent a limo for her, against her protests. He was co-hosting the event, and had to stay at the hotel. So the car, black and tasteful, picked her up and dropped her at Central Park East, and as she swept into the elegant, private room, a murmur ran through the crowd. She looked stunning. She was a new face. People buzzed.

Quinn was delighted to see her, kissing her coolly on the cheek. He stayed at her side through the cocktail hour, introducing her, his hand on her back. She knew he hated these events. He disliked meeting strangers, and was not at ease in crowds. He was restless, nervous, drinking club soda and being polite. Diane was having fun. The people there she had seen on stage or read about in magazines.

Sir Derek Shore was larger than life, a handsome, towering man, openly homosexual, whose long and distinguished career ranged from Greek tragedy to musical comedy. An icon in England, he was rarely seen on an American stage, and he was milking this event for all it was worth.

When Quinn introduced him to Diane, he threw out a dazzling smile and put his arm around her shoulders and drew her close.

"Thank God, somebody I don't know. These people bore, bore, bore me to death. You'd think the New World could come up with some new faces. And I do love a woman with glorious tits. I may be a sad old pouf, but I have excellent taste. Quinn, are you sleeping with her? You should, dear boy, after that dreary ex-wife of yours. May I steal her? I need to be protected. That bitch from the Mirror is here, and I if I'm with a woman, she won't bother with a photograph." He steered Diane in the direction of the bar, ordering scotch for himself. Diane was sipping champagne, and Derek looked her up and down closely.

"So tell me, Diane, who-no-one-has-heard-of, you know our Quinn? He does deserve someone rich and juicy. Did you ever meet the famous ex-wife?"

Diane shook her head. "No."

"Such a slut - really. I say that about a lot of people, I know, but with her it's the truth. She actually gave head to a male nurse while in hospital after giving birth to her daughter. She slept around for years. That's why it was such a shock when she fought the divorce. So ugly. Fleet Street went onto mourning when the whole thing was finally over. She really raped him. Financially of course."

"Is that so?" Diane asked faintly.

"Oh, it was such a bad show. And then the daughter turns against Quinn and sides with the mother. What a spoiled little cunt. After all Quinn has done for her. He worshipped her, and she hasn't spoken to him in months. That's the buzz, anyway. I feel terrible for him. He's one of my favorite people, you know."

Diane downed the rest of her champagne. "Why did he finally divorce her, do you think?"

"Well, everyone was looking for The Other Woman, but there was none to be found. There were lots of short term things, of course. I mean, he is a healthy, normal man, isn't he? He had to be getting something from someone. But no young thing tucked away, making demands. I suppose he finally decided to live his life on his own terms." He lifted his eyebrows. "He's a fine person. So if you are after him, you've got no one standing in your way. He'd be easy to catch, really."

"We're just friends. But he is a kind and gentle soul, isn't he?"

"Yes. And that's rare in this business. He actually believes in encouraging his actors instead of beating them into submission. Last year I did Ibsen with Gordon Prescott, and I was suicidal. Truly. Without the support of a lovely little bike messenger named Geoffrey, I would have succumbed."

"A friend of mine is working with Prescott now." Diane said. "He says Prescott is a madman."

Derek looked interested. "Gordon's finishing his film right now. They say there's smoke rolling out of the studio windows. Who do you know? I can tell you all the gossip."

"Michael Carlucci. He's doing the score." Derek looked blank. "Mickey Flynn?" Diane prompted.

"Oh?" Derek put his arm around her shoulder again. "Yes, I know all about him. A 'friend' did you say? He's quite scrumptious. The other one, Joe somebody, is getting most of the attention, especially since his wife has left our rainy isle for sunnier climes. But I know all about your little genius. He's created quite a stir. Of course our tabloids are such a load of crap." Derek leaned down, speaking into her ear. "If he's fucked half the people they claimed, he wouldn't have time to take a decent shit, let alone work for Prescott. Gordon is such a beast, really. But you, my dear," he stepped back and looked her up and down again, eyebrows arched, "you and Mickey Flynn? Well. I can see why Quinn hasn't got a chance. American rock stars are so exciting. Our British boys are mostly old, married and boring, or complete junkies. I saw him in the luscious flesh, you know, at some publicity thing, just last week He was being stalked by some bulimic blonde who couldn't keep her tongue out of his ear. Of course, I prefer my boy toys a bit taller. Pure logistics, you know. You two must be a good match, though. He wouldn't have to stoop. Ah, Harris." Quinn had come up, placing his empty glass on the bar. "I was just telling the delightful Diane here about her boyfriends' exploits in Londontown."

"And if she has a lick of sense, which I know she does, she won't believe a word." Quinn took Diane's hand and patted it. "He's a terrible liar and an incorrigible trouble-maker. Please ignore everything he said. They're serving. Shall we go in?"

The rest of the evening was a pleasant blur. Diane put Derek's words out of her head. The food turned out to be delicious, and after the dinner was finished, and the official part of the evening was over, Diane followed Quinn into a small, dark lounge, where she sat and listened to Quinn, Derek, and a few others talk about the theater. It was her favorite kind of conversation, the insiders dish. It was almost two in the morning before she even realized it.

"Quinn, what about the car?" She asked, shamefaced. "I've been sitting in here making that poor man wait."

"It's his job to wait," Quinn said mildly. "He'll take you home now. Unless you'd rather stay? We could get you a room, I'm sure." His hand had been resting lightly on her upper arm. Now, he touched her cheek. "Or we could just take a cab to my place."

Diane shook her head slowly. "No, Quinn."

He took her chin in his hand and kissed her lips. "You're beautiful tonight, Diane. It would be such a lovely end of a lovely evening."

Her lips were tingling, and she felt a slow rise of heat in the pit of her stomach. Her body was remembering another touch, Michaels' soft mouth. She could feel herself starting to blush.

Quinn kissed her again, longer this time, but she stepped back, away from him. "No, Quinn. Please."

Quinn pursed his lips, and put his hands in his pants pockets. He jingled the coins in his pockets nervously. "I'm sorry. I didn't mean to presume."

"I think I should go home now." Diane said quietly, and Quinn walked her through the hotel doors, and waited silently with her until the car came up to take her home.

Derek Shore came down the steps and stood beside Quinn, lighting a cigarette. "Is she the reason?" he asked casually.

Quinn glanced at him briefly. "What do you mean?"

"Oh, come now. I know we're not close friends, but we're in the same brotherhood. Surely I'm entitled to a few confidences."

Quinn raised his eyebrows. "Brotherhood?"

"Yes." Derek took a long drag. "We're one of the select few in theater who have worked with your ex-wife in the past five years without actually fucking her."

Quinn let out a short laugh. "Yes." He glanced at Derek again. "I met her two years ago. We fell in love. I thought it would be easy, getting the divorce. Who knew there'd be such a fight? And now it appears I've returned too late."

"Ah, yes. She and I were talking about him. I've met him, you see."

"He's younger, apparently."

"Much. And quite charming. Rather attractive too, if you like the Drop-Dead-Gorgeous-Blue-Eyes type." He stubbed out his cigarette. "Is she in love with him?"

Quinn thought. "She never said. He's in love with her, apparently."

"Well, that's not the same thing at all, is it? You've got the upper hand here, my friend."

"Really? And what's that?"

"Well, you're here and he's not, and you know what they say about love. Location, location, location."

Quinn chuckled. "I thought that was real estate."

"It's all the same, isn't it? Every time you take the plunge, you hope it will be a perfect fit and you'll stay forever. With real estate you pay up front, of course. With love, you pay for the rest of you life."

"Ah, there's that old cynicism. I thought for a moment you were getting romantic on me."

"If you want her, make her remember. Don't be such a bloody gentleman."

Derek walked back into the hotel. Quinn stood outside for a long time, looking into the darkness

Angela stopped her in the hallway on Monday. Diane was hurrying to Sam's office, her mind racing, and she went right past Angela, only stopping at the sound of her name being called. She turned, saw who it was, and broke into a tired smile.

"Angela. I'm so sorry. I'm in another world." She kissed Angela's cheek. "How are you?"

"I'm great, but you look so tired. Is everything okay?"

Diane shrugged. "The play. It's taking up a lot of time."

"Yes, I'm sure it is. I hear that Quinn Harris has taken an interest."

Diane raised her eyebrows and looked at Angela in surprise. "What?"

"In the play." Angela said quickly. Then she tightened her lips. "But of course, there are all sorts of other things flying around." Angela shrugged. "You know Merriweather. It's like a small town. Rumors, you know?"

Diane looked at her closely. "What kind of rumors, Angela?"

"About you and Quinn. About why he's spending so much time here." Angela was looking at Diane steadily. Diane swallowed a rising anger.

"Don't believe everything you hear, Angela. Quinn and I have had dinner a couple of times. That's all."

Angela threw up her hands. "Okay. I believe you. But you should know what's going around."

"Well, it's not true."

"Fine. I didn't mean to upset you, Diane."

Diane sighed. "I'm sorry. I hadn't heard, but then, I wouldn't, right? Thanks for telling me." Diane squeezed Angela's arm. "I've got to go. Tell everyone I said hello."

"Okay. I will. I'll see you later."

Angela went back down the hall, and Diane stood, staring after her. Rumors about her and Quinn? Sam would know.

But Sam claimed ignorance. He hadn't heard a thing, and he was in the thick of it all. Besides, why pay attention to all that anyway? He patted Diane's shoulder and urged her to sit. There was going to be a champagne reception after the first performance. He had just found out. Since most tickets for the first performance were usually given away to faculty, important alumni, press and guests of the cast and crew, he was able to talk the hospitality committee into springing for a rather lavish spread.

Diane tried to get excited, but she was feeling uneasy about what Angela had said. She left his office determined not to see Quinn again.

Rachel called her a few days later. "Mom," she said cautiously, "did you ever tell Emily or Meg that you and Michael were, well, together?"

Diane was startled. "No. He left for England before they came back up from the shore. Why?"

Rachel sighed. "There was a thing - on the Internet."

"What kind of thing?" Diane asked, concerned.

"On one of the sites. Do you know who Moira MacCauley is?"

"No. Should I?"

"I guess not. She's a singer," Rachel explained, "kind of New Age-y. Anyway, there was a thing, and this Moira had an interview. She said that all the English women were shit out of luck when it came to Mickey Flynn, because he was madly in love with some older woman back in the States. She knew you lived in his hometown. And that you taught at a local college."

Diane was stunned. "How did she know any of that?"

"I don't know, Mom. Maybe somebody else from the band. Who knows? You two didn't exactly keep things a secret, you know?"

"Oh, God." Diane felt sick. "Do you think Emily or Meg have seen it?"

"I don't know. Remember Chloe? From the group? She read it, I don't know where, and asked if it was about you. You and Michael came to see us a couple of times, remember? She was just curious, since you had just been there with Quinn."

Diane ran her fingers through her hair. "Can you talk to Emily, please?" she asked. "Just to try to find out if she knows. If she does, I've got to explain."

"Sure. You were going to tell them anyway, right, when he came back?"

"Of course. I just didn't think anyone would - shit, I've been so stupid. Of course, something was bound to come out. I just figured if he was over there, I wouldn't have to worry just yet."

"So, is he really madly in love with you?"

Diane took a breath. "Yes, actually."

"Oh, Mom. That's amazing. So then, what's with Quinn?"

"Nothing, Rachel. I told you, we're friends. It's possible, you know, for men and women to be just friends."

Rachel was quiet on the phone, and then sighed. "I bet this whole thing really sucks, him being away so long. It's been over a month. Do you ever, like, talk to each other on the phone? Like normal people?"

"No," Diane said softly. "It would be very hard for me, hearing his voice. It's easier when he's just a few words on a computer screen. Then missing him is not, I don't know, as real."

"I'm sorry, Mom," Rachel said. "Look, I'll try to see if I can get anything out of Em. I don't think Megan would really care that much, but with Emily, well, you know."

"Yes. I know." Diane hung up, suddenly worried.

That Saturday, Diane answered the door, and Ed, looking large and embarrassed, stood at her door with a stocky, disapproving-looking woman.

"Remember, me?" Ed asked. "Mike sent me out here back in May?"

"Yes, Ed. How are you?"

He grinned. "Good. So. Mike called, from England I guess. This is Mrs. Whitmire. She's from the New Jersey Rose Society."

Diane looked at the woman with interest. "I didn't know there was a Rose Society in New Jersey." Diane said.

Mrs. Whitmire puckered her lips. 'Yes. Apparently you need a lesson in pruning your roses and preparing them for the winter?" Her voice was shrill and condescending.

Diane looked at Ed, who was trying to keep a straight face. "Well, of course I'd be grateful for any advice. Come in."

She led them through the house and into her back yard. Leaves had begun to fall, and things were looking shabby and tired. Mrs. Whitmire walked through Diane's small rose garden, turning over leaves and clucking to herself. Diane looked sideways at Ed.

"What did Michael tell you to do, find a Rose Nazi?"

Ed cleared his throat. "He said to find an expert. If I'd known she'd be the one, I'd have grabbed the little guy from the garden department at Walmart."

Mrs. Whitmire came up to them, shaking her head disapprovingly. "Black spot, of course. Didn't you spray? No Japanese beetle, thank heaven, and your Louise Odier is suffering from iron deficiency. But, on the whole, they should survive. You have an interesting assortment." Mrs. Whitmire looked vaguely displeased. "Most people try to select roses that have some common trait."

"Well, I picked ones that smelled good," Diane said apologetically. "I didn't realize there was some kind of Rose Protocol."

Mrs. Whitmire sighed, and led Diane back to her roses, and for the next hour gave Diane a fascinating and helpful lesson in how to prune, and when, how to wrap the roses against wind, and what to do the following spring. Diane thanked her, thanked Ed, and spent the rest of the day outside, starting to clear dying plants, raking, waiting until it was late enough in the day to call Michael in England. He had been staying at Seth's, and he had given her the number there. She tried to calculate the time difference, knowing he stayed late at the studio.

He answered on the second ring, angry, tense. "Now what?" There was noise in the background, voices raised.

"Michael. Hello."

A pause, then - "Wait a minute." He yelled something, then she heard a scuffling, and the sound of a door closing. "Diane? Please tell me it's really you." He sounded hoarse. She felt a lump in her throat.

"Yes, it's really me. The rose expert from Hell was here this morning. She made me feel two feet tall, but she was very helpful. Thank you for thinking of me."

"I'm always thinking of you." He stopped. She could feel him, over the miles, reaching for words.

"It's terrible here. Prescott is a madman. He found another producer for the soundtrack. Seth and Joey are furious. Prescott still doesn't have a final cut. This movie is supposed to be done, opening in December, and he's still changing things. David Go quit twice already."

"Oh, Michael," she said softly.

"How is your play?"

"Opening in four weeks. It's going to be good, I think. It's hard for me to tell, but Sam is happy."

"How are the girls? Is Megan still in love?"

Diane bit her lip. "Yes. They're fine." She was sitting on the floor of her den, knees drawn up to her chest, clenching the phone so tightly her knuckles were white. "I miss you."

"I don't know when I can come home." His voice was so low she could hardly hear him. "I can't leave now, it's impossible. It's all falling apart. If I sent you a ticket, could you come?"

Her heart leapt. "Of course. Next weekend. Would it help?"

"The situation? No. If God himself came down, Prescott would probably tell him to mind his damn business." Michael sighed. "But it would help me. I'm going crazy here. It would be so much better if I could see you. I didn't – this was a mistake, coming here. I should have insisted on Toronto. I shouldn't have let him bully me. It's just, this is – I didn't want to blow this, you know?" He sounded exhausted, defeated. "I may have blown it anyway."

"No, Michael," she said quietly. "I know how important this is to you. You'll get it done."

"Maybe. No, you're right. I'll get it done, one way or another. I have to go."

"Yes. Good-bye."

"Diane?" She heard voices again, loud, arguing. "Diane, I have to go. Bye."

Jasper jumped lightly up, balancing on her knees. She scratched his ears absently, thinking about London. It was one of her favorite cities. She would go to London to see Michael. Jasper purred, and she sat for a long time, phone in hand.

Michael leaned his head back against the wall and let the phone drop from his hand. He could hear Seth in the next room, raging at Prescott. Seth had started doing lines of cocaine at three in the afternoon, and now, all those hours later, Michael knew Seth was totally out of control. Prescott knew it too, but Gordon Prescott thrived on tension and discord. He was one of those people happiest when all those around him were miserable. Prescott had been a happy man for weeks now.

Last night had been the last straw. Michael refused to look at what Prescott had called 'the final cut' of the film. Michael had only two days before he finished what he thought was the last bar of music that he would have to write for Prescott. But Prescott had arrived at Seth's house just outside of London with yet another version of his film, and Michael had finally, finally lost his temper. He would not re-write anything else. David had done all the orchestration, they had been recording all day. Michael could see a light at the end of what had become the longest tunnel he had been ever seen in his life. He was not doing another note.

Prescott had wheedled, promised and begged. Michael, drained and miserable, had walked out of the house. When he returned an hour later, after walking aimlessly around Seth's posh neighborhood, Seth and Prescott were locked in a battle over the soundtrack.

It had been decided, way back in June, that Seth and Joey would produce the soundtrack, including all the cuts by the other contributors to the CD. Upon arriving in London, they found that Prescott had made an agreement with a new Irish band, Daemon Spirit, who was also going to be on the soundtrack. Daemon Spirit would produce their own tracks. With the tracks for NinetySeven complete, that left only four more songs on the soundtrack, and Daemon Spirit wanted to produce those as well. Seth and Joey had been fighting with Prescott and Daemon Spirit for weeks, in and out of the studio. Michael, having written a lovely ballad to be sung by Moira MacCauley, tried to stay out of it, but it was proving impossible.

Moira MacCauley had presented another set of problems. She was a beautiful girl, just twenty-two, all ready an established star in Europe. She met the band at a party given by Prescott early in September, a vast feeding frenzy for the press. She immediately attached herself to Joey Adamson, despite the presence of Joey's wife. Joey had never considered his marriage a deterrent to any sexual detours he felt worthy of exploration. After ten days, his wife left for an extended tour of the Italian Riviera, and Moira became a fixture.

Michael, Seth and Stephanie had moved into Seth's house, but Michael did not spend much time there. He had been locked in with Prescott and David Go, grinding out what he knew was some of the most interesting and innovative music he had ever written.

He had embraced the challenge back at the beginning of the summer, but now he was worn down by Prescott's constant interference. He wanted the soundtrack completed, so that he could get back to the States. He missed Diane so much it became an almost physical effort to keep from driving to the airport and simply flying back to her.

Prescott had brought up Quinn Harris a few weeks before. Prescott, at sixty-five, considered Quinn Harris a weak upstart who would never get beyond the acclaim Harris had achieved when he directed his then-wife, a renowned actress. Prescott had read a bit in one of the tabloids about Harris in Manhattan, and had stormed into the studio to rant against him to whoever would listen. When he left, Michael casually picked up the paper and read the offending article.

It was a brief item, stating that Quinn Harris had recently spent an evening attending a performance of the 13th Street Chorus. Harris had been a guest of the mother of one of the cast members, and had taken the entire ensemble out after the performance. One of the cast later said that Harris was a 'charming, talented and generous' man. Michael knew all about the 13th Street Chorus. He and Diane had attended a few of their shows over the summer, watching Rachel. He knew that it was probably Diane who took Quinn there, and why not? Rachel was a talented girl. Being seen by someone like Harris could act in her favor.

The following week, Stephanie brought home another tabloid, whether by accident or design Michael never asked. Quinn Harris was pictured on page seven. Standing next to him, in elegant profile, was Diane. The accompanying article described a dinner at the world-famous Pierre Hotel, given for the arrival of Sir Derek Shore in New York by his soon-to-be-director. The woman in the picture was not identified. She was described only as being Harris' companion, a close one, apparently, since they were seen kissing in the lobby at two o'clock that morning. Michael spent a long time looking at Diane's face, tracing in his mind the curve of her cheek, the hollow behind her ear. Michael had learned not to believe half of what he read in some of the British press, having seen the most outrageous articles about himself published there. But a picture was something else. Harris had his arm around Diane's waist. She was smiling, obviously enjoying herself.

Michael had been in London over four weeks by then. He knew that every day was going to be a battle. He had spent very little time away from the studio. Once or twice, Seth had talked him into a drive, a half day away from London, to help him clear the cobwebs.

He was incredibly lonely. He had politely declined the countless offers of women, and men, who would have been more than happy to accommodate him in any way. He felt no conscious desire for sex. He was always tired, under tremendous stress, and was beginning to drink more heavily than he had ever before. Seth and Joey consumed vast amounts of cocaine, but Michael had always stayed away from drugs. Alcohol, on the other hand, was becoming a factor.

He began to spend time with Jane Whyte, an assistant of David's who, as far as he could tell, tried to sleep with every musician she came into contact with. She was pleasant, cheerful, and did not take his refusal of her sexual advances to heart. She just smiled and said she would have to keep trying. He didn't take her seriously. She made him laugh. He was in desperate need of someone to make him laugh.

The night he saw Diane's picture with Quinn Harris, he called the car to take him back to the studio. David was there, working of course. David was always working. David knew that if he could make a success of Prescott's movie, his career would be assured. A tiny man with huge ambition, he listened stoically to Prescott's rants, agreed with everything the director said, then went back to what he had begun in the first place. David Go knew that Michael had written music that was going to win awards, and he was determined to stick around for the payoff. He quit, then returned, at least twice that Michael knew of.

Jane Whyte saw Michael wandering down the hallway and knew at once he was troubled about something. She intercepted him before he could get involved in something that might change his mood, dragged him out the front doors, and took him to the nearest pub. He was drunk after the second pint, his brain and body too tired to offer any resistance to alcohol. Jane tried her best, supplying a comforting shoulder and a sympathetic ear as he poured out his story. She kept one hand on his thigh, the other playing with his hair. He finally turned to her, bleary-eyed, and she kissed him, a long, deep kiss that sent shivers down her back, but when she pulled back and looked at him, his eyes were so blue and sad, something in her heart twisted.

"What is it, love?" she whispered, "didn't you like it?"

"Don't do this, Jane. Please." Michael's voice was low, his shoulders slumped.

"Come on, my flat's just around the corner. Don't sit here and be all sad. So, your lady is stepping out. Just step out yourself a bit. You'll feel so much better, really."

"She's not stepping out," Michael insisted.

"Well, you told me you saw her picture, right? So, let her have a bit of fun. You've been over here for weeks. Did you think she'd just sit at home and do a bit of knitting?"

"No." Michael buried his head in his hands.

"So, come on then. She'd never know. Wouldn't you like to just stretch out somewhere soft and quiet?" She moved her hand higher up his thigh.

"Don't, Jane," he said tiredly. "I'm not going to fuck you, so just stop."

"What are you being so bloody loyal for, anyway?" Jane asked, annoyed.

"I love her, Jane."

"Then why the hell don't you get her over here?" Jane hit his arm. "If she's so fuckin' wonderful, she'll come, right? I know I would. I'd be over here in a flash."

"Would you?" Michael looked at her intently. "If I asked you to fly for hours just to spend the night with me, would you really?"

"Love, for a roll in the kip with you, I'd walk to fuckin' China. Why wouldn't she, if you two are so in love?"

"Well, that's the thing," Michael said sadly. "I don't actually know if she loves me or not."

"What?" Jane stared at him. He was beautiful to her, his eyes deep blue, his mouth soft and slightly parted, his hair falling down across his forehead. "Oh, now Mickey, how could she not love you? " She brushed away his hair and kissed him on the cheek. "You're such a darlin', really you are. Call her and tell her to come and when she gets here, fuck her brains out. Believe me, she won't mind a bit."

He cracked a smile. "Do you think?"

"Come on, let me get you home. I can't believe I'm doing this. Let's go." She pulled him off the stool and walked him back to the studio. She knew she was only one more pint away from having him naked in her bed, but she didn't have the heart. Perhaps, she thought, she could find another way.

Diane called him two days later. She would come over to London. As he sat in the darkness, listening to Seth and Gordon Prescott scream at each other, he didn't care. She was coming to London. That was all that mattered.

CHAPTER ELEVEN

Quinn called her Monday morning. "I've learned my lesson, Diane. I was out of line. Please, have dinner with me? Just dinner - I swear. It won't happen again."

"Do you know there's a rumor going around about the two of us?" she asked accusingly.

"Rumor? Oh, I can imagine. University is just one big opportunity to gossip, isn't it? Are they saying anything terribly naughty?"

"Quinn, Michael's sister is on campus. Angela Bellini."

"Oh. Blast, I'm sorry. Are you afraid she'll report back to him you've been misbehaving?"

"No. It's not that. I'm just - " Her shoulder slumped. "I don't know."

"Well, you miss him, I'm sure," Quinn said briskly. "When is he due back?"

"I don't know, but I'm flying over there this weekend to see him."

"Ah." Quinn paused. "Well then, why on earth would you worry about any silly gossip? Please, have dinner. Otherwise, I'll be forced to eat with the secretary of the Dean of Admissions again. The woman has been stalking me, I swear. Hovering outside my classroom at precisely three-fifty-six, asking what I'm doing after class. I feel positively threatened."

She agreed, laughing, and they went out after his class, and later walked back to the train station, and she sat with him, waiting for his train, talking.

When she got home, it was still early, barely eight. Emily was upstairs, music blaring, and Megan and Becca Griffen were in the kitchen, bowls everywhere, obviously trying to bake something. Diane looked wearily at her kitchen.

"Why did you feel you had to do this so late, Meg? I'm not cleaning this up, okay? Becca, how could you let her rope you into this?"

"Well, she had dinner at my house, Mrs. M., but my mom said no dessert, and Megan said you wouldn't care." Becca grinned sheepishly. "It's brownies. You can have some."

Diane shook her head, and headed upstairs. She pounded on Emily's door. The music stopped, and her daughter threw open her door.

"Gee, Mom, glad you could make it home. What was it tonight? Did you have emergency surgery to perform? Finding a cure for cancer? Rescuing some poor stranded kitten?"

Diane exhaled loudly through her mouth. "Emily, you have been a bitch on wheels for weeks now. Rachel told me that your father was taking care of the car situation. If that's still why you're so pissed off, please act out at his house, not mine."

"Did you sleep with him here?" Emily asked angrily. Her dark eyes were blazing, her thin body tense.

Diane's mouth dropped open. "What are you talking about?"

"Alison told me there was a car parked over here a lot this summer. Most times it was some junky old truck, but there was also a fancy silver car, she said. Her mom told her it was a gardening guy for your stupid roses." Emily was breathing fast and heavy, and Diane forced herself to lean casually against the door jamb.

"Rachel told me all about it, you know." Emily went on. "Tonight. She called, and I asked her about the Internet stuff. I didn't believe it was you, but Rach said that it was, that you had a 'relationship' with him. Did you?"

"Yes," Diane said calmly.

Emily's jaw dropped open. "Oh. Oh, Mom." Emily cast her eyes around the room. "I can't believe it. Is that why you were so happy for us to spend the summer down the shore? So you and your 'boyfriend' could play house all summer?"

Diane kept her voice quiet and steady. "Emily, you asked to spend the summer with your father before I even met Michael. You asked me, remember?"

"How convenient for you, though. I bet you hated the idea of us coming back." Emily's voice was shrill and harsh. Diane could feel her daughter's anger like a wave.

"Emily, I asked you all summer long to come back home to spend a few days. You're the one who wanted to stay down there. I had to drive down to see you. Is any of this sounding familiar?"

"Did he come with you? When you drove down to Long Beach Island?"

Diane shook her head. "No. He was never with me. I wanted to spend the time with you, honey - you and Megan."

"Where was he when we came up in July?"

"He went to Toronto. But if he hadn't, he would not have been here. I would not have had him stay here when you girls were in the house." Diane said emphatically.

"But when we weren't here, did you sleep with him, Mother? In our house?"

"Michael and I are grown-ups, Emily," Diane said quietly. "And what I choose to do in my own home is my own business."

"Oh, that's right. It's Michael. You're in that special little group, aren't you? The 'Call Me Michael' group." Emily spat out the words.

"He also asked you to call him that, Emily," Diane reminded her, trying to keep her own rising anger at bay.

"I wonder if that meant he wanted to fuck me too."

Diane left the safety of the doorway and lunged toward her daughter. Emily scrambled back. Diane froze. Her voice was low and hoarse.

"You will not speak like that again in my house - ever. If you do, I will throw you into the street with nothing but the clothes on your back." Diane was aware of movement behind her, and she turned quickly to find Megan and Becca in the doorway, eyes wide.

Diane swallowed hard, wondering how long the younger girls had been there. "Becca, you have to leave now," Diane said. "I'm sorry. Megan, go down and watch her from the steps 'till she's at her house. It's late. Go." The girls scurried away. Diane turned back to Emily.

"I don't know why you think you can treat me this way, Emily, but you can't. I'm sure you've imagined that I've committed some hideous crime against you, but all I did was stay in the company of a man who came to mean a great deal to me. I never once let it touch you. It never interfered with my being a mother to you. You keep telling me how grown-up you are. Well, here's your opportunity to prove it. You will stay in this room until you apologize. If that is unacceptable to you, call your father now and have him come and get you."

Diane left the room, closing the door behind her. She stood in the tiny hallway, gulping air, hands to cheeks.

"God," she whispered. "Oh, my God."

She went quickly downstairs and into the kitchen, reaching with an unsteady hand for the vodka in the upper cabinet. She poured quickly into a juice glass

228

and gulped it down. The panic in her stomach eased, but she was still shaking. She looked up. Megan had come into the kitchen and was standing quietly, her hands thrust into the pockets of her sweatshirt.

"Are you okay, Mom?" She asked shakily.

Diane nodded, and Megan crossed over to her, putting her arms around Diane and holding tightly. Diane stroked her head.

"You know Em," Megan said, her voice muffled, "she's just hard sometimes."

"Yes, honey, I know. Emily is very hard." Diane stared over Megan's head.

The front door opened, and Diane ran from the kitchen, thinking that Emily may have run out. Instead, there stood Sue Griffen, her face pale.

"Meg, let me talk to your Mom, okay?" Sue asked quickly. Megan nodded and ran upstairs. Sue came over to Diane and gave her a quick hug around the shoulders.

"Becca told me. Are you okay?" Diane nodded. "Drink something," Sue urged. Diane managed a weak smile.

"You give the best advice of anyone I know. I did have a drink. Now at least I don't want to throw up. But I still want to hit something."

Sue was looking at Diane anxiously. "What did you say to her?"

Diane said unsteadily, "I told her she had to apologize, and if she didn't she could call her father." And at that moment, the phone rang.

Diane let out a deep breath and answered. It was Kevin.

"Are you going to tell me what this is about?" he asked, concerned. "She's hysterical. I'm supposed to come and get her because you've disowned her."

229

"I have not. Oh, shit. Come and get her. I think she needs to be out of here for a few days, okay?"

Kevin sighed. "Okay. I'm on my way."

Diane hung up and looked at Sue. Tears filled her eyes. "She's going to stay at Kevin's."

Sue nodded and rubbed Diane's back. "Yeah, kiddo, maybe it's best for now. Emily just needs time, you know her. She'll be back."

Diane was nodding. "Yes, I know."

Megan came running back down the stairs, sobbing. "Em says she's leaving, Mom, stop her."

Diane caught her daughter in her arms and held her, rocking her back and forth. "Just for a day or two, honey, don't worry." She kissed the top of her head

Sue rubbed the back of her neck. "Why don't I make coffee?" She whispered. Diane nodded, and Sue went into the kitchen. Diane led Megan to the couch, and they sat together. Diane could hear a rattle of pans. Sue was cleaning.

"Megan, is it time for your brownies to come out?" Megan nodded. "Okay, honey, why don't you go on in the kitchen, okay? Sue will help you."

Megan stood up as headlights flashed into the driveway. She looked at her mother, and tears started in her eyes again. Sue came out, took Megan's arm, and led her into the kitchen. Diane stood, waiting for Kevin.

He came through the front door, took one look at Diane, and put his arms around her gently. He patted her shoulders, then pushed her down onto a chair and sat on the coffee table across from her.

"Okay, tell me quick," he said in a low voice.

"I was seeing somebody. I didn't tell her, because she was with you all summer, and then he left, but she just found out. It's complicated, Kevin. I'll explain tomorrow. Just get her, okay?"

He looked at Diane sadly. "For a woman who's tough enough to take on Tyson, why do you let her get to you so much? You know she pushes buttons. You know she's out for blood." He stood up. "Where's Megan?"

Diane swallowed hard. "In the kitchen."

Kevin took in a bushel of air and went into the kitchen. Sue came out a moment later, with a tray of coffee cups. She set them down and pushed a mug into Diane's hands.

Diane shook her head. "I can't drink caffeine this late," she said automatically.

Sue looked disgusted. "Oh, right. Like you're really going to sleep tonight. Drink up. You're white as a ghost and your hands are freezing." Sue took a sip of her own mug. "Megan seems okay, Diane, honest. She's a level-headed kid."

Diane sipped the coffee. Kevin and Megan came out and together went upstairs. Sue and Diane exchanged looks, and they sat together, drinking coffee until Kevin came back downstairs. He sat down heavily and picked up a coffee mug, spooned in sugar, and drank.

"Megan is helping her pack." Kevin said. "At least she's stopped crying."

They sat and waited. Finally, Emily came slowly downstairs, dragging a duffel bag behind her. She stood at the front door, looking at the floor, not speaking. Kevin stood up, nodded to Diane, and walked Emily out of the house.

Sue stood up. "More coffee?" Diane nodded, and Sue went and brought back the pot. They drank another mug. Diane kept taking long, deep breaths. Sue hadn't said anything. Megan came back downstairs, face red and blotchy, and sat down next to her mother.

"Why was she so angry?" she asked Diane.

"How much did you hear, Meg?"

Megan looked shamefaced. "All of it. We followed you upstairs. I knew she was mad about something. I didn't know why, though."

Diane lifted her shoulders and let them drop heavily. "I don't know why either, honey. Maybe she thought I should have told you both about Michael long before this. I would have. When Michael came back, and when we started seeing each other again, I would have told you both."

"I like Michael," Megan said.

"Yeah. Me too. He's a nice person."

"Where did he go?"

"London," Diane explained. "He's writing music for a movie over there. He'll be back in a couple of weeks."

"Is he really your boyfriend?" Megan was looking interested now. Sue began to smile.

Diane chewed her lip. "Yes, honey, he's my, ah, boyfriend."

"Oh." Megan nodded to herself. "Does this mean we'll get to go to all the concerts?"

Sue ducked her head, hiding her grin. Diane smiled and nodded.

"Yes, honey, I guess if we want to."

"That's cool." Megan stood up and kissed her mother's cheek. "I'll see you in the morning." She ran upstairs.

Sue gave Diane a quick smile. "Want me to stay?"

Diane shook her head tiredly. "No, but thank you for being here. Really."

"No problem. Call me tomorrow." Sue went to the front door. "I mean it."

Diane waved her out, then fell back against the chair cushions, pressing her hands against her eyes. She sat, exhausted, until Jasper jumped onto her lap.

She took her hands away, and pushed the cat off her lap. She walked into her kitchen. It was spotlessly clean, a single pan of brownies on the counter. Diane cut a square out of the corner of the pan, ate it, then ate three more pieces. Feeling slightly sick, she went into the den. The light on her answering machine was blinking. She played the message. It was Rachel, saying she had talked to Emily about Michael and Diane should call A.S.A.P. Diane looked at her watch. It was almost eleven. She'd call her tomorrow. Then she looked at her computer. A message from Michael - just a quick line. He had her tickets to London. She could confirm the reservation. She sat down and answered. She wouldn't be able to make London after all. There were too many problems with her play. She'd have to wait for him to come home. She hit the send button and started to cry again.

Emily did not apologize. She did not come home. She texted Megan all day long, but Emily would not speak to her mother. Kevin, having heard the story from both Diane and Emily, threw up his hands. He would not interfere. He felt she owed Diane an apology, but if she refused, he could not force her. She could stay with him as long as she liked.

For the next few weeks, Diane lived under a cloud. Michael was still in London. She had tried to call him again, but the number he had given her had been disconnected. His cell phone, she knew, had vanished his second week in London. She was desperate to speak with him, but did not want to call one of his sisters to ask how to reach him. Angela continued to be cool and aloof. Diane knew why. She was spending too much time with Quinn.

He found reasons to be outside her office at the end of her day. He would offer to take her for a quick drink, which often ended with dinner. She was tense, excited and miserable, and he was a warm and a soothing shoulder for her to lean on. She was so grateful for his presence that she pushed aside their growing intimacy, the longer looks, the softer kiss good-night. Every time she left him, she thought about what her life would be like with him, and how different it would be from her life with Michael – calmer, more dignified, none of the burning passion, true, but still full and rich.

The Monday before the first performance, Quinn came by her office. He sat across from her and waited while she listened patiently on the phone to a student, and when she hung up she gave him a smile. She was thinner than she had been at the start of the term, and her hair, longer now, framed her face in shining waves. His fingers were beating a tattoo in the arm of his chair.

"I'd like to be your date Friday," he began. "I'd be honored to sit by your side on your opening night. Unless you've heard from the mysterious Michael?"

Diane chewed her lip. "No, I haven't heard from Michael. He hasn't even e-mailed. I'm worried, actually." She looked down at her desk and played with her pen. "I, ah, don't know what to think about Michael at this point."

"Oh? Well. Then why don't you forget about him and marry me?"

Diane looked up at Quinn in disbelief.

"We're quite well suited to each other. We have the same taste in books, music, that sort of thing. We can talk to each other about anything." He leaned forward. "I'm not asking you on a whim, Diane. When I came to the States two years ago and met you for the first time, I thought, this is the woman I want to spend the rest of my life with." Diane sat up straighter.

"It took me this long," he continued, "to free myself of my marriage and get back here to find you again. I'm in love with you, Diane, terribly in love with you, and it's been torture for me to sit by and watch you wait for this phantom lover of yours. Especially since things have been bloody awful for you for the past few weeks. The whole thing with Emily, wouldn't it have been easier for you if he were here? Why the devil didn't he fly from London the minute he knew about what was going on?"

Diane found her voice. "I never told him, Quinn. And even if he were right here, what could he have done? Nothing. When I have something that I need to deal with, I don't want a cheerleader. It distracts me. I need to be able to concentrate on getting the job done."

Quinn waved her words aside. "Besides, the whole problem with Emily is Michael, right?"

"I won't have the willfulness of a child determine how I live my life," Diane said hotly.

"Well, good for you. Are you telling me that if you had to choose between your daughter and this man, you'd send Emily packing?"

Diane said nothing.

"How about this - how long have you dreamed about writing a play and seeing it performed?"

Diane dropped her eyes back to her desk. "Since I was, oh, probably ten."

"So, Friday's a fairly important night for you? Where is Michael? He does know about Friday, doesn't he?"

"Quinn, you said yourself that Prescott is crazy. Michael is drowning over there."

"And he can't get away for a day?"

Diane raised her eyes and looked at Quinn steadily. "I don't love you, Quinn."

He made a face. "You've got him locked in your brain right now. Do you remember two years ago? Do you remember how you felt about me then? We were in love with each other. Granted, it may have happened quickly, but it was real. It was the most important thing that had ever happened to me."

"It was for me too," Diane said quickly. "You know that."

"Yes. I did know. All I could think about was what the two of us could be together. I'm not talking about sex, although I had been going mad thinking about that. But we could have been magnificent. You knew it then, didn't you?"

"Yes," she said quietly. "I thought about us for a long time. I used to dream about what we would be like together." She took in a deep breath. "Michael changed me, Quinn. I don't know if I can go back."

"He hasn't been around for months," Quinn said.

"Eight weeks tomorrow," Diane corrected automatically. She looked apologetic. "So, I've been counting."

He put his fingertips together and tapped them against his upper lip. "Can I at least court you? Properly, that is. Give me a chance, Diane, a real chance. Let me touch you now and again without all those red flags going up."

Diane smiled tiredly. "How special you are, Quinn. Court me. What a lovely phrase." She covered her face with her hands, and took several deep breaths. "I need a little more time, Quinn," she said at last. She dropped her hands. "Can we wait until after Friday? Please?"

He stood up and walked around to her side of the desk and pulled her up from her chair. He took her face in his hands and kissed her, long and deeply, and she kissed him back, pushing Michael away.

Quinn broke the kiss and looked at her tenderly. "I will wait until Friday. But I will be with you Friday night, unless you tell me otherwise, all right?"

She nodded, and Quinn left her office. Diane stood there, trying to sort things out inside her head. She walked out of her office and down the hall to Marianne. The secretary waved her in. Marianne was looking through a fat computer printout when Diane came in, closing the door behind her.

"What's wrong?" Marianne asked. "Emily again?"

"No. Quinn just asked me to marry him."

Marianne pushed aside the printout and looked at Diane incredulously. "He what?"

"Yes." Diane walked over and sat down across from her friend. "Just now. He said we were well suited."

Marianne shook her head. "You are so entertaining this year, I cannot begin to tell you. He's right. You're very well suited. You two make a terrific couple. There have been more than a few people making that observation."

"Marianne, have you heard anything about Quinn and me?"

"Quinn and I," Marianne corrected automatically. "Really, Diane. And yes, I've heard all sorts of things. Are you deaf as well as blind? Did this come as a surprise to you? Don't you notice the way the man looks at you?"

"But, but, I told him," Diane sputtered, "I told him about Michael. He said he understood."

"So? He understood. That's fine. But obviously it didn't change his feelings toward you. Let's look at this for a minute. He divorced his wife, and from what you've told me, it cost him dearly, and not just money-wise. He came back here for you. He finds you mooning over another man. Fine. But did you really think he was just going to shrug his shoulders and gave up? After all that? Good God, Diane, you amaze me. Are you really this stupid about men? I've never dealt with them as romantic partners, and I thank my good Lord every night for that, but even I've figured out the way they work."

Diane slumped down in the chair. "So, now what do I do?"

"Do you want to marry him?"

"I'm not in love with him anymore."

"But you were once. You were crazy to be with him."

"Yes, I remember."

"And with Michael you've always had, well, reservations."

"I know," Diane said miserably.

"Look, Diane," Marianne said seriously, "I only want what's best for you. And I know Michael is all you can see right now. But Quinn is a good man. He obviously loves you. He's asked you to marry him. Has Michael?"

"You know he hasn't," Diane said miserably. "He hasn't said a thing in weeks. I wish I knew what was going on with him."

"So, call him."

"I tried. The number I had is no longer working. He hasn't answered my e-mails. God, I am so upset about this."

"You've got enough to be upset about with Emily. I'd forget about Michael, Diane, unless he makes a serious comeback."

Diane sighed. "Quinn is coming with me Friday night."

"Well, that will certainly be a statement."

"Yes, I suppose it will."

"I'm so sorry, Diane," Marianne said gently. "Michael was glorious."

Diane stood up. "I have the final outline done, for the grad class. I'd like you to take a look."

"Great. How about lunch tomorrow?"

"Fine. See you then."

Kevin's car was parked in Diane's driveway when she came home. It was just after four, which meant Kevin had to have taken off early from work. Diane's heart was in her throat. That was either a good thing, or a very bad thing.

Kevin was sitting at the dining room table, working at his laptop. He looked relieved as Diane came in.

"Emily's upstairs." he told her. "You'll have to ask her to come back, and I think she might say no, but keep asking. She wants to be back here, okay?"

Diane nodded and walked upstairs slowly. Emily's door was closed. Diane knocked once, and immediately Emily opened it. Diane folded her arms across her chest and waited.

"Mom, I'm sorry." Emily said in a small voice. "I was really upset and I didn't mean to say those things to you about Michael. You were right. If I'm supposed to be grown-up, I've got to stop being so selfish and stupid about stuff. I was mad 'cause I thought he should like me better." Emily had been looking at the floor, twisting her hands together. She looked up at her mother. "So, I apologize."

Diane pressed her lips in a thin line. "Sit down, honey," she said.

Emily sat on her bed, legs crossed Indian-style. Diane stood over her, arms still folded.

"If I see Michael, again, will there be a problem?"

Emily shrugged. "No. I wouldn't like it if you hated my boyfriend, so I'll be fine. Really."

"Oh, great. So you've just guilted me out of all objections to any future boyfriends you may have in this life and the next, is that it?"

Emily's mouth twitched. "No, Mom." Pause. "So you'll be seeing him again? Megan said he was in London."

"Yes. He's in London. I don't know when he'll be back."

"Oh." Emily looked up shyly. "Did you go to his house?"

Diane sat down next to her on the bed. "Yes, I've been to his house."

"What's it like?"

"Long. Elegant. He has very sleek furniture, no knick-knacks. He lives on a lake and it's beautiful. He has a studio, with a glassed-off sound booth, and all this ridiculously sophisticated equipment. He collects Japanese art."

"You like Japanese art," Emily said.

"Yes. We have lots of things in common."

"Is he really in love with you?"

"Yes, honey, he really is."

"Are you in love with him?"

"Yes. I am. I wasn't sure, for a long time, if I was or not. But I do love him. Very much."

Emily looked at her mother sideways. "Are you going to get married?"

"Honey, I don't think I want to get married again."

"Can we go to the Grammys?"

"What?"

"The Grammy Awards. Do you think we can go?"

Diane bit back laughter. "I don't know, honey. Why don't we wait on that one?"

"Why didn't you tell me?"

240

Diane took in a deep breath and let it out slowly. "I should have told you from the beginning, but I was afraid you'd have, uh, expectations, and I wasn't sure we were going to last. I was going to wait for him to come back, invite him over, and just kind of let you get used to the idea. It was a mistake. I'm sorry. You shouldn't have had to find out about this over the Web." Diane gave her a hug. "Are you ready to come home? Rachel is coming in early on Friday, and we were all going to get dressed together and see the play. Stay here. You'll be back at your fathers' that night anyway. Stay and see the play with us."

Emily shrugged again. "Yeah, okay, that sounds like fun"

Diane exhaled silently. "Okay, then. I'll tell your Dad." She went downstairs, thanking the gods. Kevin was packing his briefcase.

"She's staying." She hugged her ex-husband tightly. 'Thank you so much. I don't know what you did or said, but thank you."

Kevin kissed her forehead affectionately. "I didn't do anything. Really. I think she just figured it out for herself." He shrugged into his jacket. "This guy she was talking about." He looked at her with interest. "He's in a rock band? I mean, I don't care who you date, you know that. And I want you to be happy, Diane, I really do. But how old is this guy?"

"About three years younger than your wife," Diane said dryly. Kevin had the grace to color slightly.

"Well, I hope he's worth it. I know what these past few weeks have cost you. I'll bring the rest of her stuff tomorrow. And I'm seeing your play on Friday. I'll take the girls with me from there. Break a leg, or whatever."

"Thanks again." Diane closed the door behind him. Megan would be home from Becca's soon. It was time to make dinner. Emily was back home. Quinn had proposed. All in all, a good day's work.

Friday afternoon, Diane raced home to get ready for her play. Rachel was waiting for her as Diane emerged from her shower. Her daughter was wearing a long, flowing dress, obviously vintage. Diane looked at her suspiciously.

"I think I wore that same dress in 1986. To a fraternity dance." Diane said slowly.

Rachel looked shocked. "You went to a fraternity dance?" she asked, horrified.

Diane shrugged. "Hey, times were different then. It was free beer. You look terrific."

Rachel rolled her eyes. "So, what are you wearing? I hope you bought something incredible for your premier."

Diane pulled out a black pants suit, the jacket cut to look like a man's tuxedo, the pants wide and comfortable. Rachel examined the outfit critically.

"Are you at least wearing hot lacy underwear underneath?" she asked at last.

Diane's shoulders slumped. "Rach, why would it matter what I was wearing underneath?"

"Mom," she explained patiently. "You are about to become a playwright. This is big. Exciting. You need to dress as though you can take on the world. You're going to look like a maitre'd at a lesbian nightclub in this outfit. You should at least have exciting underwear. And spiky, sexy shoes. Besides," she asked casually, "isn't Michael going to be here?"

Diane shook out the pants carefully without looking at her. "I haven't heard from Michael in weeks."

"Oh. I'm sorry."

"Me too. Actually, I was thinking about socks and sneakers, but I think maybe just plain black flats. I am going to be an absolute wreck tonight, I know it. The least I can do is be comfortable."

Rachel was shaking her head. "Mom, how boring. Wait, what about your hair? I brought my chopsticks. We can put your hair into a French twist. You'll look amazing." Rachel started combing out her mother's hair, pulling it tight.

"Listen, Rachel," Diane said, "About tonight. You'll be sitting with your dad, right?"

"Yeah." Rachel twisted up Diane's hair and stuck in one of the chopsticks. They were standing in front of her dresser. Diane met her daughter's eyes in the mirror.

"What's going on, Mom?"

"Well, Quinn Harris is kind of my date."

Rachel worked another chopstick through Diane's hair, then put in some hair pins. She pulled a few strands of hair around her mother's face. When she was done, she kissed her cheek. "You look beautiful, Mom. I just want you to be happy, okay? Quinn is a neat guy, really. I like him a lot. If he's here for you, that's what really counts, you know?"

Diane nodded. She felt strong, glamorous. She got dressed and went out into the living room, where Emily and Megan applauded as Diane spun around, balancing on the tips of her shoes. There were roses in the living room, a massive bouquet from Quinn. She picked one, snapped the stem, and pinned it carefully to her satin lapel, then they all piled into the Subaru and drove off to Merriweather.

The curtain went up at 7:30. By ten after eight, Diane knew they were a success. The crowd laughed in all the right places, listened carefully when the dialog was serious, and half a dozen times had burst into applause. By the intermission, she was on cloud nine.

Quinn was right there, his arm tight around her waist, pushing her through the crowd in the lobby. He left her side only to bring them champagne from the tiny bar. He was incredibly proud of her, and of her obvious triumph. Sam French was ecstatic. He came running from backstage to kiss Diane repeatedly on both cheeks.

"What do you think, Quinn?" Sam asked, "Are we going places, or what?"

Quinn smiled and drew Diane closer. "There are some people here who are going to want to talk to you both," he said. "Sam Levinson from the New School has already given me the high sign. Make sure you see him after the curtain."

Sam flittered away, and Diane leaned against Quinn. Her daughters were coming toward her, happy and excited.

"Mom, this is so cool," Megan said.

"Yes, it is. How do you like it so far?"

Rachel was beaming. "It's funny, Mom. The people here are loving it. Congratulations."

The lights blinked. The second act was beginning. They filed back in, and the rest of the show went off beautifully. After the final curtain, Sam French came on stage for a bow, and called up Diane. She ran up the steps of the stage, heart pounding, and her eyes blurred with tears as the audience rose to their feet. She beamed, bowed, and saw Quinn in the third row, smiling and applauding.

Afterwards, the crowd lingered in the lobby, where a long table of champagne glasses and hors de oeuvres was set up. Diane was bowled over by the response of the audience. Quinn stayed beside her as people she had never seen before told her how wonderful she was, how talented, how much they had enjoyed the evening.

Diane didn't need alcohol to feel drunk. She was giddy with power and triumph. Every nerve was alive, every sense heightened. Quinn was more than a shadow behind her. She could feel every touch of his hand, every movement of his against her skin. She looked into his eyes and saw openly, for the first time, desire. Something akin in her answered. *This is why,* she thought fleetingly, *men must make love after war, why victory must be answered with sex.* She wanted Michael so badly the ache in her groin felt like a lead weight. Every time she turned and saw Quinn, his green eyes alive and smoldering, she felt her throat tighten.

It was midnight before the crowd thinned. Her daughters all had kissed her goodbye. Faculty and friends were beginning to leave. The cast had joined them from changing backstage and there began a serious discussion of the show, the mistakes, the triumphs. The press was still there, and a few other theater people, including Sam Levinson who began to talk to Diane about bringing her play to the New School, just as a round table reading at first, but after that, who knew?

She had turned away from Levinson for a moment, and saw, just through the glass doors that opened to the courtyard, a figure standing, backlit by the lampposts outside. A man, his breath a cloud in the cold October air. Diane knew the set of his shoulders, the tilt of his head.

"Michael." She said his name aloud, in disbelief. The night was wide and black behind him. He was wearing a black leather coat, long, almost to the ground. His hair spilled over his collar, and his face was white, haggard. He stared at her, saw her mouth frame his name. He did not smile or move toward her. He stood. Watching.

"Michael," Diane said again, her eyes not leaving Michael's face. Levinson said something, and she looked at him, her face frozen. "I'm sorry. I'll be right back." She smiled automatically. Beyond Levinson she could see Quinn, talking to someone, glancing at her, smiling, turning away. Diane looked back to Michael, but he was gone. Her eyes searched frantically, and she went across the lobby and pushed the heavy glass doors open, running out into the courtyard. She caught a flash of black and saw him, in the dimly lit building across from her, walking down an empty corridor. She ran after him, through the doors and down the hallway. Her shoes echoed against the tile floor as she half-ran into the semi-darkness. She drew a deep breath. The hallway was empty.

"Michael?"

He stepped out from a doorway, and she ran to him, heart pounding. As he caught her his mouth took hers, and everything melted away, all the weeks of darkness and loneliness. He pushed her against the slick wood of the door, and he was cold, the rough cotton of his sweater, the leather coat, but her hands were beneath his clothes, and his skin was hot and smooth.

"Michael, where were you?" She whispered roughly, hoarse with wanting. "Why didn't you tell me?"

His eyes were close, burning. "I didn't know if I'd make it." His voice was strained. "I literally ran to the airport in London. I called Angela from the plane and had her leave her ticket for me at the window. I didn't want to tell you. I wanted to surprise you." His hands were on her face, tracing the line of her lips, smoothing back her hair from her forehead. "God, I missed you so much," he murmured, burying his face into the soft of her hair.

She reached for the doorknob and turned, the door fell open, and she pulled him inside. He pushed the door shut, and reached under her clothes. He had her tight against the wall and the zipper of her pants slid open and his hands pushed her clothing away and it fell, down around her feet, and she stepped out of them to wrap her leg around his hip. She could feel him, stiff beneath his jeans, hard against her. They were silent, frantic, and her fingers fumbled as she released him, sweetly alive in her hands. His breath was ragged, their mouths locked together. Then he gripped her around her waist and lifted her, her legs came around him as he plunged into her, and a cry leapt from her, and in seconds she was coming, biting the leather shoulder of his coat. He was making a noise, deep, guttural, as he pushed her against the rough cinderblock wall, and he climaxed suddenly, a hard, violent shudder. They leaned against each other, breathing harsh and unsteady, and Diane loosened her legs and her feet touched the hard tile floor, and as she tightened her arms around his neck, she felt the warm stickiness of him trickle down the inside of her leg.

The only light in the room came through the open blinds at the window, a streetlight, and she strained to see his face. She kissed his lips, and felt tears on his cheeks.

"Did I hurt you?" he asked, his voice shaking. "Did I?"

"No. Oh Michael, no." She kissed him again, her lips against his mouth.

"The play was wonderful," he whispered. "It was so great, they loved it. I am so proud of you. I was afraid I'd miss the curtain. I raced over from Kennedy. I almost didn't make it."

She pushed his head away, trying to see into his eyes. "You saw the play?" she asked. "You were here all along? Michael, why didn't you find me? At intermission? I've been out there, all this time, talking to all those people, and you didn't try to find me?"

He stepped away from her then, and she felt the cold air rush in against her bare skin.

"Why didn't you tell me you were here, Michael?"

She could see him in the pale light, not his face, but the shrug of his shoulders.

"You were busy," he said quietly, and he turned away from her, out through the door.

She leaned back against the wall, stunned and frightened. He was leaving. She bent down and felt for her clothes, pulling them up, and she ran out after him. She felt her hair falling around her face, and she pulled out Rachel's chopsticks, flinging away the hair pins as she ran down the hall. He was at the glass doors, going back outside into the courtyard, and she followed, fear crowding with sudden anger. How could he leave?

She pushed through the glass doors after him, running, and called his name sharply. He stopped and turned, and a breeze caught his coat and it billowed around him, and the light behind him threw his face into sharp relief. He looked dark and beautiful, a fallen archangel, and her heart leapt to her throat, but she was angry now, wounded and afraid, and she stopped within a foot of him, her body shivering in the sudden cold.

"What the hell was that?" she lashed out. "Is that what you flew all the way over here for? Couldn't you find anybody to fuck while you were in England?"

"No," he shot back, "but apparently you could."

"What?" She was incredulous. "What did you say?"

She heard her name, and she glanced away from Michael to see Quinn, running toward her.

"Diane. Are you all right?" As he reached her, he took her by the shoulders, his hands gentle as they touched her face, pushing away her tousled hair. "You look a fright. Are you hurt? What happened?" He turned to Michael, angry, challenging. "Who the bloody hell are you?"

Michael pushed his hands into the pockets of his coat and squared his shoulders.

"I'm Michael."

Quinn looked back at Diane, saw the flushed cheeks, the wildness in her eye, and he knew, in that moment, that he had lost her.

"Ah. Well." He took a deep breath. "Diane, Levinson wants to know. Next summer? Will that be all right with you?"

Diane nodded.

"Fine. I'll tell him. There are some people back there, though, you should say good-bye to."

"I know, Quinn. I will. Just give me a minute, okay?"

"Yes." He looked at her, shivering, her teeth beginning to chatter from the cold. "Look, take my jacket –"

"No, Quinn." She crossed her arms, hugging herself. "I'm fine."

He turned and walked quickly back into the building. Diane watched him go, and heard Michael's voice, cold and calm.

"Well, isn't he protective?"

She turned to him. His face had closed down, click, a blank page.

"The tabloids in London were full of you two. They ran an item about the great Quinn Harris at a theater on 13th Street. You took him to see Rachel, didn't you? They didn't know who you were. Then there was a dinner, for Derek Shore. They had a picture. They still didn't know who you were. They said you were the woman Quinn Harris was kissing at two in the morning in the lobby of the Pierre Hotel. They said you were the reason he wasn't spending his time in Manhattan, working on his play. I didn't believe it. Angela told me all the rumors, but she said you denied everything. I believed you, of course. Even after you told me you couldn't come to England, I believed you."

She could see his eyes, dark and full of pain, and her mind became suddenly clear. The tears that had been threatening were gone.

"But I saw you." His voice was tight, controlled. "At intermission. After the show. I watched you. He couldn't keep his hands off you, could he?"

"I couldn't come to England because of Emily," Diane said calmly. "She found out about us. She was so angry. She said terrible things. Then she left. She stayed at Kevin's. I couldn't leave, Michael. I couldn't."

His jaw moved, clenched. "What about Harris?"

"Quinn asked me to marry him. He said we would be good together. He said we wanted the same things. He said he loved me."

Michael's voice was deathly quiet. "What did you say?"

She took a step toward him. She could feel him, the heat and energy from his body, and it soaked into her skin, pulling her. "I told him that I didn't love him. I love you. Michael." She took another step, and she was against him, and her arms crept around him, under the leather of his coat, and she felt him flinch, as though she had struck him.

"I love you, Michael." she said again. His eyes closed, and his arms tightened around her, and she could feel the tension and anger and fear leave his body.

"I should have told you," she whispered. "I never should have let you go all the way to England without knowing. I'm sorry." She pulled back and looked into his eyes. "I didn't realize until after you were gone. All I could do was wait for you to come back, and hope you hadn't found somebody else."

"Somebody else?" He asked in quiet amazement. "How could there be anyone else?"

"Because you were over there, and it was terrible and you were all alone, and you didn't know, Michael, that I loved you. I wouldn't have blamed you if you couldn't wait for me."

"Wait for you? I love you. And I will love you forever, Diane. Your loving me or not won't change that. Your being with me or not won't change it. Nothing will change that."

"Oh, thank God. I've been so unhappy without you. Please, don't leave again. There is so much I need to tell you. Are you home for good? Please say you're home."

He shook his head. "No. I'm flying back tomorrow. For another week. It's such a long story. Listen." He kissed her, hard. "You have to go back. There are people in there who can help you, right? Help with your play? I know how this business works. Go back in there and play nice. Those people are your future, you know?"

"No, they aren't. My future is right here. But you're right. I have to say good-bye to people. To Quinn."

"I'll be at the house. I've still got the key. Take your time, okay? I'll wait for you." He kissed her again. "I'll wait."

"Yes. Give me a few minutes, but I'll be there."
She pulled herself away from him and walked back into
the lights and noise, smoothing her hair. People turned
and smiled and reached for her. She answered
automatically, saying the right things. Quinn was back
at her side, not touching her. And when she finally said
good night, he held her coat for her and walked her out
across the parking lot, standing beside her in the cold.

"So, I suppose you're quite sure about all this?" He
asked her.

She lifted her shoulders and let them drop. "I love
him. Ever since I met him, I've been trying to talk
myself out of this. Really. But in spite my best
arguments, I want to be with him. Everything just feels
so much better when I'm with him. So, yes, I'm sure."

"I thought that I was the one," he said.

"You could have been. If I hadn't met him, you
would have been. You're a wonderful man, Quinn.
I'm so sorry."

Quinn hugged her gently and kissed the top of her
head. "If you need anything, you'll call me, right?"

She nodded, feeling a sudden sadness.

"I know. Thank you, Quinn." And with that, she
got into her car and drove home to Michael.

He was asleep when she got home. The black
leather coat was a lump on the floor, and his shoes were
in the hallway. He was stretched out on her bed, fully
clothed, sound asleep. She undressed carefully, pulled
on flannel pajamas, and covered him with an old quilt
from the closet. Then she unplugged the phone beside
the bed and crawled next to him, curling her body next
to his. She was exhausted, but she lay there quiet,
happy, listening to the sound of his breathing, feeling
the heat of his body next to hers.

She awoke late, slid from his side, and padded into the kitchen. She made coffee, and picked up the phone. She called Rachel. Then she called Sam French to tell him she would not meet him for lunch. Sam was still flying high and told her they didn't need to meet at all, that last night's performance had been perfect, and he would see her that evening. She took her coffee back into the bedroom and sat on the edge of the bed, watching Michael as he slept.

He finally opened his eyes, blinking against the sunlight. "How long have you been sitting here?" he asked groggily.

"A while. Coffee?"

"God, yes."

"Food?"

"Toast. Please."

She nodded, and went back to the kitchen. She was spreading butter as he came down the hall from the bathroom, and she carried the tray into the living room. She sat beside him and he kissed her.

"I tried to call you," she said softly.

"I'm sorry." He shook his head. "Seth changed the number because too many people had gotten hold of it. He never told me, of course. Then I gave my password to someone, she said she'd help with some of my business stuff, but I found out she was, ah, editing my e-mail. And after you said you couldn't fly over, I thought – " He stopped and shook his head again. "What about Emily?" he asked.

She told him, about Emily, Megan, and Quinn. The phone rang once or twice, but she did not answer it. At one point she crawled into his lap and he held her and she told him about Levinson and his plans for her play. The words came in a flood, everything she had been holding and saving just for him.

253

"Now you," she said finally. "Tell me. Tell me everything you did while you were gone."

He started with Seth, and Jane Whyte. He told her about the movie, it would be released in December as planned. They were done with the score, but there was an additional song for the soundtrack, another ballad he had written, and he had to finish recording. He was going back. He'd be home for good in a week.

She was quiet in his arms. "I love you very much," she said. "Did I tell you that?" She looked at him, and he was smiling, eyes blazing with happiness.

"Yes, you mentioned it."

"It wasn't until after you left. I was so miserable, and I couldn't figure out why. My life was the same, the girls, my job, everything. And then I remembered what you said, about having a place to belong. That's what was wrong. You weren't here, and I had nowhere that was just mine, no place to be happy. That's when I knew I loved you. Because I knew that I belonged with you."

He kissed her. "Then what are we going to do?" He asked.

"I guess you'll come for dinner. We'll talk to Megan and Emily. We'll tell them how we feel. We'll see each other as often as we can. We'll spend every weekend together. We won't be apart any more than we have to."

"Is Emily going to be okay with that?"

"I think she has big plans for you. Megan too. Be warned. And don't say yes to anything."

He was quiet for a moment. "Would you consider moving up to Mendham?"

She sat for a long time, then shook her head. "I can't. I can't live with you. I wouldn't feel right, with the girls."

He nodded. "Can we go away somewhere?" He asked her. "We have serious catching up to do."

"I know. I can't believe you're leaving again. I'll talk to Marianne. I've got days coming. We could get a long weekend, maybe. Someplace warm - just the two of us?"

"Yes. I need a long, quiet rest. I feel one hundred years old. And I've missed you so badly I thought I would lose my mind. I need days in bed."

"That sounds perfect."

"Could we start now? Do you have anyplace you're supposed to be? I need you, you have no idea." He kissed her roughly. "Can we go back to bed? Please. I need to make love to you. It's going to be the longest week of my life, waiting to get back to you this time."

"Come on."

They undressed. She was thinner, he thought, but her breasts were still full and lush, and as he slipped into her, her legs were still strong around him. He would not rush, moving slowly as she arched against him, her hands in his hair.

"I love you," he whispered at last.

"I know," she whispered back, "I love you too."

Made in the USA
Charleston, SC
19 April 2012